DON'T TRUST A KILLER

NEW YORK TIMES & *USA TODAY* BESTSELLING AUTHOR

CYNTHIA EDEN

Published by Cynthia Eden.

Copy-editing by: J. R. T. Editing

CHAPTER ONE

Kace Quick was tall, dark, sexy as every sin imaginable, and…quite possibly, a cold-blooded killer.

Bree Harlow released a slow breath as she was escorted into his office. The place was high-end, fancy. Reeked of money. Kace had plenty of money, after all. Money to burn. He owned most of the clubs in New Orleans and several casinos over in Biloxi. His name was whispered by those who feared him, and by those who wanted to bring him down—the local authorities—it was cursed.

"Have a seat, Ms. Harlow." His voice was rumbling and low, with no hint at all of the South flowing in his words. She knew he'd been raised in New Orleans, though. Brought up in the foster care system. He'd gone from having nothing to controlling one of the biggest empires in the South.

The cops thought he was as dirty as they came. Tied to every sin in the city.

He turned toward her, moving away from the window that let him look out over the busy street below. His eyes—the most electric blue that she'd ever seen—locked on her. And for a moment, all Bree could think was…

Sin.

Yes, this man knew all about sin.

His dark hair was thick and heavy, shoved back from his forehead. He didn't wear some fancy suit, though she knew he could afford anything he wanted. Everything. Instead, he wore a black t-shirt that stretched over his wide shoulders and powerful arms. Jeans encased his legs. Comfortable, faded. Still…sexy. The guy oozed sex appeal even as he gave off a dark, dangerous vibe that she was sure most women found irresistible.

She wasn't most women.

Bree finally took the seat he'd indicated. She'd play his game, because she could *not* afford to screw this up. The leather squeaked beneath her as she eased into the chair. "I, um, didn't expect to meet with you."

He headed toward her. Bree tensed but…

He just propped one hip on his desk, crossed his arms over his chest, and stared down at her. "Why the hell not? It's my club."

"Uh, right." She cleared her throat. "But I'm just here applying for the waitress position and—"

"And you don't think I care about the people who work for me?"

She hadn't thought he'd want to be in on this interview, no. She'd figured it would take her days to work her way up to him. But if fate was going to be kind and put him in her path right then, who was she to complain? Bree glanced up at him, holding his bright blue gaze. "There are a lot of...stories about you." It was a gamble to say those words.

One dark eyebrow rose. "Stories?"

"Y-yes..." She let her voice tremble.

His gaze raked over her. "Bree Harlow. Twenty-five years old. Fresh from Asheville, North Carolina." His lips hitched into a half-smile. "What in the hell are you doing in my city, Bree?"

"Looking for a job." Her hands twisted in her lap.

He laughed. Like his voice, the laugh was deep and rumbling. Sexy. The guy had the sex appeal down to an art. "There are plenty of waitressing jobs in North Carolina. I don't think you needed to come all the way down here to find one."

She slowly exhaled. "I wanted a fresh start." This was going to be tricky. Truth and lies could always be tricky.

His eyes narrowed on her. "What are you running from?"

What have you got? She'd spent the last ten years running from all kinds of things.

His jaw—square and hard—tightened. "A lover?"

"I wanted a fresh start. That meant I needed new people in my life. A new place. So, I came here." She held his gaze, but it was hard to meet his intense stare. She'd seen his picture before. Learned everything that she could about the man before she'd crossed the threshold into Fantasy, his new club.

But…

Seeing him in person was different. The guy was bigger, sexier, and a whole lot more dangerous. She'd had to pass four guards just to get into his office. Guards who'd raked her with their hard stares. The big boss was insulated, and getting this in-person meeting with him…

Hell, yes. Major score.

Now, if she could just manage not to screw up this part and actually land the job, she'd be golden.

Kace lifted a hand, rubbing it over the faint stubble that covered his jaw. The guy's face could have made him a model, if he had been into the whole not-being-a-criminal thing. High cheekbones, long blade of a nose. Sensual lips.

"When did you arrive in New Orleans?"

She was prepared for the question. "Three days ago." Truth.

"And in that three days…" His head tilted as he studied her. "What sort of…stories …have you already heard?"

Bree bit her lip.

His gaze dipped to her mouth. No warmth appeared in his eyes. Slowly his stare drifted up once more. "Ms. Harlow?"

"The lady at the bed and breakfast where I'm staying…Ms. Queen knew I was looking for a job. She told me about this club, but said I had to be careful."

"And why is that?"

"Because you're a criminal." There. Bree waited for his reaction.

There was none. No laughter at the crazy claim. No denial.

Just those blue eyes staring hard at her. Trying to see *through* her.

"And you want to work for a would-be criminal?"

Sound desperate or you'll lose him. "I just want to work. I'm down to my last hundred, and I need this job."

"A job working for a criminal?"

Her heart pounded harder in her chest. "*Are* you a criminal?"

"I don't know…are *you* a waitress?"

What in the hell was that supposed to mean? Her lips parted.

But Kace laughed again. "There are lots of stories in this town. Some people say I'm a criminal, some say I'm a savior. It's really all in who you ask." A pause. He leaned toward her. "I wonder, what will I be to you?"

His gaze had finally lit with something other than ice. She would have needed to be blind in order to miss the sudden interest in his stare. Lust. Her heart jerked. She was in so much trouble.

"Let's find out, shall we?" His hand lifted up, and he tucked a lock of her hair behind Bree's ear. "You're hired."

A smile curved her lips. "Thank you."

Kace frowned at her. "You have a dimple in your cheek."

Her smile dimmed.

His fingers slid to her cheek. "It's cute."

His touch was making her nervous. His fingers were warm and slightly callused, and… "I think there is a miscommunication here." Abruptly, she rose. So did he.

Their bodies brushed. He was taller than she was. Bree wore tennis shoes and stood at five-foot-five without heels, so she had to tip back her head to stare up at him.

"Miscommunication?" Kace repeated. He didn't back up. He didn't give her space.

"I'm not here for sex."

He laughed. The sound rolled right over her.

She didn't laugh back. "I'm looking for a waitressing job. Nothing more. If the job is contingent on me playing nice with you—"

More laughter. The guy looked as if he was truly amused. "Oh, sweetheart, I never play *nice*. That's just not who I am."

Right. Crime lord. Charmer. Killer? The stories said he was all of those things and so much more.

But he'd stopped touching her. That was something, wasn't it?

"Sleeping with me isn't part of the job, don't worry about that."

Her cheeks went red.

He blinked, as if surprised. Then his hand rose again—

Her fingers grabbed his wrist. "Stop."

"I didn't expect the blush. You surprised me."

The fact that his hand seemed to burn her—that surprised Bree. She felt an electric spark run the length of her hand, and she immediately let him go. "I'm a good waitress. I'll always show up on time, and I'll stay as late as needed. I won't cause trouble, and I'll get the job done."

"No trouble? Really?" Now he walked around her, letting his gaze slide up and down her body. She couldn't help but tense. "I find that hard to believe."

Her gaze slanted to the left. Locked on him.

"You look like trouble to me, Ms. Harlow."

No, she didn't. She'd dressed in deliberately casual clothes. Jeans and a white t-shirt. She'd wanted to appear unthreatening. A little desperate. Even though the truth was that she was a *lot* desperate. This job was absolutely necessary to her.

"Have you waited tables before?"

"Yes." Now she moved and tapped her hand on his desk. Her resume sat there. "I've done a lot of waitressing work. I've done bartending work. I can handle anything."

"I guess we'll see if that's true." He rolled back his shoulders. "Like I said before, you're hired."

Her breath left in an excited rush.

"Start tonight. Be here at seven p.m. We don't open until nine, but you'll need some training. And clothes." He motioned vaguely toward her. "All of my waiters and waitresses have a particular uniform. For the women on the first floor, it's red heels, black pants, and a black blouse. I provide the uniforms for everyone, so be sure to stop and get outfitted before you leave today."

"Thank you! I really appreciate—"

"If you fuck up, you're out."

Well, wasn't he the blunt one? Her chin notched up. "I won't fuck up."

A faint smile curled his lips. "That remains to be seen."

Then he headed back for his desk. Sat down. She assumed he was dismissing her, so Bree hurried for the door.

"I want to hear the stories."

She stilled, her fingers reaching for the doorknob.

"Before you leave, tell me, exactly, what you've heard about me."

Her tongue slid over her lower lip. Carefully, Bree schooled her features before she turned toward him. "I heard you were a killer."

Kace didn't even blink.

"Those who cross you don't get second chances. You eliminate threats to you. You make your own laws. You do whatever the hell you want."

His fingers tapped on the desk. "That all you've heard?"

No, not even close. "Two…two women were found murdered in New Orleans recently. I heard the cops think you were involved with their deaths."

His smile came slowly, and it was a strange sight to see. So charming. So warm. She imaged the devil would smile just that way. "Who has been telling you all these stories? Especially since you've only been in town a few days…Three, wasn't it? Surely, they didn't all come from the talkative lady at your bed and breakfast. Although, I do know Ms. Queen. Most of the town does. She certainly enjoys her gossip."

No, all of the stories hadn't come from Ms. Kelly Queen. "The news," she blurted. "I saw about—about the two women on the news."

"You shouldn't believe everything you see…or hear."

"I don't. That's why I'm in your club right now, asking for a job."

"From a man who many believe to be a murderer. Interesting. *You* are interesting, Ms. Harlow."

There was something about the way he said her name…

"Some women get off on danger. They like to fuck criminals."

She shook her head.

His eyes narrowed. "Is that a no? You don't enjoy that dark thrill?"

"I was shaking my head because this is the weirdest job interview I've ever had." That statement, at least, was the absolute truth.

"Ah, so you *do* get off on danger. Good to know."

Her lips pressed together.

"Relax, Ms. Harlow. I have a strict policy about *not* having sex with my employees. You'll have to look elsewhere for your rush."

"But—but those two women—" Bree pushed when she probably shouldn't have.

"I didn't have sex with those women, despite what the media says. And what the cops think. I wasn't involved with them romantically. And, in case you were wondering but weren't quite brave enough to ask…No, I didn't kill them." His hands flattened on his desk. "I didn't kill Lindsey Marshall and Ciara Hall. I didn't strangle them and dump their bodies behind the St. Louis Cathedral so that some poor, unsuspecting tourists could find them the next day."

Bree swallowed. His voice had been completely flat, dead of emotion while he spoke.

"Still want the job?" His bright gaze seemed to mock her.

More than ever. "Yes." Another swallow. "And at least now, I know my boss isn't a killer."

His eyes narrowed.

"Right?"

He didn't smile at her, but she could have sworn his eyes gleamed. "The guard outside of my door is named Remy St. Clair. He'll take you to see the floor manager and get you squared away with the uniforms. I'm sure there's some paperwork somewhere for you." His voice sounded disinterested, and he was already turning toward his computer.

"Thank you."

She waited. He didn't reply. So, Bree cleared her throat. "Thank you," she said again, louder.

He let out a little sigh as he finally looked up at her. Kace seemed confused about why she was still there.

"It's polite to thank someone," she told him in a very calm voice, "when the person does something nice for you."

A furrow appeared between his brows. "What on earth makes you think I did anything nice for you? Didn't we cover this already? I don't—"

"Do nice, right. It just *seems* nice."

Now he leaned back in his leather chair. Kace seemed to like leather. Or maybe he just enjoyed expensive things. Judging by the paintings on the walls—she was ninety percent certain the one to the left was a Jackson Pollack—Bree was going with option B.

"Ms. Harlow, I haven't done anything nice. You're hired on a temporary basis. Let's call it probation, shall we? It's the same for all my employees. If you want something permanent, you'll have to make it through the night."

Why did he make it sound as if surviving the night was some incredible feat? She could do a night of waitressing, no problem. She'd done it before. Over and over again. "I've got this."

"We'll see." He motioned to the door. "Good-bye."

The phone on his desk rang. He picked it up, not even waiting for her to leave the room.

But that was fine. She'd gotten the job, and she'd gotten a one-on-one interview with the big boss himself. Talk about a stroke of luck. Sure, he might act like an asshole, but she'd known exactly what he was before she'd strolled into his club.

Bree opened the door and found a tall, muscled, dark-haired man waiting for her. Had to be Remy St. Clair. Unlike Kace, this fellow was dressed in a fancy suit, a gray one with a white shirt tucked underneath. He stared at her from unblinking, chocolate eyes.

"You're hired." He didn't seem overly surprised.

She glanced back at Kace's office. "You could hear us?"

"No, but you've got a great ass, and he doesn't usually say no to blondes with good asses. The customers will like you, and that's good enough for Kace." He turned on his heel. "Follow me."

She'd *happily* follow him, despite the ass comment, because when he led her through the corridors, she got to see all sorts of things in the club. The VIP area was on the second floor, filled with dark, one-way glass. There were dressing rooms, storage areas, and— "Um, I'm sorry, is that a trapeze?" She'd stopped in the middle of

Fantasy's main floor, her gaze darting to the ceiling.

Remy stopped, too. He looked up. "Yep." He sounded absolutely bored out of his mind.

"Why is there a trapeze here?"

He sighed. "You're not going to be on it, so why worry?"

"But—"

Remy turned toward her. "That's the big reveal. The surprise. The club is called Fantasy for a reason. Kace is going to have performers out here doing one of those crazy Cirque-type shows. Flying through the air. Contorting. The show will start at midnight, and, according to Kace, it will be absolutely killer."

Bree glanced around the area. "Will there be a net?"

"Hell, no. That's not exactly exciting, is it? Where's the danger if a net is involved?" He started walking again. "Come on. This way."

"So, this place is—"

"A high end, very high-priced fantasy environment. Kace will have performers walking through the crowd. Performers who will be wearing very distinctive attire so they won't be confused with regular staff." He stopped before a door marked "Management." His gaze pinned her. "Something you should know. Kace doesn't tolerate anyone messing with his staff. There will always be bouncers on the floor. Guards close at every moment. If something goes wrong, someone scares you, then all you have to do is signal."

Good to know. "How do I signal?"

"You fucking scream, baby. Then one of us will come running." He swung open the door. "Hey, Abby, got some fresh meat for you."

***

Bree walked out of Fantasy, her new uniform tucked under her right arm, her steps sure and certain. The club was located near the end of Bourbon Street, just steps away from the infamous Jean Lafitte's bar. As she hurried onto the street, a horse and carriage came rolling by, the wheels churning as the driver told the family in the back all about Lafitte's haunted bar.

She didn't glance at the carriage. Instead, Bree made her away across the street. Then she turned into an alley. Slid between two buildings. Every now and then, she'd look over her shoulder and when she was sure that she was clear…

She headed for her planned rendezvous. The building she approached appeared abandoned. The windows were boarded up. A "No Trespassing" sign was attached to the old porch. She didn't climb onto the porch. Instead, Bree entered via the back of the old house. And as soon as she stepped inside…

"Excellent job, Agent Harlow."

Her team was waiting for her. The FBI agents all faced her, smiles on their faces.

Dominic Grant lowered the headphones he'd been wearing. "Heard every single word." He gave a low whistle. "Thought I'd piss myself when you said that you'd heard the guy was a killer." His green eyes gleamed. "Took some balls."

She was covered in sweat—and the sweat wasn't just from the fact that it was still humid in October. The New Orleans heat *was* like a suffocating coat, but her sweat came from the fact that she'd just had a face-off with the man suspected of being a serial killer. *The New Orleans Strangler.*

"Told you that it would be easy for you to get in," Grayson Wesley said with a slow nod. He was the special agent in charge of the investigation and the whole reason she was even involved with the case. She'd just graduated from the FBI Academy in Quantico, and Grayson had called her in. He'd specifically requested her for this case, and she had no idea why. He'd done a stint as a lecturer at Quantico, and she'd loved his profiling discussion. The cases he'd talked about, the way the agents had been able to track the killers just based on psychological assessments—

that was what fascinated her. She'd always wanted to profile. Her desire to understand and unmask killers was the reason she'd joined the Bureau. She wanted to be out in the world, stopping monsters. She'd had that one goal for as long as she could remember.

Ever since monsters destroyed everything I cared about.

And now, she had the chance do it. Her first real assignment as an FBI agent. Sure, she wasn't making the profiles just yet, but that was okay. She was working undercover. Getting close to the target. Closer than anyone had gotten before.

"I knew you'd be just his type," Grayson continued with a slow nod. His brown hair was brushed back from his high forehead, and his eyes glinted with approval.

A little shiver slid down her spine at Grayson's words. She knew what he meant, of course.

The other two victims who'd recently been found in New Orleans—Lindsey Marshall and Ciara Hall—had also both been blondes. Lindsey's hair had trailed down her back in a tangle of beautiful curls. Ciara's blond hair had been styled in a short pixie-cut, one that accentuated her delicate features…and that had left her neck completely exposed to the killer. Both women had been strangled, their necks marked with deep bruises in death.

Bree tucked a lock of her hair behind her ear. "I'm scheduled to go back to the club tonight." But they'd know that. Bree was wired, and the team had been listening to every single word she said to Kace.

Karin Miller approached quickly. A few years older than Bree, the redhead gave her a reassuring smile. "The hardest part was getting inside."

Grayson shook his head. "No, the hardest part will be finding evidence to nail that bastard. He's walked for years. Bribed the local PD. Gotten away with every fucking thing imaginable, but it ends here. Kace Quick is a killer, and we're going to lock him away." His gaze held hers. "You're the bait, Bree. Reel him in. Let's make this jerk pay for what he's done."

When Lindsey's body had been discovered behind the St. Louis Cathedral, Grayson had immediately known her case was different. When she'd looked at the crime scene photos, Bree had understood why. The woman had been strangled, a long scarf left around her neck, and her body had been perfectly positioned by the killer. Then…too soon after, the second body had been found. Ciara Hall had been murdered in the exact same way, strangled. But this time, a long length of white, hemp rope had been coiled around her neck. She'd been placed behind the St. Louis Cathedral, too.

Two dead women. The same MO. Grayson had started looking for links between them, and he'd found one major link, all right.

Kace Quick.

Kace Quick…Fifteen years ago, the guy had been charged with murdering his girlfriend, Brittney Lang. A young woman with blond hair who'd been found strangled. Kace had been eighteen years old at the time. He'd been crucified in the Press, but at the last moment, a new witness had come forward, a girl who had provided Kace with an alibi. Kace had been found not guilty.

Grayson believed that Kace *had* killed Brittney Lang. He thought that long-ago witness had lied. And he believed that Kace was killing again. That Kace had a preferred victim type.

Women who look like me.

So, when Grayson had started a task force to look into the New Orleans Strangler—a moniker the local reporters had adopted—Grayson had called her in because he wanted her to get close to the chief suspect.

Kace Quick.

Sexy. Dangerous. Killer?

Time to find out.

Bree squared her shoulders. "I'll get the job done. Count on it."

***

A soft knock rapped at the door. "Come in," Kace called, not even glancing up from his computer.

The door creaked open. Footsteps were swallowed by the lush carpet. And—

A throat cleared.

Sighing, Kace looked up and found Remy frowning at him. "There a problem?"

"I'm not sure about the new girl."

He let his brows climb.

"You want a full background check on her?"

That was typical. Kace always wanted to know exactly who he employed—and what secrets those individuals might be hiding from him. Secrets could be very dangerous. "Of course."

Remy nodded. He didn't leave.

Kace waited.

"I don't trust her, Kace."

Ah, finally. Remy wasn't normally the type to hold back. "Well, that makes two of us."

Remy blinked. "If you don't trust her, then why—"

Now Kace stood. He stalked around his desk. "You think I don't know what she is?" He laughed, but the sound held no humor. "Come now, my friend, you and I have been in this business a very long time."

Remy inclined his head.

"I could practically smell the fear coming from her." He'd seen the nervousness in her stare. Bree Harlow had been scared to death to be in the same room with him, yet she'd stayed. And she'd asked her questions. Very deliberate questions. "Our girl is green. Far too green for this case."

"You think she's a cop?"

"She's not local. I know all the local cops." Especially cops who looked like her.

Golden eyes. Golden skin. Red, lush lips. Her hair had been a sun-streaked blond and cut in a bob to fall just above her shoulders. Totally straight, her hair had emphasized her high cheekbones and framed her heart-shaped face. The woman was gorgeous. Curved in all the right places and gifted with a voice that sounded better than Saturday night sin.

And he would have bet his life that she was a Fed.

Kace rolled back his shoulders. "The FBI wants to pin Lindsey and Ciara's murders on me. They've been practically salivating, but they don't have enough to go on." They had jack shit. "So, I think they've stepped up their game."

Remy tensed.

Kace pretended not to notice. Remy could be so touchy about things…things like murder, for example. With the secrets that Remy carried,

Kace would have expected something different. But, oh well.

Remy's brows lowered. "If you think she's FBI, then why the hell would you let her even step foot in Fantasy?"

Now Kace had to laugh. *Why?* "Remy, Remy, Remy…" Kace slapped his hand on the guy's shoulder. "Didn't you look at her? The woman is just my type."

Remy seemed to stiffen even more. "Boss…"

"Don't worry. I promise, I'll just scare this one." Scare her. Maybe seduce her. Maybe do both. It all just depended on how he was feeling. He was *definitely* in the mood to teach the FBI a lesson. "Of course, she has to make it through the night first." He headed for the door.

"Kace…"

He laughed again. "The grand opening. Our big show. Bree Harlow arrived just in time." Kace threw a final glance over his shoulder. "I promise you this, the night will be an absolute killer."

CHAPTER TWO

"Perfect, you're here on time." The tall, gorgeous redhead gave Bree a quick once over. Bree had met Abby Johnson, the floor manager at Fantasy, right after Kace had given her the job. And now that she'd come back for her night shift, Bree's first order of business was to check in with Abby.

Abby waved Bree forward, her gaze sweeping over her body. "Uniform fits. You look great." She gave an approving nod. "Go get scanned and you'll be ready to learn the shift routine."

Bree paused. She'd been about to walk past Abby and head for the staff area. Now, though, she glanced at the manager and asked, "Scanned?"

Abby blinked her hazel eyes. "You weren't told about that part?"

Bree shook her head.

Abby blew out a quick breath. "Nothing really. Takes all of five seconds." She offered Bree a reassuring smile. "The security guys run a quick scanner over your body. It's just a precaution." She glanced down at the clipboard in her hand.

"A precaution for what?" Unease slithered through Bree.

Abby looked up. "To make sure you're not a cop."

Oh, shit, oh, shit. Oh, shit.

Then Abby laughed, a light, quick peal of sound. "God, your face is absolutely hilarious right now." She came closer, still smiling. "Relax. It's just standard operating procedure for Kace Quick." Another laugh. "The guy is paranoid to the extreme, but you'll learn that fast enough." She leaned toward Bree and whispered, "He always insists on every staff member being scanned before a shift. Sometimes, the business that is discussed in his club isn't exactly, well..." Her words trailed away.

So, Bree finished, "Legal?"

Abby simply stared at her. "According to Remy, there was an incident once. A waiter tried to come in with a listening device on him. Thought he'd get some incriminating tidbit on Kace. Didn't happen."

"What *did* happen to the waiter?"

"Hell if I know. You don't screw around with Kace Quick and just walk away." A shrug. "The scan is required for everyone. Seriously, they just wave a wand over your body. They don't get to touch you, if that's what you're worried about."

It wasn't. She was worried about the damn listening device that was tucked inside her bra.

"Get the scan and then come back to me. When you're all clear, I'll start giving you table assignments for the night."

Before Bree could respond, someone called Abby's name. Abby hurried away. "Seriously?" Her voice rose. "The trapeze is supposed to be *higher* than that. How many times do I have to tell…"

Bree sucked in a sharp breath. Then another. Then she tried to figure out what the hell she was supposed to do. The security guards were to the side, and, jeez, yes, they *were* scanning the other staff members. If she didn't go toward them, it would look suspicious as all hell.

And if she *went* toward them, she was busted. She'd be kicked out of the club before the shift had even started.

Her gaze darted around, frantic. There—the restroom. She made a beeline for it and—

"Hi…Bree, isn't it?" Remy was in her way. Wearing a new suit, a black one this time, and still looking like a big, brick wall.

She gave him a quick smile. "Yes, it's Bree."

"Ready for your first night?"

No. But she would be, once she got rid of the listening device.

"Abby tell you that you need to check in with security? It's standard practice, every single night."

Bree forced a light laugh. "It'd be nice if the customers had to get scanned, too."

He didn't laugh back. "We keep an eye on them. Don't worry."

"Ah, right." She side-stepped. "I have to go to the ladies' room, please excuse me—"

"Kace wants to see you."

Her heart shoved hard into her chest.

"Right now," Remy added, and his dark eyes seemed extra cold. Before she could say another word, he took her arm and *escorted* her to the big boss's office. And with every single step they took, one thought flashed through Bree's mind…

Oh, God. This is so not good.

She stumbled, her high heels tripping her. She would have gone down, but Remy caught her. He pulled her close and their bodies collided. She pushed against him and straightened up. As she straightened, Bree smoothed her hands over her shirt, slipping her finger inside and toward her bra strap. "I'm…sorry." She turned away, just for a moment. "I am so clumsy." Her hand moved to her side. Her fingers opened. She dropped the small transmitter.

"Better be careful in those heels. You don't want to get hurt."

Deliberately, she moved one heel to the right. The soft *crunch* sounded way too loud to her ears, but Remy didn't seem to notice the sound. He just took her elbow again. "You don't keep the boss waiting. Remember that."

***

"Kace, Ms. Harlow is ready for work." Remy stood just inside of Kace's doorway, with Bree at his side.

She is fucking beautiful. The thought immediately ran through Kace's mind as he sat behind the desk, and he was damn glad that he *was* sitting. Because his dick took one look at Bree and immediately jumped to happy attention.

There was something about her. Something that hit him on a primal level. He'd had the same reaction the first time they'd met. He'd taken one look at her—and wanted. Lusted.

A big problem.

"Leave us alone," Kace ordered, aware that his voice was too rough but not really giving a shit.

Remy backed out of the office without a word. He shut the door with a soft click. Bree stood there, her hands at her side, her feet encased in a sexy as hell pair of red heels. She wore the standard black pants, and the low cut, scooping black blouse—but on her…

Bree looks good in black. Good enough to eat.

Her golden skin and her blond hair were emphasized by the dark outfit. Her breasts pushed against the top of her blouse, and the pants showed off her narrow waist. Dark shadow and mascara made her golden eyes seem even bigger, and the slick, red lipstick on her mouth made him hungry to taste her lips.

"Is there a problem?" Her voice was careful, her expression guarded.

He sighed and reached into his desk. "There could be."

Bree stiffened.

He rose, pulling out the security wand—the same wand that his men used to check personnel. He'd been burned in the past, so he didn't take chances any longer. *Fool me once, shame on me. Fool me twice…*

And you'll wish you'd never been born.

His hand curled loosely around the end of the scanner. "I thought we'd do this check here."

"Why?" She backed up a step. Ah, a bad move. Didn't she know that showing fear would just make her more tempting to him? "I, uh, Abby told me that the check would be performed by the guards—"

Taking his time, he walked around the desk and headed for her. He was still aroused, and if the woman glanced down, she'd sure as shit notice the fact. But her wide-eyed gaze was on his face. And he could practically smell her fear. *Baby, you've obviously got plenty to hide.* She was truly the greenest agent he'd ever seen.

Why was he doing the check himself? The real reason was because he didn't want his guards getting rough with her when they found the listening device. He had no doubt the woman was transmitting. So, he'd decided to check her out himself. When he found the device, she'd confess her lies. He'd escort her out. He'd show the FBI that he didn't dick around. That he was on to their games.

That would be the end of his fun with Bree.

He couldn't very well fuck an agent investigating him. Could he?

"My references checked out." She seemed absolutely certain of that fact.

Too certain.

Inclining his head, Kace agreed, "They did."

Her smile came and went, the dimple an all-too-brief flash. "Then what's the deal? Why do I get special treatment?"

He stopped in front of her. His left hand lifted and touched her cheek. "Maybe because you're special."

Her breath caught.

"Don't worry. It will only take a moment."

Her lower lip trembled. She truly had gorgeous lips. He'd like to lick that lower lip. Like to suck it. Bite it.

Make her moan.

"Extend your arms from your sides for me. Then brace your legs apart." When she complied, he began to run the scanner over her left arm—

"Is this legal?" Bree blurted.

He had to bite back a laugh. "It's entirely your choice. You can walk out the door right now, if you want."

But he could see the knowledge in her eyes. If she didn't agree to the scan, then he'd know she was hiding something. And if she *was* wearing a transmitter, then sweet Bree was about to be exposed. It was a lose, lose situation for her.

"I need this job. I'm not going anywhere." Her slightly pointed chin lifted. "Do it."

Taking his time, he scanned her left arm. Then her right. When he brought the wand over her chest, he saw her tense. Kace paused. "Something you want to tell me?"

"Yes, this is a huge invasion of privacy. It's total bullshit, and you shouldn't treat your employees this way."

"A waiter came in once." Kace didn't move the scanner. "This was at another club, my place in the Quarter, Nightmare. The guy said all the right things. Did all the right stuff. And then I caught him wearing a wire as he tried to find evidence of money laundering." Money laundering, drugs, you name it—the guy had been looking for everything. "He didn't find any evidence, of course, because I'm not a criminal."

"Of course," she murmured back, her long lashes sweeping down to conceal her gaze.

"Now, a scan is part of the employment process. Should have been in the paperwork you completed."

Her lashes lifted. "I don't remember reading anything about a security scan."

"It was there, should have checked the fine print." He had to smile at her. He'd miss her when she was gone.

Wait. Where the hell had that thought come from?

And, actually, the part about the scans *hadn't* been in the paperwork. If it had been, how would he have caught her unaware? Catching her this way would be so much fun. Then he'd be able to shove the truth right back at the FBI jackasses on his trail.

"Are you going to finish? Or just keep that over my chest all night?"

She had bite. Nice. Since she wanted him to finish, he slid the scanner lower. Bree tensed, but the wand didn't make a sound.

Interesting.

He knelt in front of her, scanning up her legs.

Nothing.

Except, well, she had great legs. Phenomenal, really.

He swept her whole body, being quick now, and the scanner didn't go off even one time. He'd circled her during the scan, but now he returned to stand in front of her.

"That was painless." A wide smile curled her lips and flashed her dimple. "And I get to do this every night with the guards? How much fun for me."

"No, you'll be doing it with me." The words rapped out. Suspicion was heavy inside of him. The scanner hadn't gone off, the woman *wasn't* transmitting, but Kace still didn't trust her. Not for an instant. And when he didn't trust someone…

"Wow. I get lots of special attention." Bree retreated a step. "Better be careful, or I'll start to think you're interested in me." She turned her back on him and headed for the door. "I'll start to think you want to break that super important rule about not getting involved with employees. I'll start to think—"

"I want you."

She froze. "What?" Her head whipped toward him as she spun around.

With slow, deliberate movements, Kace strode to his desk and put down the scanner. She'd surprised him. *I would have bet the woman was wearing a transmitter.* He would have been wrong. He wasn't often wrong. "I want you." He slanted her an amused glance. "You're hot as hell. What straight man wouldn't want you?"

"But—"

"But I don't always take the things I want. And you're off-limits."

Bree sucked in a quick breath.

"I can keep doing the scans for you each night because you seemed…nervous…when you were with Abby."

"How do you know—"

He pointed to his computer. "I can see the club's security cameras anytime I want. I saw you with Abby. I saw the fear on your face when she pointed to the scanning area. I thought I'd help you. I contacted Remy and got him to intervene."

"Because you…want me."

"Because, despite what you obviously think, I'm not a cold-hearted bastard. I can be kind." He could also be very, very cruel. But he'd never be that, not to her. At least, he hoped that he wouldn't have to be. "If you're scared of the others, you can always come to me. I'll take care of you."

"I can take care of myself, but thanks." Once more, she turned away.

"Fine, then when you report tomorrow night, just have the guards scan you. You now know what a painless process it is." He was pushing her, deliberately. Because if she *was* some sort of undercover cop or agent, she'd want to be around him. She'd want to be as close to him as possible. She wouldn't pass up the chance—

"I'll come back to you tomorrow night," Bree said quickly, not looking at him.

Since she wasn't looking, Bree missed his satisfied smile. *She wouldn't pass up the chance to have one-on-one time with the man she was investigating.*

"I prefer to do the scan up here. I like the privacy." Now she did throw a hard glare over her shoulder as she added, "It has nothing to do with you."

"Whatever you say." He had a club opening that was waiting. And speaking of that opening… "If anyone gives you shit tonight, tell Remy."

"I know the signal." Her voice seemed amused.

He wasn't amused. "No one messes with my staff. Don't take shit. Don't hesitate to call out if you need help."

Her glare had vanished. Now confusion filled her stare. "You actually seem to care."

"Why the surprise? Don't you know, sweetheart, even monsters protect the things that belong to them?"

"I don't belong to you."

You could. But instead of saying that, he just shrugged.

A moment later, she was gone.

Remy poked his head inside. "Boss?"

He could still smell the faint scent of lavender in the air. Her scent. "Make sure no one lays so much as a fucking hand on Bree tonight. If some fool gets out of line, you kick his ass out of my club, got it?"

A nod. Then… "So…no wire? No transmitter?"

He smiled. "Nothing."

"Maybe she's just a waitress. Just a woman who needed a job. You tend to be so damn suspicious of everyone."

With reason. Betrayal was a fact of life for him. That was why he didn't trust anyone.

And why he would never let his guard down around the ever-so-tempting Bree Harlow.

CHAPTER THREE

"Two whiskeys, one apple martini, and a Hurricane." Bree passed out the drinks at the table. Her feet ached in the heels, her spine felt as if someone had twisted it like a pretzel, and she'd only been on the floor a few hours. Jesus, she was out of practice. "You need anything else?"

The people at the round table were already taking their drinks. Murmuring their thanks.

She backed away.

The club was bursting. Voices and laughter filled the air. Opening night was a huge success, and the big show hadn't even started yet. A quick glance at her watch showed her that it was just minutes until midnight. She'd been busting ass since her shift started, determined to prove herself to a watchful Abby and to Kace—wherever the hell he might be.

As she headed back to the bar, Bree's gaze darted around the area. VIPs were immediately led upstairs. She hadn't been up there yet. That area had a separate group of waitresses and waiters. They didn't wear the black uniform. Instead, they were dressed all in white.

Was the real action up there? The dark deeds? She'd bet money it was. But she had to start at the bottom. Had to work her way up—

A hand slid over her ass. She spun around, shoving out hard with her right hand. "What in the hell?"

The guy—looked like some frat boy—winked at her.

She pulled back her fist, ready to punch him in the face—

"You're out of here." Remy's hands slapped down on the frat boy's shoulders. "You and your whole crew."

The guy gaped. "But, but I didn't—"

"You did," Bree snarled at him. "I'm not part of the entertainment."

The security team closed in. They grabbed the whole table and kicked them out in seconds.

She saw Remy lift his hand to his ear. *He's wearing an ear piece.* "Yeah, boss," he said. "I got them."

Her gaze flew around.

She didn't see Kace.

Remy grunted. "Kace wants to know if you're okay."

"Where is he?" Watching…on his computer? Or maybe behind that one-way glass in the VIP area? Or—

"I'm right here."

Or maybe he was right behind her. Shit. Bree spun around.

He smiled at her. Looked absolutely killer. He'd changed into a suit—black. The crisp, white shirt underneath the suit coat was unbuttoned a bit, making him look sexy and casual. The shadow on his jaw was a little darker. His eyes seemed to drink in Bree. "Are you okay?"

"I'm fine," she told him. The noise around her seemed to dim. "Just taking care of my orders."

He waved Remy away and stepped closer. "The next man who touches you without your permission will get a broken hand."

"Uh…that's…" She wasn't sure what that was. Nice that he was watching out for her? Scary as all hell that he could order physical violence so easily? Both?

"Broken hands send strong messages. Word will spread that *no one* can touch my staff here again."

"You have a very *hard* way of doing things, don't you?"

"You have no idea."

The lights flickered.

He leaned toward her. "The show is about to start, Bree. When the lights go down, you don't wait the tables. Everyone just watches the performance."

Okay, right. He'd walk away and—

"Want to watch with me?"

Before she could answer, Kace continued, "I think I want to stay close to you in the dark. Just to make sure no other assholes think they can touch you."

"You giving this same attention to all the waitresses?"

"They've already cleared the floor for the show. You're the only one out here."

A quick glance showed her that he was right.

Kace offered his hand to her.

She took it. Felt that strange spark that flared when they touched.

"It means we'd be fucking incredible in bed."

Her lips parted.

"That heat you feel when we touch. Yeah, we'd probably set the sheets on fire. Something to think about." But his voice was completely mild as his fingers curled around hers, and he led her across the club. He didn't take her upstairs. Instead, they went to a reserved table, right in the front. One that was just a few feet away from the performance area. He pulled a chair out for her, surprising her with the old-school gentleman act. Something she hadn't expected from him.

How can a killer be so charming?

He sat next to her. She noticed that Remy stayed close by, slipping into the shadows.

The overhead lights turned off. A spotlight slid onto the performance area. Faint glows came from all the tables. Not real candles, but flickering light that sure appeared genuine.

"It's all about the illusion," Kace murmured as he reached out to tap the glass candle holder on their table. "The real thing is too dangerous in a place like this. All those candle flames—hell, one drunk knocks them over and Fantasy would light up. These are just battery powered. They flicker and give the appearance of real candles."

"You like illusions?"

"Everything in my world is an illusion."

Music filled the air. Romantic. Slow.

The first performer came out. A blond woman in a glittering costume, a costume that seemed to be composed of diamonds—and nothing else. She lifted her arms, and long silks unfurled from the ceiling. She grabbed the silk and immediately flew into the air. Unable to help herself, Bree smiled.

"You like the show?" Kace murmured.

"I used to be a dancer." The truth tumbled out as she watched the woman fly and twist in the air. The performer rolled up in the silk, then tumbled down, over and over in quick succession. "Studied gymnastics for a while, too." She'd had big dreams back then. Plans. Her mom had wanted her to be a prima ballerina. She'd gone to competition after competition and—

No, don't go back there.

Those dreams had all died with her parents.

The performer was stretching into a full split, holding the dark silks as wind blew against her. Bree laughed in delight. "You've got a wind machine?"

"You were a dancer?"

Her head turned toward him. He wasn't watching the show. Under the faint light, she found his gaze on her.

"I like hearing truth from you, Bree. It sounds different."

"I've always given you the truth." She'd made a mistake. Let down her guard. "I was a dancer in another life. Back when I was a kid. I stopped dancing when I was fifteen." All of that was truth. He could believe her or not.

"I bet you were incredible."

"No." Her smile felt sad. "But I did enjoy it."

The silks were gone. A man and a woman came out. The spotlight hit them, shining on their blood-red costumes right before the trapeze lowered. The man grabbed the bar, then swung down so that his knees were locked around it. Hanging upside down, he reached for his partner as the trapeze began to lift into the air.

She grabbed his hands as the crowd erupted into applause.

As the trapeze went higher and higher, the two began their act. The man flipped the woman, once, twice, and on the third loop, she landed up on the bar, standing between his legs as he continued to dangle upside down.

"They are incredible." Bree couldn't take her eyes off the show.

"This is the first club of its type down here. I'll be opening one in Vegas later this year. Everyone in Vegas loves a good show."

"I…I didn't know you had business in Vegas." Their voices were low, barely whispers, and Bree realized that she'd leaned close to him. Their heads were near, and to onlookers, it must appear as if they were about to kiss.

"It will be my first venture there. Figured it was time for a change."

Before he could say anything else, Remy emerged from the shadows. He leaned down and whispered something in Kace's ear. She tried to catch the words.

Shipment. Delayed. Trouble.

"I have to go." Kace stood. "Stay here for the rest of the show. And come to see me before you leave."

Then he strode into the darkness.

***

"How do you know Kace?"

Abby stood in front of Bree, her gaze suspicious. They were in the staff area, near the row of lockers that the waiters and waitresses used for storage. It was nearly four a.m., and Bree just wanted to slip away.

Only Abby was blocking her path.

"He's the owner of the club." Bree tried for a careless shrug. "I met him when I got the job."

Abby lifted a brow. "He doesn't let every waitress sit at his table." Her arms crossed over her chest. "You screwing him?"

"No!" The denial was fast and furious. "I'm not, I'm—"

"Easy, jeez. Chill out. I don't care if you are. I just need to know." Abby glanced over her shoulder, then crept closer to Bree. "Because if you've got a thing going with the boss, then I need to make sure you're putting in a good word for me. You know, telling him what an awesome manager I am and all of that." Abby winked.

Bree's breath expelled in a fast rush. "You *are* awesome." That was true. Abby had checked on Bree throughout the night, and Bree had seen her monitoring all of the first-floor staff the same way. "But I'm not sleeping with him."

Abby gave her a quick smile. "Yet."

"He doesn't sleep with the staff!"

Now Abby looked confused. "Why in the hell would you say that?"

Uh… "Because he told me?"

Abby laughed as she slammed her locker shut. "Don't believe everything that Kace says.

The man is a charmer." Her gaze came back to Bree. "But he's also—" Then she stopped, seeming to catch herself.

Bree wasn't about to let that go. "He's also what?"

Abby looked over her shoulder. A few other waitresses were talking just a few feet away. "He's a good boss." Abby straightened her shoulders. "You did a great job tonight, Bree. See you again tomorrow." Without another word, she hurried for the door.

Bree watched Abby in silence, then she quietly closed her locker. Were the other women watching her? She could have sworn she felt their eyes on her, but when she looked their way, they turned their heads. "Good night," she called to them as she ducked her head and headed out. Just when she reached the door—

"Wish I could sleep with the boss. He's hot as fuck."

Her cheeks burned as she caught the comment from one of the other waitresses. Great. Everyone thought she was screwing Kace. She kept her head down, and she hurried through the club. No one stopped her as she made her way to Kace's office, and Bree figured he'd spread the word that the guards weren't supposed to stand in her way. She even passed by Remy, and he just backed up at her approach.

"He's waiting for you." Remy gave a slow nod.

She offered him a weak smile, one that fled right before Bree stormed into Kace's office. Bree swung open that door with authority and—

He was on the phone.

"Right. One million and that's fucking it." He lifted a hand toward her as he kept talking on the phone. "Do I sound like I give a shit? Get it done or disappear."

What? Who said stuff like that? Uh, obviously, Kace. Kace Quick.

He ended the call without another word. Then he leaned back in his chair. Stared at her. He'd changed clothes. The suit was gone. Now he wore a t-shirt and a battered, leather jacket. Beneath the desk, she could see his jeans as he stretched out his long legs.

Her hands twisted in front of her. He was just staring. Had he forgotten that he'd asked to see her? "You said I needed to see you before I left."

His mouth hitched up. "You made it through the first night. Dammit. I'm going to lose my bet with Remy."

She blinked.

"Didn't think you would. I mean, you come in here, looking like some well-bred debutante, and carrying a total BS resume. You're fragile as shit. I think a strong wind would knock you down. I take one look and say, no way does this woman belong in my world." His gaze slid over her. "No way."

His words pissed her off. "You don't know me."

"You look like a lost princess. Shouldn't you be in some fancy world full of ball gowns and ballerinas? I mean, that *is* what you did, right? Dance?"

Pain was a thick knot in her stomach. "My parents died when I was fifteen years old. The life I'd had then died with them." She didn't know why he was grilling her, but she was going to give him the truth, then he'd better back the hell off. "A debutante? No, I was on the street."

Now his gaze jerked to hers.

"There was no family to take me in. Foster kids at fifteen? We're not exactly scooped up by willing families. We're automatically labeled as 'special needs' because of our ages. I got sent to a group home. I got locked away there until I turned eighteen, and the minute I did, I was on the street. *Gladly* on the street." She'd hated that group home and the icy cold that always seemed to consume the place. "I waited tables every single day. And night. I know how to do this job. I don't need some jerk like you giving me a hard time because—"

He rose to his feet. "I'm sorry."

Why did he sound so sincere?

Kace stalked to her side. He stood near her, and as crazy as it seemed, Bree could have sworn that his pose was…protective.

"I'm sorry about your parents." And there was sympathy on his face. "I'm sorry that you lost the life you had with them. I said you were a princess because that is what you fucking remind me of. A woman who should be showered with presents. Someone who should be protected and treasured."

Her shoulders stiffened. "I don't need anyone else protecting me." She could do that job just fine on her own.

"My mistake." His eyes gleamed. "I think I misjudged you."

"It happens a lot." She was always being underestimated, and normally, it didn't bother her. She did her job, and she proved them *wrong*. She had waited tables when she'd left that group home. She'd worked her way through college. Graduated at the top of her class. Gotten into the FBI. All on her own. All without anyone's help or *protection*.

She wasn't looking for some white knight. Hell, no. And even if she had been…that role would never go to a man like Kace Quick.

"It won't happen again," he told her softly. "There is far more to you than meets the eye."

He had no idea.

"And what about you?" Time to do her job. "Are you just the criminal or is there more to you?"

His smile had her breath catching. "Sweet Bree. Since we're both being so incredibly honest with one another, there are a few things you need to realize about me." He wasn't touching her, but she could feel the warmth of his body all around her. "First, I don't like the word 'criminal.' It implies I'm breaking laws. And, since I'm not in a jail…" His sentence trailed off. "Well, I'm obviously a law-abiding citizen. So, let's not use insulting labels with each other, hmm?" His eyes twinkled a bit, and she could have sworn he was laughing at her.

"My bad," she said, and her words indicated that clearly, it *wasn't* her bad.

"Next up, I'm not some horrible monster. I have never hurt anyone in this world. At least, not anyone who did not deserve the pain that was coming to him."

What kind of confession was that?

"I have friends, and I have enemies. You never want to be one of my enemies."

"What happens to your enemies?" Her voice had gone even softer.

He stepped closer. His body *almost* brushed against her. "Any fucking thing I want."

Her heart was pounding too fast in her chest. "And your friends?"

"I take care of them. I protect them."

"I already told you—I don't need protection."

"Maybe you don't. Not today. But if that should change..."

She had no idea what the guy meant. Nothing was going to change. Except she might find evidence to toss his ass in jail. With that in mind... "What happens to your lovers?"

His head tilted. His pupils seemed to expand.

"I heard about the friends and the enemies. What about the lovers?"

His hand lifted. Cupped her cheek. "Trust me, sweetheart, my lovers never have complaints."

"So much arrogance," she muttered. "And you need to stop calling me sweetheart."

He smiled. "It's not arrogance. It's honesty." Then he winked. *Winked.*

"I cannot figure you out." Absolute truth. "You are not what I expected."

"Then maybe we were both wrong." His hand dropped.

Why did she immediately miss his warmth?

He turned his back on her. Headed toward a closet to the right.

"You need to learn to tell people good-bye," she groused. "When a conversation is over, *tell* the person."

He opened the closet, but angled to frown back at her. "What are you talking about?"

"A moment ago, you just hung up on the person you were talking with on the phone."

"Because I was done with that jackass."

She wondered who the jackass had been. "And right now, you just walked away from me. If you're done with our chat and I'm free to go, *tell* me—"

"I'm not done with you." He pulled out a helmet from the closet. "I was just getting you safety gear." Taking his time, he returned to her. Then he pushed the gleaming, black helmet into her hands. "You ride?"

"No." Never.

"That's okay. I'll be driving. All you have to do is hold on."

"I am *not* getting on a motorcycle with you." She shoved the helmet back at him.

Kace didn't take it. "You walked here for your shift. It's four a.m. You seriously think I'm going to let you *walk* back to your place at this hour? What kind of boss would I be if I did that?"

"You are not giving all your staff members a ride on your motorcycle."

"No, tonight, it's just you. Because you're the one who walked here alone."

Okay. Why was she fighting him? For her cover, she *needed* him close. But… "You're dropping me at the door. I don't want you getting ideas. You're not sleeping with me."

He laughed.

She was starting to find his laugh sexy. That was a problem. Her eyes narrowed at him.

"What is it?" Kace asked.

"Swear to me. Swear to me right now that you did not kill those two women I saw on the news."

All traces of humor left his face.

"Because the cops think you did it. The media is running wild with the story. And now you're asking me to hop onto a motorcycle and ride off into the night with you." She shook her head. "I need some kind of reassurance here." If she weren't working a case, no way in hell would she get on the motorcycle with a man like him.

"I swear to you," his gaze held hers, no wavering at all, "that I did not kill Lindsey or Ciara. But when I find out who *did* kill them..." His jaw hardened. "You don't want to know what I'll do. They were good women. They didn't deserve what happened to them."

"No one deserves that," she whispered back. "No one deserves to feel that much fear before death. To have some bastard take your life away."

A muscle flexed along his jaw. "I'm seeing you home safely tonight. All of my staff members are taking precautions. Leaving *with* someone they trust, leaving in pairs. The tourists packed my bar tonight because half of them wanted the thrill of being in a would-be killer's club."

She still held the helmet. "And the other half?"

"They just love a good show."

Bree bit her lower lip.

"Trust me," he rasped. "I'll take care of you."

Her shoulders rolled back. "It's not my home, okay?" She turned and headed for the door. "It's just a place I'm staying at in town. A bed and breakfast. I told you that during my interview." She hadn't been in a real home, not in a very long time.

"Bree?"

He was behind her. She felt his hand brush her shoulder. She wouldn't stiffen. Would not. But she glanced back at him.

"Trust me," he said again.

She didn't reply. A few moments later, they were heading out the back of the club. A motorcycle was parked nearby. Remy waited there, glancing around the dark alley. When he saw them, he appeared to do a double-take.

"Ah, boss..." Remy began.

"I'm taking Bree home. I'll check in tomorrow." He climbed onto the bike. Had the engine revving hard and fast.

Bree held tighter to the helmet.

Remy was watching her. Was that suspicion in his eyes? It was so dark that it was hard to tell for certain.

Kace extended his hand toward her. "Put on the helmet, sweet—uh, Bree."

He'd stopped calling her sweetheart.

She put on the helmet. Squared her shoulders. Then she reached for his hand. His fingers curled around hers, and the electric shot of desire was there again. A surge of need that leapt between them. She didn't know what the hell that was about. Unexpected. Unwanted. But so very, very strong.

Bree straddled the motorcycle. She locked her arms around Kace's waist.

Trust me. His words played through her mind again. And as they shot through the darkness, Bree thought…

No way.

There was no way in hell she could ever trust a man like Kace Quick.

CHAPTER FOUR

Kace braked the motorcycle in front of the small bed and breakfast in the French Quarter. Bree's arms were still around him, her body pressed to his back. He liked the way she felt against him.

He liked her.

Too much.

She slid away from him, hurried off the bike, and pushed the helmet at him. "Thanks for the ride." Bree tucked her hair behind her ear. He liked it when she did that. She seemed nervous when she reached for her hair. Hesitant.

He was learning her tells. Learning all her secrets. And the woman had *plenty* of those. He knew that Bree Harlow was a liar, straight to her core.

He'd brought her home so that he could see where she lived. So that he could apply the right pressure on the owner of the bed and breakfast and get more information on Bree.

She'd made it through the first night at Fantasy. One night down, so many more to go.

When she turned away, he reached out and snagged her hand. His left still gripped the helmet she'd pushed at him, but his right hand circled hers. "You feel it, don't you? When we touch?"

A quick nod. Ah, more honesty.

"What are we going to do about that?" Kace knew what he'd like to do.

"Nothing." Her voice was breathless. "You don't sleep with your staff, remember?"

"Right." He tugged her closer. "I could fire you."

"And I could sue you," she shot right back.

God, he could like this woman. *I think I already do.* "Good. Don't ever take shit from anyone." He let her go. "I'll stay here until you get inside."

She blinked. It was too dark for him to see the gold of her eyes clearly, and he hated that. He rather enjoyed seeing the emotions flash in her eyes.

"Can't figure me out, can you?" Kace laughed softly. "Don't worry. I'm having the same trouble with you."

Her gaze was on his mouth. No, no way. She wouldn't—

Bree leaned forward and pressed a quick kiss to his lips. The kiss lasted all of two seconds. It was the most chaste kiss he'd ever felt in his life.

And he couldn't remember anything turning him on more.

But she immediately backed away. "OhmyGod. What did I do?"

The laughter came from him again. "You kissed me."

"*Why* did I do that?" Bree sounded horrified.

So Kace decided to help her out. "Because you want me. And I want you." They could be honest about this part, at least. "It's going to be a problem."

She snatched her hand from his.

"Be warned, Bree. Next time, I'll kiss you. It will last longer. Be way deeper. The problem is, if I start, I'm worried I may not stop."

"There is no next time."

Then she marched away, hurrying up the steps and into the bed and breakfast. All of the lights inside were off, and he didn't like that. Darkness could be dangerous. Especially for someone like Bree. In *this* town.

So he sat there, and he waited, and when the lights flashed on in the upstairs room—what had to be *her* room—he finally shoved the helmet on his head. He saw her shadow walk past the window. Bree was in safe for the night. She was—

A second shadow joined hers. A bigger shadow that surged toward her. A shadow that *grabbed* her.

Oh, the fuck, *no.*

***

"What in the hell happened tonight?" Grayson had lunged from the shadows and locked his hand around her arm. He swung Bree around to face him. "You stopped transmitting! I got nothing but static all night long, and then I find you coming home with *him!*"

The guy had been waiting in her room? The last thing she'd expected was to find her boss hiding in her closet. Okay, technically, he wasn't in her closet. He'd been standing where—near the window of the bedroom? "I had to ditch the transmitter." She lifted her chin. "Turns out, Kace Quick is a very paranoid man. He gets all of his workers scanned for listening devices every night."

"What?" Shock slackened his mouth. "Are you kidding me?"

"No, and I would have thought the FBI's *intel* would have picked up that little tidbit! I mean, I was walking in there blind. I barely had enough time to yank out the device and crush it beneath my heel." She'd deliberately stumbled into Remy so that she could pull out the small piece of tech. "Kace scanned me personally. If he'd found that tracker on me, he would have kicked me out on my ass."

Grayson was still holding her arm. "He brought you home tonight."

Yes, and things just weren't adding up. "Kace has a protective streak."

"Bullshit. He's a killer, he has—"

The door to her room crashed open. *"Get the fuck away from her!"*

Kace stood in the doorway, his face dark with fury and his hands clenched. He didn't wait for Grayson to comply. Instead, he rushed across the room and grabbed the other man.

Kace was bigger than Grayson, by a few inches, and more muscled, and when he locked his hands on Grayson—

Oh, hell. He's about to assault a federal officer! "Kace, stop!" She yanked free of Grayson and put herself between the two men. "Stop!"

His gaze flew to her face. There was so much fury in his stare. "Are you all right?"

"Yes."

"I saw his shadow. Saw him grab you."

He'd seen all of that from the street?

"Bree, are you sure that you're okay?"

He'd seen that—and then rushed to help her.

She looked over his shoulder and saw the owner of the bed and breakfast, Kelly Queen, frowning and clutching her robe to her chest. Kelly Queen had to be pushing eighty, but she usually moved with the spry energy of a woman half her age. Her bright red hair shot from her head in corkscrew curls. Ms. Queen was definitely not looking pleased. The lines on her face had thickened into an angry scowl.

This was bad. "I'm fine." Bree tried to appear calm. "I'm okay. Really."

"You aren't supposed to have visitors here. Not at this time," Ms. Queen announced, her voice a little too high and sharp. "You're disturbing the other guests."

Were the other guests all in the hallway, craning to see what was happening in her room?

"Who is he?" Kace demanded as he glared at Grayson. "And why did he have his hands on you?"

The best way to handle this—truth. Or at least, part of the truth. "Grayson is my ex."

A growl came from Kace.

Grayson's fingers slid over her shoulder.

"*Get your fucking hand off her.*" Kace's voice was lethal.

Grayson's hand tightened. "I think you're misunderstanding the situation."

"Oh, Lord," Ms. Queen said. "*Lord!*" It sounded like she started to pray.

"Am I misunderstanding?" Kace stared at Bree. "Did you know he was going to be in your room tonight?"

"No." Another truth.

"Did he grab you when you entered?"

"Yes."

His jaw clenched tight, Kace gritted, "Do you want him here?"

"I want you all to leave!" Ms. Queen cried out before Bree could answer. "Leave! I can't handle this! I know who you are, Kace Quick. I know—"

He turned toward her, and, voice without emotion now, he said, "Ms. Queen, I'll be leaving in just a moment. And I'll make sure to provide a very generous donation to make up for the trouble. If you don't mind, though, how about you exit this room and shut the door so I don't provide more of a show for your guests? Shut the door and tell everyone to go back to bed."

Her mouth gaped, then closed. Then she was scurrying out and slamming the door shut. Bree heard Ms. Queen's voice in the hallway as she instructed the other guests to return to their rooms.

"Bree," Grayson was still gripping her shoulder. "I don't know who this bozo is..." Ah, obviously, he was playing along. Like he had a choice. The only other option was to reveal the truth about who they were. "But he needs to get the hell out of here."

Kace didn't speak again. He just moved—fast. He lunged forward and grabbed Grayson's hand, wrenching it from Bree's shoulder and then whirling. When Bree blinked, she realized that Grayson was on his knees, his face was tight with pain as Kace held Grayson's hand—and arm—at a very unnatural angle.

"Let him go," she whispered to Kace.

He did. Immediately. He also moved to stand protectively near her. His attention remained fixed on Grayson. "Get the hell out," Kace ordered flatly. "Don't come near her again. If you do..."

Grayson was on his feet. Glaring. "What? What will you do to me?"

Kace...smiled. And the cold smile in itself was a promise.

Grayson turned his glare on Bree. "We aren't finished."

No, they weren't. She needed to brief him on everything that had happened, but this sure wasn't the time.

"You are finished," Kace assured him. "Bree might have been yours once, but from here on out, she's mine."

Now she jerked in surprise. "I'm not anyone's."

"Get your ass out of here," Kace barked to Grayson. "And if you see Ms. Queen, you be *nice* to her."

Grayson stormed out.

Silence.

Bree turned toward him. "You didn't..." She cleared her throat. Kace thought he'd just saved her from a jealous ex. How should she respond to that scenario? What should she say? Maybe… "Thank you."

"I'll talk to Ms. Queen. He will *not* be getting back in to see you." Kace's eyes narrowed. "What in the hell is the story? Does he live in New Orleans? Did you come down here for him? Or did—"

"I've been trying to get away from him. It's over." Their physical relationship was over. Had been for a while. It had been over almost before it began. "I'm not going back to that place with him again."

Kace's eyes studied her. "Good." He leaned toward her, and Bree thought that he was going to kiss her—

He tucked a lock of hair behind her ear. "Get some rest."

Then he walked toward the door.

She stood there a moment, gaping after him. Kace Quick was supposed to be the big bad in the city. And yet he'd just rushed to her rescue. Since when was the criminal the hero? Or…was it possible…were the others wrong about him? Because he was not fitting the profile that she'd read on him. He wasn't cold and calculating. He was white-hot. Burning with emotions. "I don't get you."

He swung his head toward her and gave Bree a fleeting smile. "If I don't leave now, I'm going to kiss you. Hard and deep, and we already talked about where that would lead." He rolled back his shoulders. "I didn't like that SOB being here. I didn't like his hand being on you. I find that—where you're concerned—I'm a bit predatory. Possessive."

"We *just* met."

"Yeah, like that matters. Some connections are primal. That's what we are. Primal. And if you try to say you don't feel it, too…" A shrug. "You should know, I've figured out how to tell when you lie."

No way. But… "I feel it." Her admission. She found herself walking toward him. Pulled to him. He turned to fully face her, putting his back against the door. "No one has ever tried to save me before." That was another truth.

"Then you've been hanging around with straight-up assholes."

She laughed. "You…are an asshole. Everyone says so." Yet she closed the space between them. Put her hands on his shoulders. Curled her fingers over his jacket.

"I am. Don't deny it." His eyes gleamed. "But I am an asshole who would *never* hurt you."

"Kace…"

"Step back, or I'm taking your mouth."

She didn't step back. And it wasn't because of the case. Wasn't because she was supposed to be getting close to him. Supposed to be learning all of his secrets. She rose onto her tip-toes. She brought her mouth closer to his because she wanted him.

Primal. Primitive. Yes, that was the way it was between them.

She wanted him.

Nothing would have stopped her right then. Nothing.

This time, the kiss wasn't chaste. She met him with her lips parted, and his tongue immediately plunged inside. He didn't kiss her softly. Didn't treat her like she was some fragile piece of glass. He ravaged her mouth. Kissed her with rough hunger, savage need. His mouth fed on hers. His hands curled around her hips, and he lifted her up, moving her higher so that she felt the long, hard length of his cock shoving against her.

She gasped into his mouth. Realized that her nipples had gone tight and that she was arching against his cock. Realized it wouldn't take much to have her raking her nails down his back—his *naked* back. Because the need was that hot. That consuming.

A firestorm, burning her alive.

"*Stop,*" she whispered against his mouth.

He did. He lowered Bree to her feet. His breath sawed in and out, and the lust was clear to see on his face. "Much better," he muttered.

Yes, that kiss had been *way* better.

"There's a bed behind you, Bree. Want to fuck?"

Well, things had been better until *then.*

"Just kidding, sweet Bree." His fingers skimmed down her cheek. "Go to bed. Alone. You're safe tonight."

It was barely night. Dawn would be there before she knew it.

"I'll see you back at Fantasy. Nine p.m. sharp."

She wished that she could understand him. "Are all the things people say about you true?"

A half-smile curled his lips. "No."

Bree was starting to think—

"The truth is one hell of a lot worse. Don't forget that." He inclined his head. "Night, Bree."

And he left her. She was still aching for him, still turned on, and still trying to figure out if Kace Quick truly was a monster. Or if maybe he could be something more.

***

When Kace got back to the street, Bree's *ex* was long gone. Too bad. He would have enjoyed beating the shit out of the guy. Why the hell did the joker think he could just break into Bree's room? *I didn't like his hands on her.*

That would be a problem. Kace knew he was getting far too involved with Bree. And they'd only just met.

He climbed onto the bike, but didn't start the motorcycle. Instead, he reached into his jacket and pulled out the wallet he'd taken from Bree's ex. The fool hadn't even noticed it when Kace had made the grab. Mostly because Kace was good with his hands. When he'd been a teenager, he'd spent his nights lightening the loads of tourists along the streets. A little bump barely felt at all by most people, and he'd had cash in his hand.

This time, though, he wasn't interested in cash. He wanted to know who the hell that bastard had really been. Because the fellow had looked familiar. Kace opened the wallet. Saw the FBI badge inside. Fucking hell.

FBI Special Agent Grayson Wesley.

Rage burned inside of him. He shoved the wallet back into his jacket. Grabbed for his helmet and then was surging into the night. He wanted Bree, but he'd be damned if he let her use him. There was no way he would fall into an FBI trap.

Maybe it was time to show the Feds just who was the real boss of this town.

***

He didn't take her body to the St Louis Cathedral. He was tempted, oh, so very tempted. But the cops were watching that location. He'd left two bodies there for the cops to find, and the uniforms had staked out the space, being ever so vigilant now.

They had no imagination. They didn't get that the whole city was his. He could do anything he wanted.

So, he chose another spot. He headed out onto the trolley tracks, picking the Canal Street Station. The first trolley wouldn't come out until closer to six a.m. He hoped the driver was paying attention. If not, maybe one of the riders would find his lady.

He carried her across the tracks. The darkness hid him so well. He didn't put her *on* the tracks, that seemed too obvious, so he put her on the side. Spread her out.

Her hands were still bound together. She'd been a fighter. A surprise, that. His gloved fingers trailed over her cheek, and her eyes flickered open.

"Hello, there." He was glad that she'd woken up for this part. This was the best part, after all.

Her lips parted. He knew she'd scream. They always tried to scream, so he jerked tight the rope that he'd wrapped around her neck. Only a wheeze slipped from her lips as he pulled that rope so taut. Her body jerked and twisted as she strained against him, and he just kept his fierce grip on the rope. Her mouth was wide open, her eyes so wide. The light from the Canal Street

Station provided him with just enough illumination to see—

"Hey!" The shout had his shoulders stiffening as he glanced over his shoulder and saw a bum staggering toward him. "What are you doing?"

Fuck. No one should have seen him. No one should be there, but some piece of shit bum was staggering his way.

He let go of the rope around her neck. She pulled in a gasping breath. *Still alive.*

The bum was ruining *everything*. Hating it, he pulled out the knife from his boot. And he shoved the blade into her chest. Her blood poured out, wet and disgusting, but he'd done the job.

He whirled and ran as the bum screamed out after him. The bum was screaming as loud as he could, and for a moment, he thought about killing that bastard.

Then he saw the flash of police lights in the distance.

Get away. Get away. He leapt across the trolley tracks and ran fast for the vehicle he'd stashed nearby.

His victim had been found *before* she'd taken her last breath. But he didn't worry. She wouldn't survive. There was no way she'd live to tell the world who he was. He'd aimed for the bitch's heart. She'd bleed out.

I have her blood on me.

Shit. He had to get rid of the evidence. He'd made his first mistake that night. His first and his last.

The Feds won't touch me. I'm invincible. They can't touch me…

CHAPTER FIVE

Her phone was ringing. Over and over again. Bree let out a ragged groan as her hand slapped toward her nightstand. On the third try, she managed to actually hit her phone. Bree pulled it toward her, squinting at the screen.

Grayson.

She shot up in bed and put the phone to her ear. "What's happening?"

"He took another one." Fury vibrated in his voice. "The bastard dumped her near the Canal Street trolley tracks."

Bree's breath heaved in and out as adrenaline fueled her body, pushing away the remnants of sleep.

"Only someone saw the perp this time. Homeless guy caught him in the act."

What?

"The vic is at the hospital. She's still alive, Bree. Do you hear me? *Still alive.*"

Bree jumped from the bed.

"If she survives, she'll be able to ID her attacker. We'll be able to throw Kace Quick in jail for the rest of his life."

Bree stumbled as she reached for her jeans.

"Get down to our Lady of Saints hospital, right the hell now. Come meet me."

He hung up the phone.

And Bree realized that a cold, heavy knot of fear had formed in her stomach.

***

Chaos. When she burst into the ER, Bree felt as if she'd stepped into a madhouse. Nurses and doctors were running everywhere, and patients crowded the small space. Some were bleeding, some were vomiting, some were—

"Bree, back here!" Grayson barked.

He stood near the swinging ER doors. Dominic was at his side. Bree hurried through the crowd toward them.

"Freaking food poisoning on a tour group," Dominic muttered as his gaze swept over the crowd in the waiting room. "The place is a zoo."

Bree squared her shoulders. "How's the vic?"

"Not good." Grayson turned and shoved open the swinging ER doors. Dominic motioned for Bree to go in next, and she followed their team leader.

"The docs don't think she's going to make it." Grayson's steps were fast, and Bree had to double-time it in order to keep up with him. "The perp was strangling her, but when our witness interrupted, he pulled out a knife and drove it into her chest."

Jesus. "Using a knife wasn't part of his MO."

"Guess he got desperate," Dominic said from behind her. "Bastard knew he didn't have time to finish her off by strangulation, so he pulled out a blade. Our witness said he could hear police sirens coming in the distance, and he was yelling for all he was worth."

"Karin is with the vic now," Grayson added as he turned right when the corridor branched. "I wanted an agent with her at all times. If she says *anything,* I want to know about it."

A nurse started to approach Grayson, but she took one look at his angry expression and halted in her tracks. Then he made another turn, one that took them toward an operating room. They didn't enter the room, though, but just watched from behind a large window as—

One of the doctors backed away from the table. Blood covered his gloves. He shook his head.

Inside the room, Karin turned away from the table, her solemn gaze sliding toward the window and immediately locking on Grayson.

Her lips moved, and Bree could clearly see the other agent say—

She's gone.

"Fuck," Grayson snarled.

Beside Bree, Dominic let out a rough sigh.

Bree didn't say a word. Her attention was focused on the woman who lay so still on that table. She could see the woman's blond hair. Could see her neck and the purple bruises. The vic's chest was soaked in blood.

"We don't have an ID on her yet," Dominic noted softly to Bree. "But she fits the Strangler's victim profile. Early twenties, blond hair, pretty."

"I'm sure we'll find a connection to Kace," Grayson snapped. Then he whirled on Bree. "We need to interview the witness. I want him talking to a sketch artist and giving a *full* description of the killer. I want—"

"The guy is higher than a kite." Dominic shook his head. "Boss, I already tried talking to Hank Cannon twice now. He says the boogeyman attacked the woman."

Grayson's hands clenched and unclenched at his sides. "Then we talk to him a third time. And a fourth. A fifth. We talk to him as long as it takes, until we get more than a description of the boogeyman! A real sonofabitch did this. A flesh and blood killer, and I want him."

Bree's gaze darted toward the victim. The machine beside the woman showed a long, flat, green line.

"He stole my freaking wallet, Bree."

Her head swung toward Grayson. "What?"

His jaw was set. "When he was playing the alpha asshole at your room, Kace Quick swiped my ID. So he knows I'm FBI. And that means he'll be suspecting you." His eyes narrowed with warning. "Get a cover story in place. And get ready for the asshole to grill you."

Dammit.

"We have to bring Kace Quick down. There are three dead women in this city now. *Three.* I won't have anymore. Not on my watch."

***

At nine p.m., Kace sat behind his desk, waiting for Bree to make an appearance. He'd given orders to Remy that as soon as Bree arrived, he wanted her escorted to his office.

His orders were always followed at his clubs. Actually, his orders were followed everywhere.

So, at nine-oh-one, there was a brief knock at his door.

"Come in," Kace called.

The door swung open. Bree stood there, dressed in her black uniform, looking far too sexy with her wide, golden eyes and her slick, red lips.

Remy waited just behind her, and Kace's right-hand guy looked far from pleased with his tight jaw and angry eyes. The guy knew all about Bree's so-called ex. Remy had been the one to tear into the special agent's life that day. And he'd found more than a few surprises. Kace wouldn't be revealing all, he did like to keep some secrets close, but it was time to see just what truths he could shake from sexy Bree.

Kace didn't rise. He waved his hand toward Bree. "You going to keep standing there?" He tilted his head. "Are you going to come closer?"

Her tongue swiped over her lower lip. "I feel like the fly. And you're the spider, inviting me into your web."

A pretty apt description.

She crept into his web. Remy didn't follow her. Instead, Remy shut the door, giving Kace the privacy he needed.

Her steps were a little uncertain as she advanced, and her scent teased his nose when she sat in the chair across from him. Lavender. Must be the body lotion she used. He rather liked it.

"I guess I'm here for the scan, huh? That the way we'll be starting every night?"

"Not time for that just yet." He leaned back in his chair. "I'm assuming you saw the news."

Her long lashes flickered. "Y-yes."

"The Press and the cops haven't made the connection yet, but they will." He watched her carefully, wanting to see what she'd give away. "The woman who was murdered today—I know her. Just as I knew the other two victims."

"On the news, she's listed as a Jane Doe—"

"Her name is Amelia Sanderson. She's twenty-five years old. And a year ago, she worked in my club, Nightmare."

Her breath came faster. He could see the quick rise and fall of her chest.

"She became obsessed with me." He kept his voice low and easy as he spoke. "Fixated, if you will. I would find her waiting for me in my office. Naked. Once, she even snuck into my bedroom. She didn't understand my rule about not fucking employees." Not that he would have fucked Amelia. She'd already been like a broken flower. So desperate to survive. Her life had never been easy. He'd wanted to help her. Unfortunately, he'd just hurt her worse.

"I had to let her go," he continued carefully. He didn't add that Amelia had been hooked on drugs. He didn't allow his employees to use. He'd sent her to a clinic, but Amelia had disappeared days later. That was why he didn't think the cops had identified her yet. Amelia had been hiding, living on the streets, for months.

But someone had found her. Someone who'd wanted to use her…in order to hurt him.

"I let her go," he said once more. "I didn't kill her."

"I-I never said—"

"So, you can go back to your FBI lover, and you can fucking tell him that *I didn't kill her.*"

Her expression didn't change. There was no stunned shock that he'd straight up called her out. No fast flushing of her skin to show that he'd gotten to her.

She kept her control. Rather impressive. He waited for her to speak, but she didn't. Bree just kept staring at him with eyes that were too freaking gorgeous.

He was the one to finally prompt, "Bree? Don't you want to say something?"

"Grayson is FBI. And I'm sure this isn't the first time you've come across someone in law enforcement who might be…" Bree seemed to search for words before finally saying, "Less than perfect."

He'd come across some straight-up assholes and crooks before. He'd also been lucky enough to find some cops he could trust. Though they probably shouldn't trust him.

"How did you know he's FBI?" Bree asked as she tilted her head to the left. Her hair brushed over her shoulder.

He reached into his desk drawer and tossed the stolen wallet toward her. "He might be missing this."

She reached for the wallet. "Grayson was a mistake."

You think? "He's FBI. The FBI and the NOPD think I'm a killer. They want to throw me in a cell and never let me out." He shrugged. "Unfortunately for them, that's not happening." Though they could certainly try their hardest. "A serial killer is at work in this town. That's obvious to everyone. But I'm not that guy."

She opened the wallet. Stared down at the ID inside.

You think you know him, Bree? Trust me, you don't.

"The reporters said the latest victim was killed around five a.m. this morning." Her gaze rose from the wallet to pin him. "Where were you then?"

"You're asking about my alibi? Seriously?" Anger twisted in his gut, but his voice was ice cold.

"You say you're not a killer—"

"No, sweetheart, I said I'm not *the* killer that they are looking for." He'd never claimed that he hadn't killed before.

And he saw that understanding flash in her eyes. Understanding and a flicker of fear. Now she was catching on. This green agent was in way over her head. She'd gotten stuck in a battle she didn't truly understand. But he could be kind to her, in his way.

Kace smiled. "You're done here, Bree. Clean out your locker and get out of Fantasy."

She dropped the wallet onto the top of the desk. "You're firing me?"

"Yes, that would appear to be what I'm doing." Good thing she was following along.

Bree shot to her feet. "Because I once fucked an FBI agent? *That's* why you're firing me? It was a one-time thing, I can assure you of that. I didn't realize who he was at the time. When I learned the truth, I wasn't going to let it happen again."

Those words sounded honest. The fire in her eyes looked real, too. Interesting.

"One time," Kace murmured. "And yet he was in your room last night." His gaze raked her. "You must be pretty unforgettable."

Her chin notched up. "You have no idea."

Okay, shit, now she was just turning him on more. Because the woman *would not* act in a way he could predict. When he'd told her to collect her stuff, she should have folded in on herself. Given up. Not told him that sex with her would be insane and unforgettable.

Which he already knew it *would* be. The things they could do together…

"I did a good job last night. I waited all my tables. My customers had no complaints."

Except for the jackass who'd gotten handsy. He'd had complaints—when they shoved him and his buddies out of the door.

But Bree wasn't done. Her eyes blazed as she declared, "So I slept with a Fed. What does that have to do with anything?"

"Bree Harlow doesn't exist." He dropped bombshell number two.

Then waited for her denial.

None came.

The woman was so damn *interesting*. "Care to explain why it is that when I dig deeper into your past, nothing is there?" Kace prompted. This should be good.

"Sure. Fine. Whatever. It's because I wanted a fresh start. Because I left my old life behind when my parents were killed." She swallowed. "Because I got tired of having my name flashed in every headline out there. I reinvented myself, okay? And I'm glad I did. Sometimes we need to escape our past."

He rose from his chair. Stalked around the desk. Stood right beside her. "Who were you?" Now he was curious. He should have kicked her out by now. He *knew* she was a Fed, and yet—

"When I was fifteen years old, I came home to find my parents stabbed to death in the living room. I screamed and screamed, and then I realized the killer was still in the house with me."

Every muscle in his body locked down. "What?" That was *not* the shit he'd expected to hear. The anger in his gut transformed into something much more dangerous.

"I realized the bastard was still there when he put his knife to my stomach." She jerked up her shirt, revealing a long, thin scar that slid from her belly button to her right side. "The blade cut into me. I-I hadn't heard him approach. I just felt his knife while I was staring at my parents on the floor."

He wanted to *destroy.*

Instead, Kace's fingertips lifted and lightly traced the scar. "What happened?"

"I don't think he expected me to fight. I think…I mean, to him, I was just this kid. This hysterical kid who'd walked into a blood bath. He probably thought I'd be easy pickings."

Not you.

"I drove my elbow back into him. I hit him as hard as I could. He let me go, probably because he was more surprised than anything else. I ran. I ran as fast as I could for the front door. And I didn't stop running. I didn't stop until a police officer found me in the middle of the road. His lights hit me, and I realized I had blood covering me."

His fingers traced the scar.

"By the time the police went to my house, the killer was gone. And…" Now her voice trailed away.

But Kace wanted to hear more. "What happened?"

"My parents were dead. We'd fought earlier that night. A stupid, ridiculous fight because I wanted to go out with my friends, and my dad didn't want me to. The neighbors heard us arguing. I left, and when I came back, they were dead." She bit her lower lip. "But the Press went with a different story. They thought *I'd* killed them, that the knife wound in my stomach was a result of either my father or my mother fighting back. You see, their killer was never found, and as time passed, I became a pariah in my city."

His hand slid to her hip. Her skin felt like silk beneath his touch.

"Josie Shepard died when I turned eighteen. I killed her. I buried her. That girl had nothing but pain in her past, and I wanted a fresh start. So yeah, Bree Harlow doesn't exactly have a full background that you can dig up online, but she's real. She's standing right in front of you."

And he realized he was staring at someone who might actually understand him. Someone who'd felt the same staggering pain and rage.

If she was telling the truth.

His head bent toward her. His lips pressed to hers.

Kace felt the jolt of surprise rock through her, and her hands flew up, pressing to his chest.

"I spill my dark secrets to you," she whispered, "and you kiss me?"

"It was barely a kiss," he rasped right back. "Let's try harder." And he did. Her lips were parted, and he took full advantage. His tongue swept into her mouth, and her taste ignited him. She gave a little moan in the back of her throat, one that made the lust spike higher and darker inside of him. His dick was rock hard, shoving against the front of his jeans, and he wanted to strip away her clothes and sink *into* her.

His hands curled around her hips, and he lifted her up. Still kissing her, he spun them and sat her on the edge of his desk. Then he moved in between her spread legs, even as he pulled her closer to him. His mouth feasted on hers. He'd always enjoyed kissing, the sensual feel of lips and tongue, but with Bree, it was something different.

Everything felt different with her. Hotter. Wilder.

Fucking her would feel fantastic.

"Wait!" She pulled her mouth from his. Her breath came in quick pants. "I didn't…I didn't think we were doing this. You don't get involved with employees—"

She was so freaking adorable. He kissed her lips again. "Sweetheart, don't you remember? I just fired you." They were free and clear to commence fucking right then and there. The first time would be on his desk. The second would be against the wall. For the third, maybe he'd take her back to his place.

But she shoved against him. Hard.

He stepped back. Exhaled on a long, rough breath.

"You can't fire me! And you sure can't screw me right after you do it!" She jumped off his desk, glowering, and stabbed her index finger into his chest. "My ex is a Fed. What-the-hell-ever. I'd think that you might actually like that."

Now his brows lifted. "Why would I like that?" Kace was genuinely confused, a first for him.

"Because he's investigating you!" The words blasted out. "That's what he was telling me in my room last night! That he thought you were the man who'd murdered those women behind the St. Louis Cathedral. He wanted me to stay away from you!"

Kace shrugged. "Maybe you should heed the guy's advice."

"Did you kill them?"

He stared her straight in the eyes. "No."

Her gaze searched his. Was she trying to see if he was lying? Telling the truth? She'd never be able to read him. No one ever could.

"Screw him over," she urged softly. "You don't like the Feds. I don't like him. Grayson lied when we hooked up. Pretended to be someone else. I wouldn't have slept with him if I'd known the truth."

She was good. He had to give her that. He suspected that Bree mixed just enough truth and lies together that she sounded…believable.

"Piss him off. Let me keep working here."

"It would probably piss your ex off more if I fired you, but then had mind-blowing sex with you." He smiled at her.

Her brow furrowed. "You're crazy, you know that?"

Another shrug. "You aren't the first to make the claim." She could join the line on that one.

"I'm a damn good waitress."

Actually, she was. But… "You were the last hire, sweetheart. Even if it weren't for the FBI, it turns out that I don't need you. I need a bartender, not—"

"I can tend bar. I can do that job, no problem." A desperate edge sharpened her words. "I can wait tables. I can even spin from those silks that you've got hanging from your ceiling."

His smile faded.

"I can do *anything,*" Bree threw at him. "You name it. I am not losing this job. I won't let you kick me out."

My, my, someone was determined. Time to see just *how* determined. "Then I think you have yourself a *new* job." He rubbed his jaw as he considered this new development. "Can't wait to see you in the air, but you're going to need a new uniform."

"Uh, what?"

He turned away from her, the better to conceal his expression. "You said you could do the silks, didn't you?"

"I—" Just that, nothing more.

He headed for the door. Yanked it open. Remy was waiting a few feet away. "Change of plans," he told his buddy. "You won't be escorting Bree to her locker and then kicking her ass out."

A gasp from behind him. "You jerk! You were going to have Remy—"

"She'll be doing the silks tonight," he added with a firm nod. "So she'll need a costume."

Remy blinked at him. "Want to say that again?"

"The silks." He flashed his killer grin and finally glanced back at Bree. Ah, yes, now the lovely color was in her cheeks. "You *did* say you could do them, I believe? Because if you didn't, I'm afraid there is no other job available." He was calling her bluff. No way would Bree be able to—

"I thought you said you needed a bartender."

Sparring with her was too much fun. "I was wrong. I only need an aerial performer. If you can't do that job, there's nothing here for you."

"What about Marie?" Remy asked. "I thought she was doing the silks."

"Marie quit. She texted Abby and said she was done."

Frowning, Remy pulled out his phone. As his fingers swiped over the screen, Bree marched toward Kace. "I can do the silks. I told you last night, I used to be a dancer. I also competed in gymnastics until I was fifteen years old."

Until her parents had died. He swallowed. "Bree—"

"I still work out. I can do the silks. I *will* do them, and you won't be able to take your eyes off me."

Kace had a flash of Bree wearing one of those tiny outfits that the performers used. He could see her limbs winding around the silks as the lights focused just on her. On her legs. Her breasts. "Uh, wait, Bree..." *Maybe this is a bad idea.*

"Get a good seat." Her finger jabbed into his chest. "You don't want to miss this show."

CHAPTER SIX

"Tell me you know what the hell you are doing." Abby put her hands on her hips as she glared at Bree. "Because there is no way I'm sending you up there if you are just going to fall and break your neck." The floor manager stared at Bree as if she'd lost her mind.

She hadn't.

Bree eased out a slow breath as she stared into the mirror. She'd been scanned per Kace's rules, and now she was in a costume. *Not* the first costume that she'd been offered. That one had been a nude costume with some carefully placed faux diamonds. From a distance, it had looked as if her breasts, ass, and sex were just covered by the glittering gems. Bree had wanted more coverage, thank you very much.

So now she wore a black leotard with a back that crisscrossed with strips of black lace. Her legs were bare, the better for her to move and twist during the act. Basic, and probably not at all what Kace had in mind, but screw him. This was the costume she'd wear during her performance.

"Bree?" Abby prompted. Her eyes showed her worry.

"I'm not going to break my neck." She would have liked more rehearsal time—she'd gotten two hours backstage with the other performers. More time would have been *great.* But she did know what she was doing. Before the waitressing job had become available, the FBI had actually planned to send her in for the aerial silk performer spot, only that spot had been taken before Bree could apply.

"What happened to the other girl?" Bree asked. "The one from last night." She adjusted the leotard on her shoulder. "She was fabulous."

"She texted me and said she was quitting." Anger hummed in Abby's voice. "Marie Argeneaux better not think of ever working in this town again."

Bree could clearly see Abby's reflection in the mirror. The other woman looked *pissed* as she spoke of Marie.

But then Abby released a long breath. "I guess it's a good thing we have you," Abby murmured. She patted Bree's shoulder. "Way to be a team player, Bree."

Right. She was all about the team. Her FBI team. No way was she going to let them down.

Abby turned away, and Bree's hand flew out to touch her arm. "Did you hear about the woman who was killed near the trolley tracks?"

"The police released her name." Fear flickered in Abby's eyes.

"You knew her."

A nod. "Amelia was…troubled. She needed help."

Bree decided to push a little more. "Kace told me about her. Said she'd gotten obsessed with him."

The fear vanished from Abby's eyes, and a coldness took its place. "Some women will do anything to get a little power in this town. But Kace isn't a man that you screw with."

Bree let her hand fall. "He wants to fire me."

"Then I hope your show is really spectacular tonight. Don't give him an excuse." Abby nodded briskly. "I'll be on the floor watching." She hurried away.

Well, so much for getting an ally or any good intel from *her*. Bree glanced back in the mirror—

And realized why Abby had been so quick to leave.

Kace was there. Standing a few feet behind Bree. She gave a little jump when she saw him. "Jesus!"

"No."

She frowned at him. Did he think that was funny? "I'd say you're more like the devil."

Now he strode toward her. "Far more accurate."

Her heart was racing because he'd startled her and *not* because any part of her was glad to see him.

"You can back out." He stood behind her, his larger body seeming to dwarf hers in the mirror. "You don't have to do this. When I made the suggestion, I was fucking around." His voice roughened. "You don't need to—"

"I spent the last two hours rehearsing. I've got this." She stared at their reflections.

His hand lifted, and his fingers slid down her arm. Goosebumps followed in the wake of his touch.

"I…I used to teach some aerial classes." Another truth. And an understatement at the same time. She'd taught every year during college. "When you have a talent and you need to make money, you use whatever you've got." She wasn't as good as the girl from last night. No freaking way was she on Marie's level. But she wasn't about to fall to her death, either.

"You look sexy as hell."

Her lips parted. "It's…um, the most concealing costume that was in stock."

"I know. It's still too damn small." He shook his head. "No, you just look too good in it."

She fought a smile. "Is it hard to give compliments? Like, do you have some issue that stops you from saying nice things?"

His head cocked. He stared into the mirror, stared at *her,* and said, "You are the most beautiful woman I've seen."

He sounded as if he meant those words.

Then Kace shook his head. "Don't go onto the silks."

She had to go onto them. Losing her position at Fantasy wasn't an option. "I have to perform tonight. My boss is a real asshole." But she smiled at him in the mirror. "Don't worry. I'll be fine."

"I was screwing around. I thought you'd tell me to fuck off. You didn't."

Her fingers rose and pressed to his. "I know what I'm doing. Don't worry."

Abby appeared again. Cleared her throat. "Ah, it's time."

Great. Abby had caught her cuddling with the boss. Another faux pas, but whatever. Bree had a show to do. She pulled away from Kace. "Don't forget to get a good seat," she called over her shoulder.

Abby's face was tense. "Please don't fall," she whispered to Bree.

Obviously, no one had faith in her. Maybe Abby or Kace should have come to watch a bit of the rehearsal. They wouldn't have been so nervous if they had.

But she didn't have time to think about them any longer. The lights had gone out in the club. Midnight. Showtime.

And she was the first act, the warm-up for the better performers. After pulling in a deep breath, Bree squared her shoulders. When the haunting strains of the song she'd picked out began to play, she walked forward. The aerial silks were already lowered for her. She reached up for them. They were white, a perfect contrast to her black outfit. She wrapped the silks around her forearms…and when the silks lifted, she flew into the air.

***

Remy gave a low whistle as he leaned back in his chair, the better to watch the show. "I did not expect this from her."

Kace's fingers tightened around the glass of whiskey in his hand. He didn't look away from Bree. He couldn't. Her body was twisting and turning as she rose and fell with the silks. Incredibly graceful and incredibly gorgeous. She moved with a fluid elegance that was one of the sexiest things he'd ever seen. When she dipped her body down, angling so that her legs were twisted around the silks but her head was pointing toward the ground—

"Damn, that woman is *limber.*"

"Shut the fuck up. I'd hate to break your face."

Remy shut up. Smart man.

Kace kept watching the show. She was rising again, pulling herself up as if the motion was totally effortless. Then she began to spin, over and over, faster and faster, like a ballerina whipping around and around. He couldn't believe what he was seeing. He'd just been pushing her, tossing out total bullshit when he said that she'd have to take the aerial job if she wanted to stay on at Fantasy. His intent had been to get her out of the club. Despite Bree's story about her past, he knew the woman was FBI. Yes, she'd sounded honest, and maybe that shit *had* happened. He had a PI checking for a double-murder that matched the description she'd given him. But he didn't trust Bree.

He did want her, though. More with every single moment.

She'd wound herself up in the silks. She was high above them, and his jaw clenched. When the other performer had performed a similar trick last night, he hadn't even given it another thought. The silks had her, so she'd be safe, right?

Only…the silks seemed too thin as they held Bree. The trick far too dangerous. And when she let go, when her body began to spin as the silks unraveled and she hurtled to the floor, Kace realized that he'd leaned forward. His entire body had gone tense.

Then the silks gave a little jerk. She grabbed them, lifted herself up, and then she was surging forward as the crowd erupted into applause.

The spotlight hit her as Bree's bare feet touched onto the floor. She let go of the silks. The light showed her gorgeous, smiling face.

Then the room plunged into darkness.

He knew she'd disappear into the darkness. The routine dictated that the aerial silk performer went to the back while the next act prepared. Kace rose to his feet.

But Remy's hand flew out and his fingers wrapped around Kace's wrist. "I thought you didn't get involved with employees."

"I'm the boss. I can make any rule I want." Right then, every cell in his body was demanding that he get to Bree.

"You know she's here to bring you down."

Remy sounded legitimately concerned. He smiled. Remy had worked his way up to Kace's inner circle. The guy wasn't just a bodyguard. He was Kace's right-hand. "I can let her try. And while she's trying, we'll have one hell of a good time."

"Dammit, man, be careful."

Wasn't he always?

Remy let Kace go. As if he'd had any choice.

Kace stalked through the crowd, the other members of his security team making sure no one got in his way. He headed for the backstage area.

Each of the performers had been given a small dressing room. When he reached Bree's room, he turned to the guard who'd tailed him. A tall, wide-shouldered guy named Franco Wyels. Franco had plenty of tats and plenty of attitude. He was also one of Kace's most loyal guards. Franco had worked with Kace for years. "Anyone tries to get inside," Kace told him, "kick their asses."

Franco smiled. "Consider them kicked," he said with relish. Franco liked it when things got rough.

Kace figured if some horny bastard had just watched Bree's show and now had plans to make a move on her, the jerk deserved an ass beating.

Of course, I'm a horny bastard, too. But he wasn't going in there to fuck Bree. At least, he didn't think that was the plan.

Kace didn't knock. He owned the bar, so why knock? He headed inside, and Bree spun toward him with a gasp.

"What in the hell?" Bree demanded. "I could have been naked!"

She was far too close to that already. He grabbed a robe from the back of the door. Stalked to her. Stuffed her arms in the sleeves and—

Bree jerked away from him. "What are you doing? I can dress myself."

She *should* do it. He spun so that his back was to her. "Cover up."

There were rustles behind him. "You're a prude." Now she seemed surprised. "I heard a million different stories about you being a badass, but not one single story about you being—"

He turned back to face her. "I'm trying not to fuck you."

"Well, since I haven't *offered* you anything, it's not an option."

He sucked in a breath, but just caught her lavender scent. "No more silks."

"Wasn't I good enough?" There was a flicker of something in her eyes. Uncertainty?

He stepped toward her. "You were too good. Every guy in the bar is lusting after you. I had to put Franco at the door because I was afraid one of those fools would come in here, wanting more."

Her gaze swept over him. "Hate to break it to you. One guy did come in..."

"And I want you more than all the others." A truth that he didn't even hesitate to give her. The way his life worked—when he saw something he wanted, he took it. And, yes, even knowing that Bree was probably working with the Feds, he still wanted her. Though he'd been trying hard not to take...

The timing was wrong. Worse than wrong. Dangerous. Because there was a twisted freak out there, killing the women that many assumed Kace had fucked. Women who all looked far too much like Bree. So, if he let the attraction between them explode…

I could be putting a target on her.

Kace squared his shoulders. "I'll have Franco take you home."

"You're not *still* firing me?" Before he could speak, she stepped forward, closing the last bit of distance between them so that her body brushed against his. She'd put on the black robe, belted it, but it only hung to mid-thigh on her. "I just worked my ass off on the silks for you tonight! And you're going to—"

"There won't be another silk show until next Friday night. The performances at Fantasy are only on the weekends." And they charged more for admission when there was a show. "If you stay, we'll work on a practice schedule with the other performers." He swallowed. "But you're getting a different costume. One that covers way more."

"Prude. I'll wear whatever I want. For your information, this one is good for me because it lets my legs wrap around the silks better."

Of course, that made him think of her legs wrapping around *him*. "I'm not a prude." She should drop that assumption. "I just don't like sharing."

Her eyes widened. She'd added extra make-up to her eyes before the performance. Her lashes were long, dark, and black liner had been applied to give her eyes a cat-like appearance. Her lips were red and sexy.

"I'm not yours to share."

He'd shared her with the whole crowd that night. It had been all he could do not to punch Remy in the face. *Limber.* Horny sonofabitch. "There are a few things you should know about me."

She stared at him.

"I'm possessive." One of his worst traits. But it came from having nothing. When you grew up fighting for every single thing, you held tight to what did matter. "When I'm with a woman, it's just me. I never share."

"I'm not—"

"I'm jealous." Because so much had been taken from him over the years. "I'm a possessive and jealous bastard, but I am a damn good lover."

"Bragging—"

"I'd have you screaming in two minutes." Not bragging. Just stating a fact. "And you'd be coming harder than you ever have before."

Her eyes widened. "You are so full of yourself."

He smiled at her. "I never make a promise I can't keep." That was also true.

She shook her head. "I don't get you."

No, most people didn't. But he wasn't done warning her. And that's precisely what his words were—a warning. "I don't forgive enemies. Betray me once, and you're dead to me."

Her breath hitched.

"I'm a terrible enemy to have." His hand rose and curled against her cheek. "But I'm the best lover you'd ever want."

He waited for her response. For her to tell him to screw off or—

Bree's hand lifted and her fingers wrapped around his wrist. His heart pounded harder. His reaction to her was off the charts, and that worried him. When he wanted someone this badly…it wouldn't end well. Couldn't.

"I'm possessive." She stared into his eyes. "I don't share my lovers. And I don't have casual sex. I tried that once. I hooked up with a stranger in a bar. Let the chemistry take over, and you know what happened?"

His jaw had clenched. *Jealousy*. He'd warned her—

"I found out that I'd had sex with an FBI agent."

"Do you want me to kick his ass?" Or, even better, make the guy vanish? He'd be more than happy to do both.

She blinked at him. "Do you do that a lot? Kick ass?"

"I do whatever is necessary." She could read between the lines there. She was undercover, the woman would know his hands were far from clean. He couldn't remember the last time they'd been clean. Probably when he'd been a kid. Before he was tried for murder. He'd been eighteen the first time he'd been dragged into a courtroom and accused of a brutal crime.

He wondered what she knew about that old case.

He'd been found not guilty, of course. In the eyes of the world, he was an innocent man.

Or not.

"I don't want you kicking his ass," she finally said, softly. "Grayson and I are over. Ancient history."

The piece of history had been in her room the night before.

"I didn't come to Fantasy because I was looking for a new lover." Her fingers stroked inside his wrist. "But I'd be lying if I said I didn't feel this…connection between us."

He waited.

"I'm not here to fuck you, Kace."

No, sweetheart, but if you're undercover, you are definitely here to fuck me over. Yet he just smiled at her. "When you change your mind, you let me know." Kace backed away.

Her lips parted. Those sensual, cherry red lips. "I've still got a job here, right? And if I keep working for you—"

"I can make my own rules. With you, I will." Or maybe there wouldn't be any rules. Just lots of pleasure until their world burned down around them. Only time would tell. "But you have to make the call. When you're ready for me…" Now he reached into his pocket and pulled out a phone. "You'll be able to reach me anytime, day or night." He put the phone into her hand.

"I don't need a phone. I *have* a phone. I—"

"This phone reaches me, only me. Wherever I am. I don't let just anyone know how to get in touch with me that way."

Her fingers tightened around the phone. "Guess I'm special?"

She was.

Instead of telling her that, Kace said, "Franco is going to take you home."

"What? No motorcycle ride with you tonight?"

Did she sound disappointed? "No, I have some…business that I must take care of." He gave her a slow smile. "But it's nice to know you're already missing me."

"I'm *not*."

"Liar."

He headed for the door, but as Kace's fingers reached for the knob, he stopped. Glancing back at Bree, he told her, "You were absolutely phenomenal tonight. The most graceful and beautiful thing I've ever seen. I underestimated you. I was trying to drive you away, but you showed me that you are capable of more than I imagined." He inclined his head. "I won't underestimate you ever again." He hadn't dug deep enough into her past. The woman had skills he hadn't expected. The silk routine had been freaking phenomenal—and a serious turn-on.

"You'd better not underestimate me. If you do, you'll regret it."

God, that woman… "If we do fuck, be warned, I don't think I'll ever be able to let you go."

"Kace?" Uncertainty flickered in her eyes.

"When you find something special, you do whatever it takes to hold tight to it." He opened the door and went out to speak with Franco.

CHAPTER SEVEN

"Boss said I should come up with you." Franco had just opened the passenger side of the SUV. He was big and intense-looking. His head was shaved and his arms sported lots of twisting tattoos.

She hopped out of the SUV, her bag slung over her shoulder. "I'm good. I don't need company upstairs."

Did his cheeks flush? "Boss wanted you safe."

"I'm totally safe. Thanks so much for the ride."

"I'll wait here, until you get inside."

"Thanks, Franco." He was actually kind of sweet. She'd seen him talking to the other waitresses, always making sure no one was bothering them at the club. The guy was hulking and huge, but…maybe that was just all on the outside.

She hurried into the bed and breakfast. She'd managed to sneak out earlier without having to face Kelly Queen, so that was a good thing. The last thing she wanted was to piss off her temporary landlady. When she climbed up the stairs, Bree tried to keep her steps as soft as possible. Waking up the other guests in the middle of the night would hardly endear her to them.

A few moments later, she'd unlocked her door and stepped inside. She turned on her light.

And just froze. Shock consumed her as her gaze jerked to the left and to the right.

Her clothes had been cut to shreds and tossed onto the floor. Her bed—the sheets, the pillows, the mattresses—everything had been slashed. Bree rushed to the closet and yanked it open. Her laptop was gone. Her suitcase hung open, with her extra shoes tossed onto the floor of the closet.

She backed away slowly, not wanting to touch anything else in the room. There could be fingerprints inside. Grayson could get a team there to—

An engine growled outside. Bree ran to the window and yanked back the thin curtains just in time to see Franco driving away. Her heart pounded against her chest as she hurried to the small dresser against the right wall. She opened the top drawer.

Her gun was gone.

Her breathing was too rushed and hard as she pulled out her phone. Actually, Bree found herself pulling out the phone Kace had given her.

Not her own phone. She wanted to call him. Wanted to let him know what had happened. *He* was the first person she wanted to call for help.

But the truth was…

He could have been the one to trash her place. If he thought she was FBI like Grayson, then maybe he'd sent his men to search and trash her room while she'd been working at Fantasy. *He* was the suspect she was after. Coming into her room, searching for the truth…maybe he'd done it.

But I don't think he did. And that was based off pure instinct.

She didn't call him, though. She shoved his phone into her bag. A few moments later, she'd used her phone to call Grayson.

"Good night?" Grayson drawled. "Tell me you learned something useful—"

"My place was searched. Trashed. Looks like someone took a knife and cut up everything I own." Her words were flat. "I need a team over here."

"Are you serious?"

"Yes, I'm serious." Why in the hell would she joke about something like this? "My place is—"

"Call Kace," he ordered immediately. "The guy was alpha fucking insane for you last night. Give him a sob story. Play the victim."

That wasn't the response she'd expected. "Uh, I don't think—"

"Tell him you need a place to stay. Somewhere safe. The bastard is so hot for you that he'll probably move you right into his house."

Okay, this call was definitely not going according to plan. "I'm not sleeping with him for the job."

"What? No, no, don't sleep with him. That's not what I meant. But you can get close to him, and this is the perfect opportunity—"

"Someone trashed my room," she angrily cut through his words. "The place looks like it was hit by someone with a whole lot of rage." She could practically feel the fury. "We need to interview Kelly Queen and the other guests. Find out if any of them saw anything. Then we need to get a team down here to search for prints."

"Yes, yes, we'll do *all* of that. *After* you call Kace Quick. Play the role, Bree. Think about this! If you're scared, if you were just a normal civilian, wouldn't you be freaking the hell out?"

She would be freaking the hell out. *I am freaking the hell out.* If she wasn't an FBI agent, she'd be calling the police, not a local club owner.

"Call him first," Grayson urged her, voice tense. "Let the guy think you depend on him. That you need him."

"Kace could have been the one to do this. He's on to me," Bree said with certainty. "I told him that you and I had just hooked up once—a mistake."

Silence. The uncomfortable kind.

"He could have done this," Bree said again as a shiver slid over her body.

"Yeah, he could have—and that's why it will seem odd to him if you don't contact him and tell the guy what happened. If you play this too cool, he'll know you're a Fed." He exhaled heavily. "Just call the club. If he's still there—"

"I don't need to call the club. I have his direct line. I can get him anytime I want."

"Then play the victim and do it! Use this. And then I'll get Dominic and Karin to talk with the owner of the bed and breakfast and to interview the others guests. But our first goal has to be getting closer to Kace Quick."

Once more, her gaze trekked over the wreckage of her room. Would Kace really have done this? *So much rage.* "If it wasn't him," Bree licked her lips, "who would have done it?"

"Could have just been a robbery. You know, stuff like that happens in this town, especially in tourist spots—"

"There is *rage* here. Hate." The scene was classic. Not just about a theft, but about destruction. "This isn't some robbery."

A pause. "What are you saying, Bree? You think…what? You've attracted the attention of the serial killer?"

Her grip on the phone became a painful clench.

"Because if that's the case, we both know all signs point to the Strangler being Kace Quick."

She licked her lower lip. The Strangler's MO didn't include B&E and destruction *before* he took a victim.

"Do your job, Agent Harlow." Tension had entered Grayson's voice. She was now *Agent* Harlow, not Bree. "The point was for you to go in undercover. To get close to Kace. Play the victim here, and he'll pull you in tight. *Even* if he was the one to destroy your room. And if he is the serial killer, if our suspicions have been right all along, this gives you the chance to play bait. You can take him down Bree, before we have to send another woman's body to the morgue."

An image of the last victim flashed through her mind. The ER. The chaos. The blood on the woman's chest.

"Do your job," he said again.

The call ended.

"Fuck you," Bree whispered. "And yeah, by the way, I'm fine. Thanks for asking." She tossed her phone onto the mess that was the bed. She pulled in a deep breath and reached into her bag to grab Kace's phone. He was the only contact programmed in the phone. Her finger pressed to the screen. The phone rang and then—

"Missing me already?" His voice seemed to purr into her ear.

"Something happened." Her own voice came out wooden. "I-I'm in my room, but everything has been slashed to pieces. My clothes, the sheets, the bed—"

"Get the hell out of there, right now." Lethal fury hardened every word. "Get out of your room. Go find Ms. Queen. Stay in her room until I get there." He swore. "Guessing Franco has already left?"

"Yes…"

"I'm texting him now. He'll be back at your side in three minutes, or I fucking fire him."

Her heart was still racing.

"Baby, are you all right?"

She grabbed her bag and the phone she'd dropped onto the bed. Bree hurriedly made her way to the door. "I'm okay."

"You'll be okay when you're with me. I'm on the way, got me? I'm coming for you. Now get with Ms. Queen. Stay with her. *Stay safe.* I'm coming for you," he said again.

***

Her clothes had been slit with a knife. Systematically destroyed. Stuffing hung out of her bed. Feathers from the pillows littered the floor.

Fury filled Kace. A dark and dangerous rage. Someone was going to pay for this.

"We should call the cops."

He turned away from the scene and headed into the hallway. Bree stood there, nervously shifting from foot to foot. A steely-eyed Ms. Queen was at her side. Franco lingered just steps away.

It was Bree who'd spoken, and, yeah, sure, they could call the cops. For all the good that would do. He pinned Ms. Queen with a hard glance. *Ms. Queen.* She'd been a fixture in the city forever. He knew she told folks she was eighty, but he thought she was closer to one hundred, and her mind was as sharp as it had been when she was twenty-one and raising hell. "You didn't see anyone?"

She shook her head. "I-I went to bed around eleven. Didn't hear a peep until Bree came banging on my door."

Great. "The other guests? What about them?"

"There's only two others here tonight," Ms. Queen said quickly. "They're one floor down. An elderly couple. And they didn't see or hear anything."

He glanced down at the lock on the door. Saw the faint marks that told him the lock had been picked. Those small scratches were a dead giveaway. His head tilted back as he studied Bree once more. "You talk to your FBI ex lately?"

She flinched. "What?"

"He broke into your room last night. Maybe he got pissed and came back again."

But she shook her head. "No, Grayson wouldn't do this."

"Don't be too sure, sweetheart. A badge doesn't make a man good. He's either good or he's bad *before* he picks up the badge." Kace raked a hand through his hair. "Franco, stay here. Talk to the cops."

"Yes, sir."

"*I* should talk to them," Bree began, her cheeks flushing.

"I'm getting you some place safe. For all we know, the man who did this is outside, waiting and watching right now. I want you away from here until we can figure out what's going on." He marched toward her and took Bree's hand. Her hand felt so small against his. Fragile.

And he thought of the damage the knife had done to her room.

A knife could do one hell of a lot of damage to her skin…

His gaze cut to Ms. Queen. "If anyone comes around looking for her, you let me know."

"This is a nightmare." Her eyes were huge. "If word gets out about what happened, my business will be—"

"I'll give you enough money to get by. Don't worry about that."

She blinked quickly.

"You just remember to call me if *anyone* comes asking about Bree."

She nodded.

He was done there. His fingers tightened around Bree's. "Come on." She had her bag, and there was nothing else in the small room that she could use. They hurried down the stairs and then toward his motorcycle. He'd hauled ass getting there to her. It was a lucky thing she hadn't been there when the intruder broke in. If she *had* been there…

He pushed a helmet toward her. "Hold tight." He climbed onto the bike and had the engine growling in moments.

She didn't immediately get on behind him.

His head turned. "Bree?"

The small bag was still slung over one shoulder. She was staring at him, biting her lip, and the helmet was curled under one arm.

"Baby," he softened his voice. "Climb on the bike. It's time to take you home."

She seemed a little dazed. "Home?"

"My home." The engine growled again. "Top of the line security. No unwelcome guests will get inside, you can count on that."

"I can't just go to your house. I mean—"

"I'm not asking you into my bed." Though she could certainly come there any time she wanted. "Got plenty of extra rooms at my place.

You'll stay in one of them until we figure things out."

She still didn't get on the bike.

What the hell? "Bree?"

"Tell me you didn't break into my room."

The fury inside of him flared higher. "That's why you're hesitating? You think I did this? You think I took a knife and slashed all of your belongings?"

"Tell me you didn't break in."

His jaw clenched. "I didn't destroy your clothes, Bree. I didn't slash them to pieces. I didn't take a knife and wreck your freaking bed. And, no, I didn't have my men do any of that shit, either. Not really how I operate." He gave her a grim smile. "But you don't have to believe me. You can think I'm a liar. Go right ahead. But this *liar* is offering you protection. My protection. You come with me tonight, and everyone in this city will know that you're off-limits. If someone wants to screw with you, they'll have to go through me in order to do it."

She inched a little closer to the motorcycle. She was definitely within grabbing range. "Why?" Bree demanded. "I don't understand why you're helping me!"

"Because even the devil can do something good once in a while." His fingers were around the handlebars. He waited for her to choose—

She climbed on the motorcycle. She chose *him.* He gave her time to put on the helmet and adjust her bag. Then her hands slid around his waist. "I don't trust you."

He smiled. *Good. You shouldn't.*

The motorcycle raced into the night.

***

Before she'd stepped foot inside Fantasy, Bree had carefully researched Kace Quick's life. So, she wasn't surprised when he pulled up in front of the mansion on Saint Charles Avenue. Tucked behind a tall, wrought-iron fence, the stately Victorian boasted two levels of ornate, wrap-around porches. Lights blazed from inside—illuminating window after window after window in the massive structure. Kace leaned toward a keypad and typed quickly. Bree caught sight of all the security cameras right before the gates swung open.

Then they were heading up the drive. The house just got bigger and bigger as she approached. She counted at least three—no, four chimneys sticking out of the house's roof.

He braked the bike. She climbed off quickly, pushing the helmet back at him. The house was worth over four and a half million dollars. A figure she'd gotten during her research on Kace. The man had money to burn because the nearly nine thousand square foot home only had one resident—him.

The guy hadn't been lying when he'd said that he had extra bedrooms. He'd been extremely understating things.

Bree didn't speak until they were inside. The minute she walked through the entranceway, her gaze was captured by the massive chandelier that hung overhead. The ceiling stretched up so high that the place felt almost cavernous to her. Keeping the home heated must be a real bitch.

The hardwood gleamed beneath her feet. A long, thick rug stretched forward, and as she advanced, her shoes seemed to sink into the expensive material. For some reason, she almost felt as if she should be whispering as she asked, just to make sure, "We're alone here?"

Kace stopped walking. He frowned back at her. "Yes. Completely alone."

Then he turned to the left. He entered what looked like a small den—one equipped with a very huge and ornate fireplace. To the right of the fireplace, along the wall, there were over a dozen monitors. "As you can see," Kace was staring at the monitors, "I have a full security feed for the exterior as well as many interior sections of the house. No one will be getting in here without me knowing."

Okay. She rubbed her hands over the front of her black pants. She was so nervous in there. *His home.*

Kace swung toward her. "I'm going to put you in a bedroom on the second floor. I know you have to be exhausted, and you should get some rest."

Actually, adrenaline was pumping wildly through her blood so rest was the last thing that she felt like getting, but Bree still trailed after him. When she caught sight of the staircase…

Holy mother.

The staircase was massive. No other word for it. Made of heavy, gleaming wood, it led to a landing that stopped in front of a gorgeous, arched, stained glass window. Then the stairs turned back, stretching higher until they reached the second floor.

Kace had paused mid-way up the stairs. He turned back to her, one dark brow raised. "Is there a problem?"

"This place." Did her voice echo? Bree was pretty sure it did. "It's a lot to take in."

"You get used to it."

She wasn't so sure about that. "It's just you living here?"

Kace nodded.

"You don't think it's…too much? I mean, for one person."

"Maybe one day I'll have a family."

An image of a little boy, a miniature Kace, flashed before her eyes. She almost smiled.

"Maybe I won't always be alone." He shrugged. "Guess we'll have to see." His head cocked as he seemed to consider things. "I grew up with nothing. Less than nothing. I suppose you could say that gave me a desire to possess everything."

Judging by the house, Kace was certainly succeeding on that end.

He motioned with his hand. "Come on, I'll show you to your room for the night."

Her hand trailed over the thick banister as she followed him. The fourth stair squeaked beneath her feet. She couldn't get over this place. It was like being in a castle. And Bree felt like an absolute fraud as she followed him to the second story. He turned to the right, and then he was opening a door for her.

"This is where you'll be sleeping."

She brushed past him and tried really hard not to let her jaw drop. A chandelier hung over the bed. Like everything else in the house, the cherry four-poster bed was massive. To the right of it, a huge, white stone fireplace waited. A fireplace in the bedroom. Of course, because, why not?

"The bathroom is in there." He pointed. She didn't look. "And I'm right next door, should you need anything."

He was—Bree spun toward him. "Why are you doing this?"

He lifted a brow. "Offering you a separate bedroom?" Kace shrugged. "I thought you weren't ready to slip into my bed, so I was being a gentleman."

Bree felt her cheeks sting. "I'm *not* getting into your bed."

He gave a knowing nod. "See? Didn't think you were ready."

Her hands fisted at her sides. "You don't have a reputation for being *nice.* I don't get why you're playing the hero and moving me in here. I mean, you could have just dumped me at the nearest hotel. You didn't have to come and pick me up at all. You didn't—"

He stepped closer to her. She swallowed and tipped back her head.

"I've told you, don't believe all of the stories you hear. Some are bullshit."

"But some are truth." And it was her job to figure out which ones were truth.

He gave her a fleeting smile. "Some are."

Her gaze was on his mouth. The man had a mouth that was far too sexy, damn him.

"I'm being *nice,* as you call it, because I don't want you hurt." Such low, deep, rumbling words.

Now her gaze rose. He was staring straight at her, and she couldn't look away.

"I want you." Very blunt words. "Having you in my house gives me an advantage. When you suddenly realize how much you want me, too, I'll be right next door."

The man didn't stop.

His gaze burned. "You're under my protection. By bringing you here, as far as the rest of the world is concerned, you're mine."

Her heart pounded faster. "Is that supposed to keep me safe?" From who-the-hell-ever had broken into her place and trashed it?

His face hardened. "Actually, I'm afraid that, if anything, it will put you more at risk."

"Because of…the killer out there." She wasn't going to dance around this. After all, wasn't she there because of the Strangler? Because of those women who'd died?

"Because of him." His hand lifted, and the back of his fingers brushed over her cheek. "Someone is trying to make me look like a monster."

A shiver slid over her.

"I won't let you be hurt. You'll stay with me until I catch the bastard."

Wait… "Until *you* catch him?" Her surprise was real. Since when was he hunting a killer? "Don't you mean until the police catch him?"

His hand dropped. "No, sweetheart, because the cops and the Feds are only looking at me. They're too blind to see the real killer. So, I have to stop the SOB. And my way of stopping him will be far better than theirs."

Because he was planning to kill the guy. She understood exactly what he was saying.

"Get some rest," Kace urged her. "Tomorrow, we'll get you new clothes and anything else that you need."

Again, being the hero. Being kind.

He turned and headed for the door.

That was it? The biggest bad guy in the city was just walking away? She'd expected…something. Maybe an attempt at a kiss. Maybe at least a better push for—

He glanced back at her—and laughed. "Bree, baby, why do you look disappointed?"

She didn't. Did she? Oh, hell. Bree immediately schooled her features. "I'm just trying to figure you out."

His gaze turned assessing. "And I'm trying to do the same with you." He waited a beat, then admitted, "I want you in my bed."

Her breath came a little faster.

"But when we fuck, I want to know exactly where your loyalty lies."

Shock rolled through her. No, he didn't mean—

"You'll have to choose, you know. Eventually."

"I-I don't know what you're talking about." She would have liked to say the stutter was a deliberate touch, an effort to look uncertain, but in reality, she *was* nervous, and the stutter just slipped out.

"Yes, you do." But he inclined his head. "Good night, Bree. Have good dreams. Really hot, sexy dreams about me."

Her lips parted.

He was already gone.

***

Kace shut the door with a soft click. For a moment, he thought about locking the door. Having Bree free to wander his house might not be the best idea but…

The lady was full of surprises and, he figured she'd just be able to pick the lock. Besides, he wanted to see what she'd do now that he had her in his home. He figured it was past time to call her bluff. The game she was in had become increasingly dangerous.

Kace made his way back down the stairs. He avoided the fourth stair, knowing that it would give a telling creak. There wasn't an inch of the house that he didn't understand. From the moment he'd seen this place, he'd known that he had to possess it. He'd understood it was meant to be his. The boy who'd grown up on the streets, performing for the tourists in Jackson Square before he'd graduated to stealing from them—

that boy now owned one of the biggest houses in the city. He *owned* the city, for all intents and purposes.

Yes, he'd seen the house, wanted it, and he'd gotten it.

He always got exactly what he wanted.

I saw Bree, and I wanted her.

It was only a matter of time until he had her.

A few moments later, Kace entered his study, being sure to shut the door behind him. Kace sat in his leather chair behind the desk, and he pulled out his phone. Remy answered on the second ring.

"Boss, what's—"

"You fucking screwed up," he snarled. "I wanted her place *searched*. I didn't want it destroyed." He opened his desk drawer. Her gun was in the top drawer, just beneath a fake bottom. The gun that they'd already traced back to the FBI. "This is a huge clusterfuck. Tell me why the hell I shouldn't end your ass right now."

***

"Hello, Marie."

The voice came to her in the darkness. Low, whispering. She whimpered because the voice scared her, and she tried to hunch her body against the wall.

"I didn't plan to take you. At least, not so soon. But I didn't get to finish with the other girl. I didn't have all the time I needed." The voice had gotten closer. "And when I don't get what I need, it's hard for me to focus on anything else. I realize…I like what I'm doing too much."

"Please…" Her lips and tongue were so swollen. "Let me g-go…"

He laughed.

Her hands twisted against the rope that bound her. He'd tied her wrists together and tied her ankles together, too. Her wrists had become raw and bloody as she'd fought to get free.

"You were beautiful on the silks. I loved watching you up there. Gave me such a good idea…"

A light hit her, shining directly in her face. After being in the dark for so long, the light hurt, and she had to shut her eyes. What was that? A flashlight?

"You like being in the spotlight, don't you?"

"Please…"

"They always beg. It never does any good."

Her eyes were still squeezed shut. She was afraid to open them. She hadn't seen his face yet, and he kept whispering. "I can't…I can't identify you." Her breath came faster. Her words were rasping because her throat was so raw. She'd screamed and screamed, but no help had come. "Just let me go. I-I won't tell—"

"I know you won't. You won't be able to tell anyone anything." His hand reached out to her. She felt his fingers on her throat.

Her eyes flew open.

The light was still on her. One hand held the flashlight. The other was touching her neck—

"By the time I'm done, you'll never be able to tell anyone so much as another word, not ever again."

She tried to scream, but a whimper came out. She lunged forward—

And he slammed the flashlight into the side of her head.

CHAPTER EIGHT

Bree cracked open her door. She poked her head out, glancing down the hallway. Heavy shadows hung everywhere and a deep, heavy silence seemed to cloak the house.

She'd waited two hours before making her move. She'd heard Kace going to bed. She'd been far too tense when he finally entered his room. Every rustle had reached her ears. And she'd wondered if he'd been getting into a four-poster bed like the one in the room she'd been given. She'd wondered if he slept nude…

She wasn't supposed to be obsessed with her target. But she'd never encountered anyone quite like Kace. *Villain or hero?* That was the problem. She wasn't sure. When he'd swooped in and gotten her away from the bed and breakfast, when he'd been so concerned while Grayson had only wanted to use her…

She'd doubted. Doubted all of the intel that she'd been given. Maybe he wasn't the monster.

Then, after she'd been in her room for less than ten minutes, he'd come to her door.

Knocking softly. He'd given her one of his t-shirts to wear. An over-sized, soft cotton shirt that still held his scent. He'd apologized for not having something else for her to sleep in.

Apologized?

Then he'd left her. Nothing was making sense. The bad guy didn't protect his prey. Did he?

It was time for her to find out. The FBI wasn't going to get another opportunity like this one. She crept down the hallway, moving on her tip-toes. She'd go to his study. Bree had caught a glimpse of the room when she'd first entered the house, after they'd left the area filled with the security monitors, and she'd thought—pay dirt. Now her mission was to search the house. To learn everything that she could about him.

Some serial killers kept trophies from their victims. Grayson believed this killer was the type who'd like to relive his crimes over and over again. She knew Grayson would want her to search the place and see if she could find anything to link Kace to the murders.

And I want to search because…

Maybe she wanted to prove Kace's innocence.

She didn't step on the fourth step near the bottom of the stairs. Bree didn't want the tell-tale creak to possibly give away her plan. The borrowed t-shirt slid over her thighs as she descended the steps. She stilled at the bottom, glancing up to make sure there was no sign of movement from above. Her heart galloped in her chest as she made her way to the study.

Her fingers closed around the doorknob, and it turned easily. He hadn't even bothered to lock his study? Was he that confident? Or perhaps Kace just didn't have anything to hide.

Bree slipped inside but didn't turn on the lights. Her eyes had adjusted to the darkness, and she could see the outline of the furniture. She skirted around the chairs and couch and made her way to the desk. The computer monitor glowed, giving off a faint light as she sat behind the desk.

Bree reached for the top desk drawer. Locked.

Her eyes narrowed.

The second drawer opened easily. When she reached inside, she found a file folder. She pulled it out, bringing it closer to the computer screen. There was a neatly typed name on the file. It was—

Her name.

The lights flashed on. Bree gave a little gasp as her gaze shot toward the door. Kace was there, dressed in a pair of jeans that hung low on his hips. As she stared at him, trying to figure out what the hell to say, he leaned back against the doorframe and crossed his hands over his chest.

"Caught you."

He sure as hell had, but her chin notched up. She hadn't opened the file yet. She could play this as the injured party. "Why do you have a file on me?"

"Because I don't trust you, sweetheart." Now he moved away from the wall. Stalked toward her with a slow, languid stride.

"So, you had me investigated?" Did she sound affronted enough?

"I investigate everyone who is close to me."

She flipped open the file.

And found a pic of her official FBI photo staring back at her. Oh, fuck.

"The first day you were in my office," Kace murmured, "I got your fingerprints. Call me suspicious, but I like to be prepared."

The drumming of her heartbeat filled Bree's ears.

"I didn't get the full report back until tonight. Right after you were on stage, in fact. And that's when I learned that—surprisingly—you'd told me many truths."

"You got my fingerprints…"

She'd been fingerprinted after her parents had been killed. Then again when she'd joined the FBI. And he'd gotten access to her prints? To her records?

Bree flipped through the files—and froze when she saw the clippings of her parents' murders.

"I'm sorry for your loss," he told her quietly.

He sounded so freaking sincere. Her head snapped up as she glared at him. "Save me your bullshit."

He'd put his hands on the desk, and Kace towered over her. Not happening. She surged to her feet and leaned toward him. "You've been jerking me around!"

"No, sweetheart, you're the one who has been playing the games. You're the one who tried to trick me." He shrugged. "But Remy led the investigation on you. He pulled up your past faster than I expected. I knew, you see, that the FBI was sending someone into my organization. I got a tip from a very reliable source."

"Oh, yeah? And who is that source?"

"You sure you want to know? Because once you go down this rabbit hole…"

"Who is your source?"

"Ciara Hall."

She shook her head. Shock flew through her. "What? But Ciara—"

"Ciara Hall was the second victim of the New Orleans Strangler." He leaned even closer. "And I found it so fucking odd that the very day after she warned me that the FBI was planning to send an agent after me—an agent who'd try to trick me in order to gain my trust—that poor Ciara was murdered."

This was a new piece of the puzzle. Something that hadn't been in any of the files.

"So odd," he rasped, "and so coincidental. Almost as if her murder was planned. Almost as if someone in the fucking FBI is trying to set me up."

"No!" Bree shook her head. "That's not what's happening!" She rushed from behind the desk and went straight toward him.

His hands wrapped around her shoulders. "You're an FBI Agent."

"Yes." Not like she could lie now. Not when he had all the evidence lined up on her.

"And your job is to send me to jail for the rest of my life."

"My *job* is to find the serial killer responsible for the murders of three women in New Orleans! Yes, you are the chief suspect, or else I wouldn't be in your life right now. You have ties to all the victims. You were the last person seen with Lindsey—"

"I took Lindsey home because she was drunk, and I wanted to make sure she got to her place safely."

Bree exhaled slowly. "No one else saw Lindsey after that."

"No, her *killer* saw her."

Did he understand how much she *wanted* the killer to not be him? "Witnesses saw the two of you arguing."

"Yes, because drunk people can be helluva belligerent." He lifted a brow. "That the best you've got?"

No, but she wasn't supposed to reveal all of her evidence to him.

Kace laughed. "Come on, Bree. You're not standing before me because I have *ties* to the victims. That's BS. An agent doesn't get sent in undercover for such a flimsy reason. The FBI has more evidence, something that has you locked on me right now."

Yes, they did.

"You know about Brittney, right? I'm sure she figured into this grand profile that was created for me."

For a moment, her heart stopped. He was voluntarily going to talk about Brittney Lang?

"I was eighteen years old. So was she. Young, wild, and crazy. That was both of us. I had a good time with Brittney, but then I found out she was having sex with someone else." A shrug. "Two days later, Brittney was dead."

"Not just dead. Strangled." Like all of the current victims. "Strangled and left in Jackson Square." Beautiful, *blond* Brittney. A woman who'd been a slightly younger version of the current victims.

His jaw hardened. "I was tried and found not guilty of Brittney's murder."

Yes, he had been. Though there were still plenty of people—like the very judge who'd been on the bench during his case—who thought he'd gotten away with a cold-blooded killing.

"You're looking at this all wrong, *Agent* Harlow." His voice was a rough, angry growl.

"Then tell me how to look at it the right way."

"I'm not the killer you're after. I didn't kill Brittney. I didn't kill Lindsey or Ciara or Amelia. But someone is trying to frame me. The same freaking way I was framed for Brittney's murder. Someone wants to take me down." Each word was rougher, angrier than the last.

"Someone is *killing* women in order to get to you?" Now she shook her head. "No, that's not the profile that the FBI has on the perp—"

"Then your profile is wrong because I'm telling you that I'm the target. Some asshole out there thinks he can ruin me by making me look guilty as sin, but it's not going to happen."

"Kace—"

"Because *you're* not going to let it happen."

"What?"

And his smile came again. The sexy, charming, warm smile of…a killer?

"I let you into my world, Bree. And now that you're inside, I don't plan to let you go."

The words sounded like a threat. His hold had tightened on her shoulders.

"You wanted a job with me. You've got one. But it's not waiting tables or spinning on the silks. Your *real* job is going to be helping me…to catch a killer."

He looked dead serious, but… "This isn't funny."

"Good. Because it isn't a joke. Your cover is blown. It pretty much was, from the minute you walked into my office. I'm very good at spotting cops, and I spotted you from the first instant."

Her chin notched up again. She wasn't a cop. She was a Fed. "Then why the charade? Why—"

"Because you keep your enemies close, and you keep the undercover agents and cops who want to take your ass down—you keep them even closer."

She was very, very close to him in that moment. So close that the heat of his body had wrapped around her.

"I'm going to use you to prove my innocence. I'll let you into my world. You'll help me. I'll help you. We'll find the real killer because the other pricks out there—the fools on your team? They are only looking at me. And while they are doing that, women are dying."

This was crazy. He was crazy. "You're the suspect, you don't get to—"

"Don't get to tell you how things will work?" Kace interrupted silkily. "Oh, darling, I'm Kace Quick. Haven't you heard? I do whatever the hell I want." His gaze dropped to her mouth. "Whatever. I. Want."

He was staring at her as if he wanted to devour her.

His gaze rose. His eyes smoldered with a barely banked fire. "It will work my way or no way at all."

"What's that supposed to mean?" Why was her voice husky? Why was she leaning toward him?

"It means you can call your FBI buddies. You can tell them your cover is blown, and I can kick your sweet ass out of my home."

"After what happened to me tonight? After my room was—"

He let her go, laughing. "God, you do perform well. I'll have to remember that." He marched away from her, headed for the window, and peered outside. "I'm sure your team is close by. Probably parked in some incredibly unimaginative van under a tree."

Actually, they could be doing that very thing.

"I know about the set-up."

Yes, obviously, he knew that she—

"Your team-mate—and I believe, your *ex-lover*—Grayson? He staged your room. Very dramatic. I didn't expect that, so it threw me for a moment. But, really, Bree, you didn't have to go to all of that trouble in order to get into my house. I would have brought you in if you'd simply asked—"

She'd crossed to him in an instant. Bree grabbed Kace's shoulder and whipped him around. "What are you talking about?"

His stare sharpened as he took in her expression. "Didn't you know?"

No, she didn't know.

Kace shook his head. A little sadly. "Remy did some digging. Turns out, someone *had* been a witness to the destruction of your room. And your buddy Grayson was identified as the culprit. He crept in while you were performing at Fantasy, and he sliced your room to hell and back."

No. "That *can't* be true."

A muscle flexed along his jaw. "You didn't know. It's interesting. I've learned to tell when you lie so easily now. Didn't take long at all for me to figure you out."

"Stop it. This isn't a game. Grayson didn't—"

"Is he truly your ex? Did you have the bad taste to fuck him?"

Her hands clenched into fists. She debated punching him—hard.

"You did." His jaw tightened. "Regrettable, but we all make mistakes."

"I'm about to kick your ass, and it *won't* be a mistake."

Now he flashed her a grin. "That's what I like about you. The fire you can't quite contain. Makes you different from all the dumbass cops and agents who've tried to take me down before." He nodded. "Soon enough, you'll see the truth."

She was trying to see past her fury right then—as she stood in front of him, trying not to take a swing and wearing *his* shirt. "What truth is that?"

"Why, that you're not meant to be with the FBI. That you're not another cog in the wheel." A wide smile split his face. Taking him from handsome to absolute sin. "You're like me, sweetheart. You'll realize just how much before all of this is over."

"I am nothing like you."

He sighed. "You're just mad because I played you. Don't be. I've been at this game for a lot longer than you have. According to your file, you just graduated from the Academy. Went to college. Got a degree in psychology—first a bachelor's and then a master's. And you *did* work your way through college by waitressing and teaching aerial classes." He gave a little whistle. "I am impressed. I respect someone so much more when she works her way to get everything she wants. Don't really care much for folks who get the world handed to them on a platter."

To push him, Bree said, "You don't think I slept my way to this job? Grayson is the senior agent. He's the one who pulls the strings and makes the team. You don't think—"

"I absolutely don't think that about you. I read your file. You're smart and you're capable, and I believe you'll be hell on wheels when it comes to finding the *real* killer. That's why I want you on my side, not working against me." He rolled back his shoulders. "So what if you had the bad taste to fuck Grayson once? Don't worry, I'll make sure you forget him. Though I suspect he can't quite get over the time he had with you." Now Kace swept his gaze over her body. "It was in the eyes, you know. The desire that he still feels. If the jerk can't keep that shit in check, I'll have to hurt him."

"You're insane, aren't you?" She spun away from him and started to pace. "That was in the FBI files, people suspect—"

"Crazy like a fox, baby."

She stopped her pacing to glare at him.

But he just looked all smug and satisfied. Like he'd already won their battle. "Are you going to take my deal? Going to keep your close proximity to me while we hunt this killer? Or do you plan to run back to your little FBI group with your tail between your legs and let them know that their all-access pass to my life has been revoked?"

No, he had *not* just said that. Bree pulled in two slow breaths. She squared her shoulders, straightened her spine, and stalked toward him. When they were a foot apart, she flatly stated, "I don't run to *anyone* with my tail between my legs."

His eyes seemed to light up.

"When I was a teenager, I survived the world thinking I was a killer. I survived everything they threw at me, and I came out stronger for it."

She could have sworn that he looked at her with…pride?

"We are so alike," he murmured. "The world has thought I was killer since I was eighteen years old. I took everything they threw at me, and it made me stronger." He reached for her hand. Brought it to his lips. "Be careful."

"Why? What will you do to me?" What was he threatening—

"I might just fall in love with you."

And she'd thought finding his file was shocking. "What?" *Say it again.*

"If that happens, there will never be any escape for you." His fingers slid along her inner wrist, and a shiver chased down her spine. "More alike than you realize," he said, eyes thoughtful on her.

She was leaning toward him again. *Why* was she leaning toward him? Why was she suddenly trapped by his eyes? And why was she thinking about his mouth being on hers? About how well he could kiss and how the attraction between them was so powerful that it seemed almost unnatural.

Terrifyingly so.

"Get some sleep," Kace told her, voice almost tender. "You're not finding out my secrets tonight. But if you stay close to me, well, who the hell knows what you might learn tomorrow?"

True. Tomorrow, she could grill him. They could go back to being enemies or…partners?

His hand slid to her elbow. He escorted her out of the study, moving like he was some old-school gentleman as he kept perfect pace with her. But at the foot of the stairs, he paused and turned toward her. "You know what I think would scare you the most?"

She couldn't look away from his eyes.

"If you came to love me…if you loved me, even though you thought I might be a killer. I think that would terrify you."

Ice seemed to surround her heart. "I'm not going to love you."

Maybe her words would make him angry. Maybe—

He smiled at her. "We'll see about that."

CHAPTER NINE

"Ah, hello, sleepy head," Kace murmured as he moved away from the stove. He'd heard the pad of her footsteps as Bree entered the kitchen. "I was starting to think I needed to drag you out of bed."

And the idea had certainly tempted.

He turned toward her—and drew up short. How could a woman look that gorgeous? Her hair was wet, her face completely make-up free, and she was wearing the clothes she'd had on the night before.

Absolutely gorgeous.

"What?" She tucked a lock of wet hair behind her ear. "I didn't have anything else to wear."

"Total lie." He made his voice brisk. "I had Remy bring by new clothing and personal supplies for you this morning."

Her brow furrowed.

He waved a hand vaguely in the air. "Personal supplies. You know, deodorant, make-up, all of those hair items that women seem to—"

"I know what personal supplies are. I'm frowning because I'm surprised you got all of that for me."

"I told you that I'd take care of them last night." He pushed a plate of eggs across the marble bar top. "You should learn I'm a man of my word."

Her gaze swept the kitchen. "There are three chandeliers in here."

Yes.

"The fridge looks bigger than the first car I owned."

"You must have owned a small car."

Her lips twitched. "You know this room has more square footage than some of the restaurants in this town."

"True." A shrug. "So?"

"So, you're in this massive, expensive as hell kitchen…making me eggs?"

He put another plate next to hers. "I'm making myself eggs. I had extras, so doing some for you wasn't a bother."

"You're lying." She sounded surprised. "I can…tell. You specifically made these for me."

Whatever. He sat on one of the bar stools. "I like cooking. Can't bad guys enjoy doing that every now and then?"

Bree gaped at him.

"Your eggs are getting cold."

"Explain this to me." She sat on the bar stool next to him. Their knees brushed. "All of it. The house—okay, you said you bought it because you grew up poor, you—"

"No." His hand tightened around a fork. "I grew up with nothing. There is a difference between being poor and having nothing." His head turned as he pinned her with a glance. "I had nothing. I had to fight for every single thing that I now possess. Understand me, I learned to fight dirty, and I learned to fight hard."

Bree nibbled on her lower lip for a moment. "I—"

"There were times when I had no food. Times when I was so hungry that I could feel my stomach knotting and cramping. It was on those days that I swore things would change. One day, I'd have any kind of meal I wanted. I'd have a kitchen as big as a fucking restaurant." He smiled at her. "And I'd be the chef."

Her gaze seemed to soften on him.

"Careful, Bree," he murmured.

"Why?"

"You're starting to look at me as if I'm not a monster."

Because that was part of his plan. If he told her about the dark parts of his life…about how he'd been an enforcer when he was sixteen years old, about how he used to beat the shit out of people who tried to screw him over…

Well, her gaze wouldn't go soft.

And if she knew about the things that he *still* did…

Bree certainly wouldn't be on his side. That couldn't happen. He *needed* her on his side. If he was going to come out as a victor in this particular battle, he had to get an FBI agent to vouch for him. To be willing to trade anything for him.

I'm going to use you, Bree.

Maybe they'd use each other. Maybe they'd have one hell of a time along the way.

Or maybe they'd both be burned to ashes. Only time would tell.

"We're going to the crime scenes today," he announced.

"We are?"

"Yes, you're still here. You haven't run out the front door, so I take that to mean you've decided to accept my offer." He reached for his coffee. Enjoyed a slow sip. Some things should be savored in life.

Bree was one of those things. When he got her in his bed, he would absolutely savor her. Every single delectable inch of her.

"You didn't really give me a choice."

No, he hadn't. "We're going to hit the crime scenes first."

"Why?" Suspicion was heavy in her tone.

Sometimes, she was so cute. "No, baby, it's not because the guilty party likes to go back to the scene of the crime."

Her golden eyes were almost slits. Someone was angry in the mornings.

"It's because I want your take on things." This wasn't just about her having access to his world. It was about Kace being about to use the expertise of an FBI agent on *his* investigation. "I want to know what you see when you look at the crime scenes. I want to know what you think of the killer."

She glanced down at the plate of eggs. She hadn't eaten a bite. "I'm not the one who made the profile for the New Orleans Strangler. I'm the junior agent. Grayson is the one leading things."

Well, no wonder the case was so messed up. "Maybe you *should* have made the profile."

Her gaze darted to his. "What makes you think I'm more qualified than Grayson? He's been in the field a whole lot longer than I have."

"You graduated summa cum laude with your Bachelor's, then did the same damn thing with your Master's. All while working two jobs. According to the intel that Remy collected, you were at the top of your class in the FBI. Every single thing I've thrown at you, you've handled." He wished she'd eat. Her eggs were getting cold. "I don't want that dipshit Grayson controlling anything. I want to know what *you* see. I want you to create a new Strangler profile for me. We're starting from scratch. I want to find out what's in your head."

She seemed to consider his words. "Okay."

Grudging but…it was something.

Finally, Bree reached for her fork. She loaded up the fluffy, scrambled eggs and took a bite. Her eyes widened. As soon as she swallowed, Bree enthusiastically declared, "Those are amazing!"

"Of course, they are." A shrug. He was Kace Quick, after all. He didn't do anything half-way.

"You are not what I expect."

No, baby, I'm exactly what you think I am. He smiled at her. *I'm a killer. And when I find this bastard who thinks he can mess with my world, who thinks he can target women I know…I am going to make him beg me before I end his life.*

***

The jeans hugged her legs and the white shirt billowed around her as Bree kept her arms locked around Kace's stomach. The motorcycle's engine was growling, the wind whipped against her, and she realized that she'd just joined the side of the bad guy.

He braked on a side street, a narrow little crook of a space near Pirate's Alley.

Pirate's Alley.

The small lane was nestled on the side of the St. Louis Cathedral. Tourists strolled up and down it, some pausing for photos, some intent on reaching the performers who filled nearby Jackson Square.

But she and Kace didn't follow the tourists to the Square. Instead, Bree climbed off the motorcycle. Kace secured the bike, and then he took her hand. To others, they probably just seemed like a couple taking a romantic stroll.

They weren't. They were hunting a killer.

They headed to the rear of the St. Louis Cathedral. Tall, green bushes provided some privacy, and she knew the killer had used those bushes to his advantage.

Kace swung open an old, wrought-iron gate, and they entered the small courtyard there.

"The first body was here," Bree told Kace as she pointed to the ground. "A silk scarf was still around her throat. Red. So it looked like blood trailing from her neck. There were rope burns on her ankles and her wrists."

"You're not telling me anything I haven't already read in the newspapers." His gaze raked her. "Tell me what you *feel* here. Tell me why the killer chose this place. Tell me why he put her body in that spot. Tell me—"

"He chose the spot so that she could look up and see the shadow of the statue." The tall statue of Jesus that held such a place of prominence. At night, the statue's shadow was illuminated on the back of the Cathedral. To some, it was a heavenly sight. To others, it seemed a bit…foreboding. Intense. Ghostly? "He positioned her so that Lindsey was staring right at the statue."

"And what does that mean?"

"Judgment," the word slipped from her.

Kace gave a long, slow blink.

"I think it was a sign of judgment." That hadn't been in Grayson's profile, but she believed it. The scene, the placement of the body—"Her final moments were being judged."

"And I guess she was found guilty, since the bastard killed her here."

She walked toward the spot where Lindsey's body had been discovered. "There was no sexual assault. With strangulations…the crimes are usually deeply personal, often sexual, so it's possible the killer still found a release, even if he didn't violate her body."

"He violated her body plenty," Kace growled. "He fucking killed her."

There was so much rage in his voice. Bree's gaze jerked to him.

"You really thought I could do this shit? Strangle a woman because it was personal and sexual? And get off on her death?"

Tread carefully. "It is believed you fit—"

"I don't give a rat's ass what Grayson believed with his profile. Do *you* believe I could do that?"

Could he strangle a woman, get off on seeing the life drain from her?

"It's all because of Brittney." Again, his voice was little more than a fierce, rough growl. "Maybe we should clear that shit up, right now. No other cops ever cared about my side of the story, but I'll tell you."

The bells of the church rang. Service was in session. It was a Sunday, after all. Plenty of people were inside, but only she and Kace were behind the Cathedral.

"She cheated on me. I found out, and I left her. Turned my back on her and hooked up with someone else. Two days later, Brittney was dead. The bastard who killed her had used one of my old shirts to strangle her. So, my DNA—yeah, it was everywhere. The fact that I'd been snagged by the cops too many times as a kid made me a perfect suspect. They were ready to throw me in a cell and lock me away for the rest of my life." His eyes burned with emotion. "But they overlooked one small point."

His alibi. She'd read this. Turned out, he'd been with another girl at the time. One who'd finally come forward—even though her too rich family had tried to keep her relationship with Kace quiet—and offered up her testimony on his behalf. “The girl you were with,” Bree whispered. “Susannah—”

“They overlooked the fact that I was innocent. And there was no way I was going to prison for a crime I didn’t commit. If the cops catch me for the things I’ve actually done, if they actually get a jury to agree to lock me away—fine. I’ll do time for that. But I will never be locked up for crimes that I didn’t commit.” Each word vibrated with a dark intensity. “I won’t.”

“That’s why we’re here, right? To look for proof of your innocence.”

His shoulders stiffened. “We’re here so that you can make me understand the killer. I understand him, then I can destroy him.”

A few other people milled into the courtyard.

He stepped closer to her. His arm curled around her shoulders as Kace brought Bree against his body. “Was Ciara’s body positioned the same way?”

“No.” She turned closer to him, pulling in his rich, masculine scent. “She wasn’t posed to stare up at the shadow. She was positioned so that she was looking away from it.”

“And what does that mean?”

“Grayson said—”

His left hand slid under her chin as he tipped back her head. “Fuck Grayson.”

Her brows lifted.

"Actually, don't," he snapped. "Don't ever do that again."

She smiled.

His eyes widened just a little. "You've got a gorgeous smile. I love that dimple."

"Um…thank you."

He gave a small shake of his head, as if to focus himself. "I don't want to hear what Grayson thinks. I told you that already. I want to know what you think. Why did the killer leave one victim staring up at the shadow? But he turned the other away? What do *you* think?"

"I think he did it because he felt guilty. With the second kill, he felt like he was being judged, and he didn't like that."

"Why would he feel guilty?"

"Because something about Ciara was different."

He took her hand, threading his fingers with hers, and led her out of the courtyard. "He knew her."

"Well, ah, the team believes the perp knew all of the victims—"

They'd cleared the courtyard and were now back in Pirate's Alley. Kace spun toward her and pinned her against the wall of an old building. "Your team thinks I'm the killer. And it's obvious I know all of the women. But if you look at this differently, if the guy was really showing guilt over Ciara, then it's because he knew her. Maybe he targeted the other women just because of their association to me. Maybe he didn't really *know* them. But Ciara was different. He had an actual acquaintance with her. Maybe even some kind of relationship. That's why he felt guilt."

"You might make a pretty good profiler yourself," she whispered.

"I'm just good at understanding killers." His mouth moved closer to hers. "Why do you hunt killers, Bree? Is it because of what happened to your family?"

"Yes." She swallowed. "No one ever found the man who hurt them."

"The man who hurt *you*." Anger there, dark and insidious.

She nodded. "I want to help other families so they don't have to live every day, always looking over their shoulders."

"Is that what you do? Always look for the man who hurt you?"

She wouldn't let her fear show. "Yes." And sometimes, she still woke up, screaming, because the nightmares never stopped.

"You help me find this killer, and maybe I can help you find yours."

Now he'd surprised her. "What? How can you do that?" Did he think she hadn't looked for that bastard? She had. Over and over again.

Kace closed the last bit of distance between them, and his lips brushed lightly over hers. "You'd be surprised at the connections I have."

Another soft kiss.

Her hands rose and pressed to his chest. "What are you doing?"

"We both know I'm kissing you."

And he did it—again.

"Why?"

"Better question, sweetheart, why are you kissing me back?"

Oh, hell, she was. She was leaning toward him. Parting her lips. Wanting a much deeper, harder kiss. But at his words, her whole body went tense. Why was she kissing him back?

"Because you want me," he rasped. "And I want you. Soon enough, we'll have to do something about that desire." His eyes were on her mouth. "I'd like a real taste."

So, would she. For a moment, she imagined sinking her fingers into his dark hair and pulling his head toward her. She could already feel the thrust of his tongue in her mouth, the hunger in his kiss. The need that would sweep through them both.

"But if I kiss you the way I want, we might wind up fucking on the streets of New Orleans."

She shoved against his chest. "In your dreams."

"Absolutely." He backed away. "And in reality, anytime you're ready."

Bree pulled in a couple of deep, bracing breaths. "Do you want to go to the other crime scene or not?"

"We're going." This time, he looped their arms together. "Let's take a walk, shall we? The scene isn't too far away."

"No, it's not. He's keeping his kill zone tight."

"Kill zone." He seemed to mull that over.

"Three murders, all in the same tight, geographic area. The perp feels comfortable here. He knows the city well. When he took his third vic to the trolley station, he knew the place would be closed down for a while so he could…work." She stumbled over that last bit. God, it felt cold to say things that way. "He didn't count on the homeless man. Because of him, the perp's MO had to change. He couldn't finish strangling his vic, so he went for the quick drive of the knife." Bree fell silent as she thought about that…an interrupted kill. A serial's twisted desires. Since the guy hadn't been able to kill his vic the way he'd intended, what kind of reaction would the perp have?

They passed the Square. Performers were already set up outside of Jackson Square. A man polished his saxophone. A young kid covered in silver paint danced in his tap shoes.

The shop fronts were decorated with pumpkins and skulls. Since Halloween was closing in, the whole town seemed to be celebrating. The grinning skulls stared at Bree as she passed them. An artist had just set up his paintings nearby, and they were all dark. Twisted. With deep shadows and ghostly figures filling the canvases.

"Halloween in the Big Easy," Kace murmured. "Always an interesting time."

She wouldn't know. "Do things get crazy here?"

"Crazier. The ghosts come out stronger then."

Now she laughed. "I don't believe in ghosts."

He wasn't laughing. "This city is built on more blood and death than you can imagine. I wouldn't blame the ghosts if they decided to come back and raise some hell."

They were near the front of the Square. The carriages and their horses were all lined up and ready for tourists.

"Haunted Tour!" One driver shouted, "I'll take you to all of the city's darkest and most dangerous spots…"

"People love death and danger." Kace didn't slow his pace. "People love to be scared."

She didn't.

They hurried across the main street. Walked past more shops. More skeletons, spiders, witches. A man with vampire fangs and bloody lips tried to pull them into his store. Kace just waved the guy away and didn't slow his stride.

Then they were leaving the busy hub and heading closer to the river. In the distance, Bree could see a steamboat's wheels turning. They crossed the trolley tracks, and yellow police tape flapped in the wind near the Canal Street Station.

Other people were there. Snapping pictures. One teen was even sprawling on the tracks, feigning death.

"I told you," Kace's breath blew lightly over her ear, "people like death in this town."

She shivered. "Death isn't something you play with."

"No, it isn't."

Her gaze slid over the scene. She ignored the people with their phones and their excited voices. She focused on what the scene would have been like when the victim had been there. She'd seen crime scene photos when she'd gone to the hospital and met with her team, so she knew what the layout of the scene had been like when the victim had been there.

The killer had put her near the tracks. Not *on* the tracks, but near them. He hadn't wanted the trolley to hit her. He'd kept her hands and feet bound. The coroner believed the victims had all been restrained until after death because there were no signs that the victims had been able to fight back.

So, Amelia Sanderson had been near the tracks. Hands bound. Feet bound. The killer had wrapped a white, nylon rope around her neck. He'd been squeezing, pulling tighter and tighter.

Then he'd heard a shout...

She could see it in her mind.

"His back was to the man who'd called out. The perp knew he didn't have time to finish the job with his rope, so he reached for his knife." Her head tilted. "He shoved the blade into her chest, aiming for her heart, but missing, going a little to the left because she was struggling to survive."

Kace was quiet.

"He didn't finish the way he wanted." She bit her lower lip. "That scares me." Her gaze rose to lock on Kace's.

"Why?"

"Because most serial killers follow a pattern. A precise manner of killing. It gives them—relief, if you will. The need builds up in them, and it explodes, driving them to act."

"To take a victim." His voice was low, for her alone.

Bree nodded. "And they kill, usually in a very specific manner, and with the death of the prey, control comes back to the perp." Her gaze slid to the tracks. "He didn't get to kill his way."

"What the hell does that mean?"

"It means he was interrupted." A soft sigh escaped her. "And it means he's going to be killing again, very soon."

CHAPTER TEN

"I want you to stay here, Bree," Kace announced, his voice careful because he didn't want to give away just how badly he wanted her at his home. Night was starting to fall again. She'd spent the day walking crime scenes with him, following leads, and telling him everything that he wanted to know about killers.

Turned out, Bree knew one hell of a lot about them.

"I have to take care of some work. I won't be out long." He shoved his hand into his pockets. The better to not reach out and touch her. Being close to her all day had been the biggest temptation of his life. The woman he wanted most was right there.

He shouldn't have kissed her in the alley. He knew that. One wild kiss had just made him want so much more.

Everything.

Would a woman like Bree ever give a man like him *everything?* Probably not. But a guy could wonder.

"Stay here," he urged her. "Plenty of security. Plenty of food. I'll be back before you know it."

She cocked her head to the right. "The minute you leave, I'll search your house."

So fucking cute. As if he hadn't realized that was exactly what she'd do, but he appreciated her honesty. "Go ahead. You won't find anything." Nothing that he didn't want her to find, anyway.

A spark lit her eyes.

"When I come back," he added, "we'll have dinner together. Anything you want."

Bree gave a slow shake of her head. "I'm not your new roommate, Kace. I'm the FBI agent investigating you."

The FBI agent working with me. But he didn't correct her. "During dinner, you can grill me. Ask me every burning question that you have. It will just be me and you—no lawyer in sight."

She looked interested, just as he'd hoped. "You'll actually answer my questions?"

"Most of them." Would he confess to his darkest crimes? Hell, no.

He'd buried those bodies too well.

"But before I go…" Kace moved to stand right in front of her.

"Kace…"

"No kiss good-bye?"

Her gaze locked on his mouth.

"Tempted, aren't you?" Kace teased.

"Yes."

He hadn't expected such a direct response. He also hadn't expected her hands to rise. To curl around his shoulders. For Bree to push onto her toes and bring her mouth toward his—

He met her. His head bent, and his mouth took hers. There was nothing teasing or gentle about this kiss. Maybe because the need had been building all damn day. Maybe because the instant his lips touched hers, an inferno of need seemed to consume him. His tongue thrust into her mouth. He tasted. He took. When she moaned, the sound made his dick twitch. He was rock hard and ready, his cock shoving against his jeans, and he wanted *in* her.

He lifted her up. Took two steps and pressed her back to the nearest wall. Her legs wrapped around his hips as he held her there. He feasted on her mouth. Her taste was driving him *insane* with hunger. Kace pulled back, but only so that he could nip at her lower lip.

She moaned again. That soft little sound was pure temptation.

"Kace..."

Her head turned away. Rejecting him, again.

Fuck that. Did the woman know how many others would beg to be in his bed?

"You need to make a choice," he told her. "You need to make the call."

Her legs slid from his hips. Her ragged breathing filled the air. Wait, maybe that was his breathing. Lust was a dangerous beast inside of him.

He made sure she was steady, then he stepped back.

"There's the case," he told her flatly. "Then there is us. You can fuck me and still do your job."

Her eyes were so wide and deep.

"You can find the real killer, and you can give in to this burning lust that we feel. You and I both know this kind of hunger doesn't come along all the time. We touch, and everything else fades away."

"The last time I fucked a stranger, I almost had to kiss my career good-bye."

He smiled at her. "I'm not a stranger."

"No, you're the bad guy."

"Not to you." She should understand this. "Never to you."

Her lips were red and swollen from his mouth. He wanted to kiss her again, but because he wanted that so badly, Kace took another step back. "Make sure you set the security system when I leave." He'd shown her the settings earlier that day. Just handing over all of his passwords and his home to an FBI agent? Sure, some people might think he'd lost his mind.

Remy would certainly think that.

But Kace was just playing the game. Sometimes, you had to roll the dice.

Kace grabbed his jacket and headed for the door.

"What business are you taking care of on a Sunday night?"

He glanced back at her and winked. "Just a little matter of life and death."

"Kace—"

"Missing me already?"

Her cheeks flushed. He would never get tired of Bree's sweet blush.

"Better hurry, love, and get to work," he urged her. "I won't be gone long. Don't you want to see how much of my place you can search in that time? No warrant required."

He opened the door and slipped into the growing darkness.

***

When the door closed behind Kace, Bree became aware of the heavy silence in the house. She looked up, her gaze darting to the imposing staircase.

Alone.

She turned away from the door and ran upstairs. She'd left her phone on the bed, and now she made a beeline for it. She hadn't checked in with the team all day long, and there were sure as hell some choice things she needed to say to Grayson.

She snatched the phone from the bed and made her way to the room next door. Kace's room. She called Grayson—

"What in the hell are you doing?" Grayson snarled. "We had eyes on you all day. You were freaking making out with the guy in public! You were—"

"I was staying close to the target." Bree stilled just outside of Kace's bedroom. "That's my job, isn't it?" Anger burned inside of her. "And that was your plan. I mean, it *is* the reason you trashed my room at the bed and breakfast, isn't it?"

She waited for a denial. Kace had to be wrong about Grayson. Lying to her, that was it, he was—

"The guy found out about that, did he?"

All of the breath left her lungs in a long whoosh. "You did that?"

"Had to make the scene look real, Bree. Especially after he sent his man to investigate. Knew he was getting suspicious. Had to do something to tip the scales our way. And it worked, didn't it? He moved you right into his home."

Her temples were throbbing. "You destroyed my things?"

"I set a scene. I knew how to make it look like a crazed attacker had been there."

So much rage. She'd seen rage and hate in her room, and, yes, Grayson would know how to duplicate that set-up perfectly. It had been like so many scenes she'd studied when learning about violent behavior patterns. Now that she thought about it, the scene had almost been textbook perfect. "Sonofabitch," she gritted out.

"Don't be mad, Bree. I needed you to have a real, visceral reaction or Kace wasn't going to take you in. Didn't you hear what I said before? He'd already sent his man to search the place. I only made my move after Dominic saw Kace's right-hand slipping inside your room."

The throbbing in her temples got worse. "What?"

"The big guy, Remy. He broke into your room at Ms. Queen's. I had to react. Who the hell knows what Remy found in there? I was sure Kace had figured out you were FBI."

Remy had broken into her room, too? Had everyone in the whole world broken into her place? "He did figure it out." Her left hand reached for the doorknob. "He caught me when I was searching the house last night."

A low whistle. "Dammit. Tell me you found something useful—"

She didn't open the bedroom door. "Kace says he's innocent."

Grayson gave a rough laugh. "That guy has never been innocent a day in his life."

Said the man who'd just confessed to destroying all of her property.

"We have eyes on him," Grayson snapped abruptly. "He's leaving the property." A pause. "You're there alone?"

"He told me to search the whole place if I wanted."

"Find me something I can use, Bree."

"If he told me to search, that means Kace knows I won't find anything. There's nothing here." She'd already realized that—why hadn't Grayson? "He says someone else is behind the murders, that he's being framed, and I'm starting to believe him."

"Bree," her name was a frustrated sigh. "The man is a liar. He's cold-blooded. He's *the* crime boss of this city."

"He wants me to help him find the real killer."

"Fuck, that's such bullshit!"

She wasn't so sure. "I agreed to do it. We're working as partners. I get access to his life, and he gets to pick my brain."

Silence. Then… "No."

"It's not your call—"

"I'm the senior agent, and you are blinded by him. The guy is a charmer, a scammer, but I thought you could see through that. He wants to know what the FBI has on the Strangler. He wants to make sure we're not about to take him down. That's why he wants to pick your brain. He's using you, Bree."

So are you.

"Don't trust him," Grayson ordered curtly. "Not even for a second."

***

"Are you comfortable?" He smiled at her. "Those ropes were terribly rough, weren't they? The silks are much better." He let a long trail of silk drift from his hand.

She didn't speak, but a tear leaked down her cheek.

He bent to check the knots he'd tied on her wrists. His gloved fingers slid over her bruised skin. Perfect. The silk would hold.

Then he bent to inspect the silk he'd twined around her neck. Not tight enough to kill. Certainly not…yet. He had plans. Wonderful, brilliant plans.

He pulled back and drew out his knife.

She whimpered.

"Don't worry. I really don't like using this thing." He stared at the blade. Was that a drop of blood still on there? From Amelia? "I don't enjoy blood. Far too messy for me." When he thought of Amelia, his whole body tightened. That scene had been a cluster. And now he had to worry about the witness. No matter, he'd find the guy soon enough.

No one would notice when a homeless man or woman vanished. No one had noticed the others he'd practiced on before he'd taken Lindsey. Practice made perfect.

He caught a chunk of her blond hair in his hand. He brought the knife in and began to saw off her hair.

"Stop it! Stop!"

Now she screamed? Women could be so vain.

He dropped the knife, tightened the silk around her neck, and cut off her cries. "Not another sound."

More tears. She cried so much. He liked the tears. They made him strong.

She'd brought this all on herself. Did she realize that? "You should have stayed out of Fantasy." He picked up his knife. Went back to sawing on her hair. Blond chunks fell to the floor. "Once you came inside, you were mine."

He kept working until she was absolutely picture perfect. Then he tucked his knife back in the sheath that was strapped to his ankle.

She stared at him with her wide, desperate eyes. Eyes that were the wrong color, but, well, he didn't want to cut her eyes out. Too messy.

Then he reached for the silk that he'd twined around her neck—he'd looped the silk around the slender column of her throat two times.

"Please," she whispered.

It was the last thing she said. He tightened the silk, yanked the edges hard so that his hands became fists. Her eyes were wide open, staring at him. He loved to watch the eyes change as his victims fought. *Look, look…not so blue any longer. Now they're red.*

Her eyes changed without him having to use his knife.

Her body twisted and bucked, but there was no escape. He had her exactly where he wanted her.

And soon, soon she wasn't moving at all.

CHAPTER ELEVEN

When Kace unlocked the front door, the house appeared to be in darkness. Unease slithered through him. "Bree?" He moved to quickly reset the alarm.

"I'm in your study." Her voice was low.

He stalked toward the study, pulling off his leather gloves and tossing them onto a nearby table. He kept his jacket on, and when he approached the study, he saw the lamp shining near his desk.

Bree was seated behind his desk.

And her gun was on top of his desk.

Kace paused inside the doorway and smiled.

"You think this is funny?" Bree's voice seethed. "That's *my* gun."

"I'm smiling because I'm impressed you found it."

"It was hidden beneath the fake bottom of your top desk drawer. Hardly a challenge."

He propped his shoulder against the doorframe. "You're mad."

"You broke into my room. Wait, no, you didn't do it, did you? Why get your hands dirty?"

He glanced down at his hands. "They've been dirty for years."

She shot out of his chair. "You sent your flunky Remy to do the deed, didn't you? You had him search—"

"Haven't *you* just spent the last two hours searching my home?"

Her lips parted.

"We're even." He nodded. "Why do you think I gave you permission to search? I wanted us to be even. Now, let's have dinner. I'm starving." He turned away. "What do you feel—"

"We are *not* even."

A sigh slipped from him. "No? I'd hoped we would be." Kace glanced back at her. "Yes, I sent Remy to search your room. I suspected you were FBI. I wanted hard proof. His search ended right before I got the lovely dossier on you. Presto, proof." Kace shrugged. "Then I felt bad about the search. Especially when your overzealous ex went fucking insane and destroyed the place, so I figured it was only fair for me to let you have a turn exploring my house."

She marched away from the desk. "There is nothing fair here. You know there is nothing incriminating in this house!"

"No?" He crossed his arms over his chest. "That's where you're wrong. I just handed you the means to have me locked away."

Bree's gaze darted to the gun that sat on his desk.

"Breaking and entering," he murmured. "An FBI agent just found her stolen weapon in my house. You don't get a better slam dunk than that. You want me locked up? I gave you the means right there."

She tucked a lock of hair behind her ear. "Kace…"

"It's about building trust."

Bree shook her head. "It's about you breaking into my room!"

"You lied to me, Bree." He kept his voice calm and low. He knew how important this scene was. "You deceived me from the very first moment that we met."

She strode toward him, stopping only when their bodies were almost touching. Her lavender scent wrapped around him.

"You were in Fantasy to take me down. So, I had to do my own research. I sent Remy into your room, yes. I wanted to get real evidence on you before I got in over my head."

"Over *your* head?"

"Sweetheart, isn't it obvious?" When she didn't speak, he uncrossed his arms and reached for her hand. Such a small, delicate hand. He lifted it up. Tapped her pinky. "You've got me wrapped around your little finger."

"Bullshit."

He wouldn't smile. But, damn, he liked her.

"I should lock your ass up," Bree threatened.

Kace just nodded. "The local cops have been wanting to do it for years. They'd call you a hero. Maybe even throw you a parade."

She didn't smile at him. "Do you *want* me to lock you up?"

"I want you to stop looking at me like I'm a villain. I want you to judge me for yourself." Okay, now he was getting a little too honest with her. He needed to back up and slow this shit down.

"I am judging. I have been judging you from the moment we met." She huffed out an angry breath. "I don't need someone else to tell me what to think. I can do that on my own."

Now he was curious. "Then what do you think of me?"

"I think you're dangerous."

True enough.

"I think you're a powerful man with a lot of enemies."

Again, no denying it.

"You don't let anyone close because despite what you're telling me right now, you really don't want to let others know you too well."

All right. They could stop this little game now—

"You're cold and you're calculating, but you're also protective. You don't like it when people you consider to be *yours* get hurt."

He didn't speak.

"You think I'm yours."

He did. Dammit.

"But I'm not. I'm my own person, and this—this attraction that we have? I know it's not normal. It's probably due to the danger, due to the intensity of this case."

Is that what she was telling herself? Nah, he didn't buy it. "Maybe it's just due to the fact that we want to rip each other's clothes off."

She stared into his eyes. "I'm not fucking you tonight."

"A man can dream." He turned away. "Come on, baby, I want to make you dinner."

"I'm not done."

He rolled back his shoulders, but he didn't look at her. He was a bit worried about the mask he might be wearing—or not wearing. Kace was starting to fear that Bree could look beneath his surface too easily.

"You project this image to the world. You say you don't want me to see you as a villain, but I think…I think that is precisely what you *do* want people to see. Because you don't think you're better than that. You think that you're still the guy who got tried for murder. The guy that all the cops and the Press said was trash."

"I don't like it when you profile me."

Her steps hurried toward him. Her hand locked around his arm and Bree spun him back to face her. "Too damn bad."

Her eyes were blazing. The woman was beautiful.

"You're not that same man. The reporters were wrong. The cops were wrong. You're not the same, I'm not the same. I'm not the girl who stood over her parents' dead bodies and then *ran* from the house."

"You ran to survive."

"And you became the bad guy to do the exact same thing."

Holy shit. She'd just straight-up called him out.

"So why don't we both stop pretending?" Bree demanded as she searched his gaze. "If we're going to work together, really work together, then the games stop. You be honest with me, I'll be honest with you, and maybe we can stop the sonofabitch out there from killing any other women."

They needed to go back over one very important point. "You believe I'm not guilty?"

"No, I think you're guilty as all hell." She smiled at him. Her dimple winked. "But not of these crimes. You didn't kill those women."

"How do you know?" He shouldn't push. He should just accept the gift that she'd handed him and let it go.

"Because I built a profile on you. I started that profile before we ever met. Grayson thought you were guilty, but I didn't. And I took the case because I wanted to prove that I was right, and Grayson…he's freaking wrong."

He was going to kiss her. Going to fuck her. Going to never, ever let her go. She was staring at him, believing in him, and he hadn't even needed to lie. Well, not lie too much, anyway. She was—

"Now let's get that dinner, Kace. Because I am starving."

***

They were dead. Bree stared down at her parents, soft, desperate cries breaking from her lips. There was so much blood. Her mother's white robe was covered in blood. And her father—God, what had happened to his neck?

She reached toward them. "Dad?"

A blade pressed to her stomach. "Isn't this what you wanted?"

A scream tore from her. Wild and desperate. No, no, she'd never wanted this! She'd never—

"*Bree!*" The lights flew on. Kace stood in the doorway, clad in a loose pair of jeans that were unsnapped. His eyes were blazing, and his face was locked down in hard, dangerous lines.

Shit, *shit.* She'd screamed. Another one of the endless nightmares that wouldn't leave her alone. Bree grabbed for the bed covers and pulled them up to her chest. "I'm fine." Her voice sounded brittle, even to her own ears.

"The hell you are." He rushed forward and sat on the edge of the bed. His hands reached out and wrapped around her shoulders. "What in the hell happened? You sounded scared to death."

She didn't usually talk about the dreams. Not with anyone. "It's nothing. I'm sorry I woke you."

"Fuck that sorry shit. This is *me.*" His hold tightened on her. "You were scared, and I want to know why."

Her heart was still racing. "Just a bad dream."

But Kace shook his head. "You were afraid. *Talk* to me."

And…she did. When she'd never talked with another man, she told him… "It's the same nightmare I've had for years. My parents are dead. I'm standing in their blood, and then a man shoves a knife into my stomach."

He stared at her. Just stared. A muscle flexed in his jaw. "How often does that dream come?"

"Usually once or twice a month." Sometimes more often. Especially if she was stressed.

"And you wake your lovers up with your screams? What do they do to make you feel better?"

Feel better? What an odd question. "Nothing."

"Fucking sonsofbitches."

"There are no lovers with me. They don't stay the night. I don't—I don't have a lot of lovers, okay? Grayson and I were a mistake. Before him, it was a guy from grad school. But Max never stayed the night. I didn't let him." She tried to focus on deep, even breathing. The non-panicky kind of breathing. "I didn't want them to hear my screams."

"I heard your screams."

It wasn't just about the screams, though, it was about what she'd been afraid she might say. "You can go," she managed to say in a semi-normal voice. "I'm okay, really. Sorry I woke you up."

"Screw that." He moved away from the bed.

He'd leave now. He'd—

He scooped her into his arms. Lifted her up and held her easily against his chest.

Her whole body jolted. "What are you doing?"

"Taking you into my room."

"But—"

She stopped. She'd been about to say...*But if you take me into your room, we'll have sex.*

Because her control was too thin. She was scared, coming off the edge of her blackest fear. It was the middle of the night. She was shaky. She was—

"I'll just hold you, baby. Unless you want something more."

He carried her into his room. The bedroom she'd searched earlier, and Bree was surprised to see that all of the lights were on. And a bottle of whiskey sat on the bedside table.

Carefully, Kace placed her in his bed.

"You weren't asleep," she said softly.

He shook his head. Moved back to pour some whiskey in a glass. "Hard to sleep when the woman you want most is just on the other side of the wall." He pushed the glass toward her.

The bed carried his scent. The sheets were silk and felt like heaven against her skin. He'd had clothes brought in for her—and Bree could have worn anything she wanted to bed.

She'd chosen to wear his borrowed shirt.

Her fingers closed around the glass of whiskey. She lifted it to her mouth. Took a sip and felt it burn down her throat. "He talks to me." She hadn't meant to say that.

Kace was standing beside the bed, staring at her.

"I can't remember if he actually said the words to me that night…" Another sip. Another burn. "Or if I've just put them in my head because of all the questions from the cops. All the accusations that came at me. But lately, in my dreams, he says…" Now she didn't take a sip. Bree gulped the whiskey because she was about to make the biggest confession of her life.

To a man she should never trust.

But we're more alike than we are different. Kace had been right about that. The connection was there. It was more than skin deep. She was starting to think it might be soul deep.

"What does he say to you?"

Her shaking fingers made the glass tremble.

His hand closed around hers. He pulled the glass away. Set it back on the table, then he eased onto the edge of the bed. His hands came down, pressing to the mattress on either side of her body.

She swallowed. "Since I've come to New Orleans, he says, *'Isn't this what you wanted?'*"

"Fuck."

Now her eyes squeezed closed. "I didn't want it." Bree shook her head. "I didn't. I don't care what he said. I don't care what the newspapers said, I don't care what—"

"Bree."

Her eyes opened.

He stared straight at her. "I know."

Just that. Only that.

She surged toward him. Her hands cupped his jaw, feeling the hard rasp of stubble against her palms. Her mouth took his. The kiss was desperate and wild, and she didn't care.

I know.

He did. She had the uncanny feeling that he knew her, far better than anyone else ever had before.

His arms closed around her. His mouth opened against hers. His tongue slipped into her mouth, and he gave a low growl.

She could taste the whiskey on his tongue. Knew he could taste it on hers. It made her feel a little drunk, a little out of control.

A lot out of control.

There were a thousand reasons why she should pull away. And only one reason to hold him closer. *Because I want him.*

He tumbled her back onto the bed. She was on top of the covers, and the t-shirt hiked up a bit when he pushed her against the bedding. Her hands slid down his body, moving to hold his shoulders. Powerful, wide shoulders. His chest was broad and strong, and the way he was working his mouth…

Kace Quick could kiss.

He tore his mouth from hers, but then he began to kiss a path down her neck. Kissing, licking, lightly biting. Her hips surged up against him.

"Easy…"

No, she wanted hard. Fast. Oblivion.

His hand moved to her hip. Down, down to her thigh. Her skin was too sensitive, every touch had her on edge, and when he lifted up her t-shirt more, Bree tensed. Her nails bit into his shoulders.

His fingers stroked over the edge of her panties as he caressed her through the thin cotton. Just a touch, and she was wet for him. Her hips arched again, rocking against his hand. She didn't want this light, tentative caress. She didn't want the cotton between them. She wanted his fingers on her. In her. "Kace!" His name was a cry of demand.

His fingers eased under the edge of her panties. Stroked her clit. Had her gasping and tensing, and he kept caressing, strumming the most sensitive spot on her body and driving her toward orgasm.

She thought he'd get her to come that way. Just with his fingers. With his thumb stroking over her clit and then his fingers sliding into her core. But he pulled back.

Bree bit back her protest.

In the next moment, he'd shoved her legs apart. Ripped away the panties. She actually heard them tear, and the sound just turned her on all the more. She wasn't normally wild during sex. She'd never had a lover who was the honest-to-God, panty-tearing type, but Kace was different.

He put his mouth on her. She almost flew off the bed. But his hands clamped around her hips, yanking her toward his mouth, holding her there as he licked and sucked, and there was no holding back her orgasm. She came on a wild eruption of release. Came against his mouth, shuddering and aching in the most powerful release of her life.

In the aftermath, her heart pounded frantically. She couldn't pull in a deep breath, and her lips were desert dry. She licked them and realized she'd shut her eyes. Bree opened her eyes.

Kace was staring at her. She'd never seen such a look of dark lust before in her entire life.

"Delicious."

Her legs were still wide open. And judging by his white-hot stare, the man was very much still aroused.

But…

He pulled down her shirt. *His* borrowed shirt. He rose from the bed. Poured himself a whiskey. Downed it in one gulp.

Her thighs were trembling. She could feel aftershocks of pleasure in her sex, little contractions deep inside. "Kace?"

His hold tightened on the glass. "You go well with whiskey."

It was way too hard to breathe. "You…you didn't…"

He sat the glass down. *Hard.* "Because I want you to be sure. There's time to walk away, right the hell now. There's that final line we haven't crossed."

Um, he'd just gone down on her. She considered that a pretty big line.

"You can walk away. Say you haven't fucked the big, bad criminal of New Orleans. You can tell your other agent buddies that. Pretend your hands are perfectly clean because you never touched me."

She wanted to touch him all over. "And what will you do? Go tell all your buddies that you screwed an FBI agent?"

His eyes narrowed. "No."

Just that. Nothing more. "Kace?"

"I'm not the type to kiss and tell, Bree. What happens here in this room, I won't tell a soul. These moments are mine. I'm not the sharing sort, I warned you of that before."

He had. And he was also giving her a chance to run away. To stop before things went too far between them.

Too late.

She reached for his hand. "I want you." It wasn't because she'd woken from a nightmare and was scared. Wasn't because she felt vulnerable. Wasn't because she'd had whiskey. She just wanted him. There would be no pretending that this night was about anything other than need.

Desire.

Bree brought his hand to her mouth. Pressed a kiss to his knuckles.

"Bree..."

She liked the way he said her name. With such stark hunger and raw need. Her lashes lifted as she gazed up at him. "What is it that you're waiting for? Because I don't like waiting."

He moved fast, climbing back onto the bed, onto her, taking her mouth and kissing her with a fierce intensity. His hips were between her spread legs, the rough fabric of his jeans sliding against her inner thighs. As he kissed her, his hand reached between them. The hiss of the zipper reached her ears as her hands stroked down his back.

This was happening. They were happening.

"Let me...get condom..." Kace gritted out the words against her lips and then he was reaching for the bedside table, fumbling with the small drawer there and pulling out a condom.

When he started to roll it on, Bree pushed him back. He went willingly, and she took the condom from him. She pumped the long, thick length of his cock, and Kace bit out a curse. She had to smile and pump again before she ripped open the small wrapper and put the condom on the head of his cock. With a careful touch, she rolled the condom down his erection, savoring every touch.

"You like to tease."

Her gaze met his. "You have no idea."

He didn't know all of the things she liked. She didn't know what he liked, but Bree was ready to find out.

She climbed on top of him, straddling his lap. His hands had clamped around her hips again. The head of his cock brushed at the entrance to her body. She was wet and eager from her climax, and Bree wanted to sink down on him.

"Get rid of the shirt," Kace growled. "I want to see all of you."

She lifted the shirt up and tossed it away.

"Fucking beautiful."

Bree took him inside in one long, slow glide. They both groaned. He felt so good, filling her completely, stretching her. Already sensitive, the slide of his cock had her nearly coming again. She lifted up, pushed down—

"You feel like heaven."

She should say something back. Speech was just a little too hard. She was moving up and down, and his hand was on her breast. Squeezing her nipple, teasing her, and her climax was so close, already so close and—

"Again? Hell, yes, baby, *hell, yes*."

He leaned up, took her nipple into his mouth, and his hand moved between their bodies. He found her clit and stroked, and she came, her whole body clenching as the pleasure hit her on a furious wave of release.

He tumbled her back onto the bed. Lifted her legs up higher and pounded into her, his rhythm fast and rough and exactly what she wanted.

"Heaven…feels so good…so good…" He stiffened against her, his hips jerking, and Bree was staring right into his eyes when they went blind with pleasure. Her sex clamped greedily around him as he came, and her whole body seemed tuned to him.

He shuddered again, and the pleasure on his face deepened.

Her own body was still lost in a post-climax haze, but fear was sliding into her heart. Fear because…

Holy shit, those had been the best two climaxes of her life.

His mouth pressed to hers. She expected a tender kiss. One of those after-sex pecks. Instead he feasted on her again. Kissed her with the same wild hunger and need he'd shown her just moments before. As if they hadn't just pounded their way to climax.

"Want you again," he growled.

He did. She could feel him getting thicker inside of her already.

"Want me?"

Bree nodded.

He pulled out of her. She hated his loss, but he headed for the bathroom. She started to call after him. She definitely wanted him again. And again. When you had sex that good, you could get hooked—

He was back. He'd ditched his condom, but he was already reaching for another. His blue stare was blazingly bright.

"It's going to be a long night," Kace told her.

And all she could think was…

Hell, yes.

***

Bree hadn't checked in again.

Grayson sat in his office. It was close to one a.m.

And Bree hadn't checked in.

He'd ordered her to search Kace Quick's home. To tear the place apart. She should have found something they could use.

But he hadn't heard a word from her. No call. No text. Nothing.

A light rap sounded at his door. "Boss?" Dominic stood there, looking tired, his hair tousled. "I just got back in," Dominic said. "Spent the last few hours retracing the crime scenes. Figured if Bree and Quick were there today, maybe there was something I'd missed."

"Was there?"

Dominic shook his head. "Tourists have turned the Canal Street scene into photo central. They're posing on the damn tracks, and that's going to get someone killed."

Yeah, it would.

"Karin is at the morgue," Dominic continued. "She's hoping some DNA evidence can be found on Amelia Sanderson. Of all the kills, her crime scene was the least organized."

Organized—this perp *was* organized. Until Amelia, the scenes had been perfect, absolutely pristine. But he'd screwed up with her because of the homeless man who'd interrupted his kill. And things had gotten very, very messy.

"Maybe we'll get lucky with her," Dominic added with a roll of one shoulder.

"Well, Amelia sure as shit didn't get lucky, did she?" Grayson swiped a hand over his face. The dead woman's image was in his head, along with too many others. Another ghost to haunt him.

"No." Dominic shifted from foot to foot. He wiped his hands against the front of his thighs. "You heard from Bree?"

"She's still staying with the suspect." *And, no, she didn't check in after her search. She should have –*

"With respect, I didn't like that you trashed her place," Dominic's chin lifted. "Didn't seem right, especially the way all of her stuff was destroyed."

"I was setting a scene—"

"She should have been told." His green eyes were angry.

"Then her reaction wouldn't have been the same." Why the hell was he having to explain this to an agent under him? Grayson shot to his feet. "Because of our plan, she's now in the house of Kace Quick. She has better access to him than anyone has gotten before."

"And she's in more danger." Dominic straightened his spine. "*If* he's the killer, then she could be his next victim. It's like we put her on a silver platter for him."

This was BS. "Bree is a trained FBI agent. Would you rather have the killer targeting her or a civilian? At least Bree can fight back. She can bring the bastard down."

Dominic just shook his head. "FBI agents can die, too. And she's in there with him, all alone. Who knows what could be happening to her?"

***

His hands linked with hers as Kace lifted Bree's arms over her head. His eyes were on her, his body driving in and out of hers. Every thrust and glide had his cock pushing against her clit. Her legs were clamped around his hips, and she arched against him, meeting him wild thrust for thrust.

The sex was out of control. She was out of control. The pleasure wouldn't stop—she felt drunk from it. From him. Another orgasm was building, rising up faster and faster, and when he bent to kiss her, when his tongue dipped into her mouth—

The pleasure hit. Another eruption that shook her whole body.

He was right there with her. He drove deep into her, held her tight, and she felt the shudder of release that ran the length of his body.

Her heart was thundering. Or was it his? She couldn't tell. Maybe it didn't matter. He withdrew, and she didn't even open her eyes. Exhaustion pulled at her.

His steps shuffled toward the bathroom. She just pulled the covers closer, and then Bree realized—

Maybe I should go back to my room.

Her eyes opened. If the sex was over, then he probably didn't want her staying there. And she didn't want to stay, did she? It had just been about pleasure. A physical need. It had—

He was back. He slid into the bed. She started to rise, but he just curled his arm around her stomach and pulled her against him. "Going somewhere?"

"Um, my bed. I might—I might scream again so—"

"If you do, I'll wake you up, tell you everything is okay, and then you can go back to sleep." His head turned so that he stared at her. She was on one pillow, he was on the other. Their faces were just inches apart. "Or, if you want, we can fuck again."

Her breath caught.

His hand lifted. Stroked over her cheek. "Either way, you don't need to leave."

Eventually, she would have to leave. The case would be over. Whatever was between them—that would be over. But for the moment, she didn't move. She stared into his eyes, and Bree wished that she knew his secrets. Every single one of them. "Are you really as bad as people say?"

His hand lingered against her cheek. "Sometimes, I'm worse."

Hardly reassuring.

"But I would never hurt you, Bree. I hope you understand that. And if any fools tried to hurt you…"

"What?" She tried a faint smile. "Would you kick their asses?"

He didn't smile back at her. "I'd kill them."

CHAPTER TWELVE

When he woke up, Bree was gone.

Kace jerked in the bed, sitting upright. "Bree?" The space beside him was empty. He stretched his hand toward her pillow, but it was cold to the touch.

Maybe she was just showering. Or maybe she'd gone downstairs to grab breakfast. Sunlight drifted in through his curtains as he yanked on a t-shirt and a pair of jeans. He checked in the bedroom he'd given her, but she wasn't there. The bed had been made, though. The bedcovers pulled up, the pillows neatly arranged.

He hurried down the stairs. Kace thought he caught the faint scent of lavender, but when he went into the kitchen, she wasn't there. A note was, one that she'd put on the refrigerator with a magnet.

Had to check in with my team.

He pulled out his phone. He'd grabbed it on his way out of the bedroom and shoved it into his pocket. Now he sent Bree a fast text.

You left without saying good-bye.

And he didn't like that. He'd wanted to wake up to Bree. He'd liked the idea of her being beside him. She probably had no idea, but he didn't typically let his lovers spend the night in his bed.

Bree was different.

His phone dinged as he received a text.

It's not good-bye. It's just me checking in with Grayson.

She included a devil emoji.

Kace found himself smiling. *Tell him to fuck off.*

Her text came back immediately. *Nah, I want to keep my job.*

And Kace wanted to keep *her*. He stared at the screen. *I'm going to Fantasy. Meet me there when you're done?*

Why was he so eager to see her again?

Not because he thought she might have more intel on the case but…

Because he just wanted her.

I'll be there.

He nodded. Started to tuck the phone away, but then…*How did you leave? Tell me you didn't walk to meet that bozo.*

Three dots appeared on his phone. She was typing something and—

No, you were right. This morning when I woke up, they were in the ever-so-obvious van down the road.

Now he did smile. *I had fun last night.*

Three dots. She was going to send him something…

Me, too.

***

"Your face changed."

Bree shoved her phone back into her pocket, frowning at Karin's words. "What do you mean?"

"Whoever sent you the text." Karin motioned to the phone. "You like him. Your face softened. You smiled."

Oh, jeez. How to handle that one?

"I'm big on body language," Karin added as she reached for the coffee pot. They were at the FBI's main New Orleans branch office, back in the cramped conference room with a murder board behind them. The pictures of the victims stared back at Bree every time she looked at the board.

"I am, too," Bree admitted carefully. This was her first time to really talk to Karin. "Words can lie, right?"

Karin inclined her head. "But bodies never do."

A sharp knock sounded at the door. "They sure as hell don't."

Bree's gaze darted to the door. Grayson was there, staring at her with a hard, fierce glare.

"And when the techs are done collecting evidence from Amelia Sanderson's body, I'm hoping we'll be able to get an arrest warrant for Kace Quick."

She squared her shoulders. "I don't think it's him."

Karin took a slow sip of coffee. "Couldn't find anything at his place, huh?"

"No, nothing that implicated him in the murders." Her word choice was very deliberate. Because Karin was right. Words could lie, words could twist the truth so easily.

"He's just smart enough to hide the evidence," Grayson snapped.

"Or maybe we need to stop looking at him as the perp and consider that he's another victim here, too."

"What?" It sounded as if Grayson might be strangling. It looked that way, too. His face had gone all blotchy.

Karin took another slow sip of her coffee.

"These murders are too much like Brittney Lang's, and maybe that's because the real killer wanted us to see the connection. He wanted Kace to be linked to the crimes. The perp is targeting women that Kace knew—maybe he's doing that—"

"You let him get to you," Grayson cut through her words with a growl of disgust and frustration. "I thought you'd be better than that."

Her spine straightened. "I'm looking at the evidence. I'm looking at the profile *I* created."

She could feel Karin's gaze on her, but the other woman wasn't speaking.

"I think the killer is someone who hates Kace. Someone who wants Kace to suffer, so he's picking women that Kace knew. Women that he thought Kace was sleeping with—"

"Thought?" Karin interrupted, the one word curious.

"Kace said he wasn't involved with them. He had a strict policy about not sleeping with his staff members." A policy that he'd broken with her.

"He's lying," Grayson said flatly. If anything, his skin was redder. "He's tricking you, Bree. You're too green. You didn't—"

He was pissing her off. "You sent me in because you thought I could get close to him. I *have* gotten close to Kace. I did my job. And everything I learned is telling me that Kace isn't the man we're after. Someone is setting him up. Someone is trying to punish Kace by making him look guilty as sin."

Grayson stalked toward her. "Maybe he *is* just guilty as sin."

Bree shook her head. "He wants to work with me. He wants us to hunt the killer together."

"Bullshit." Grayson huffed out a breath. "He wants to know what the FBI has on him. You're not getting close to him. *He's* getting close to you."

I had fun last night.

She would not let Grayson shake her. Bree kept her voice steady as she revealed, "Kace knew I was FBI from the first moment. Pegged me on sight. He could have shut me out then, but he didn't. He wants to stop this killer. He knew those women. He's not so heartless that he doesn't—"

Grayson's laughter cut her off. "Yes, he is. He is *absolutely* heartless." He shook his head. "You don't get it, do you? Didn't you read all of the files? I mean, what is it? Do you not understand what he's done?"

"He's—"

"Sheldon Taggert."

The name was familiar. Mostly because she *had* read the files, and Grayson could shove his superior tone where the sun damn well didn't shine. "He's the guy that Kace said…During the trial, Kace said Sheldon was sleeping with Brittney."

"Right. Kace always believed that Sheldon was the real killer." A deliberate pause from

Grayson. "You know what happened to Sheldon Taggert?"

She did. "He died a year after Brittney's death."

Karin cleared her throat. "A year to the date. As in…exactly." She put down her mug. "Some would say that was biblical justice…or cold-blooded revenge."

Cold-blooded revenge? Bree shook her head. "I read the report on Sheldon. He was in a fatal, one-car accident. An accident, nothing more."

Karin and Grayson shared a long look.

"What?" Bree demanded.

"A *one-car* accident," Grayson stressed as he raked a hand through his hair. "Late at night. And because of the way he was pinned in the car, Sheldon Taggert asphyxiated. He died of strangulation, the exact same way that Brittney did."

Bree felt her stomach tighten. "Hardly the same way."

"You're right." The faint lines near Grayson's mouth deepened as he grimly said, "He was pinned in the car, his head somehow crushed between the steering wheel and the driver's seat. His seatbelt was found wrapped around his neck. Did you read that detail in the coroner's report? So fucking strange…the coroner had never seen anything like that in all of his time working in the parish."

Her heart was racing faster. "You're saying his death was a murder." That *hadn't* been in the files.

"And who do you think killed him?" Grayson pushed.

"Kace?" She laughed but… "You're saying he staged that whole scene? That he killed a man without leaving any evidence behind?"

"I'm saying he sure as hell *could* have done it."

Karin took a step forward. Her attention was on Grayson. "No one ever ruled Sheldon's death a homicide, Agent Wesley. You know that. Taggert's blood alcohol level was through the roof."

Yes, Bree had read *that.*

"Sheldon could have gotten drunk, and he slammed his fancy Ferrari into the side of a light pole. When he realized he was trapped behind the steering wheel and the deflating air bag, the guy could have struggled to get out." Karin's gaze drifted to Bree. "In his panic, Sheldon fought the seatbelt. Instead of getting free, he tangled himself all the more. He was trapped, and he died. An accident."

Exactly what Taggert's cause of death had been listed as by the coroner.

"An accident," Bree repeated. "There's no way Kace could have staged that scene. He would have been only—"

"He was nineteen, and well on his way to running the city by then." Grayson's voice cracked with a hard rage. "The minute he walked out of the courtroom, found not guilty by the men and women who should have sent his ass to jail for the murder of Brittney Lang, Kace's life changed. He took over New Orleans. He destroyed. He did anything necessary to succeed in this town."

"You're talking about a kid—"

"He was never a kid. He was a killer. Still is."

Her breath came too quickly. "We're tearing his life apart. There is no evidence that he's murdered anyone."

Grayson stepped closer to her. "You and Kace are tight now, aren't you? He moved you in to his house?"

"Because you trashed my room." The fury still flared in her.

A muscle flexed in his jaw. "Ask him about Sheldon. You think you know Kace so well now. Stare into his eyes and *ask* him about Sheldon Taggert. See what he says to you. Then you come back to me, and tell me if you believe his lies."

"I will."

Their angry gazes held.

Karin shuffled toward them. "Um, I think we all need to take a breath here. I mean, we're on the same team, right?"

Grayson's eyes glittered. "Bree is blinded by her chief suspect. She can't see him for what he really is."

She could see just fine. Twenty, twenty. "Why are you so convinced he's the bad guy? Why can't you consider that maybe Kace was framed?"

"Because he told me that he was going to kill Sheldon Taggert! He told me, and I fucking didn't believe him."

What?

Grayson turned away, marching angrily toward the far wall. "Shit."

Karin and Bree exchanged a confused glance.

"I think you need to tell us more, boss," Karin said, her voice curt. "Like, *now*."

He whirled back toward them. "I started here in the NOPD, okay? I grew up on these streets. Born and bred here." He exhaled and straightened his shoulders. "I was one of the uniforms working the Brittney Lang case. The day that Quick was found not guilty, I was there. I saw the way he glared at Sheldon all through the trial. I saw the hate in his eyes. And when the prick was found not guilty, I was one of the officers assigned to protect *him* as Kace walked through the crowd of reporters." He rubbed the back of his neck. "The last thing Kace said to me…the *last* thing…was that Sheldon Taggert would pay." His hand dropped. "Every bit of intel I've ever gotten on Kace Quick says that the man is a greedy, controlling bastard. He doesn't share—not with anyone. Sheldon was screwing Brittney. So Kace killed her. He killed her because she'd cheated on him. She'd betrayed him. Even as a young punk, Kace couldn't handle betrayal. Then he waited, and one year to the date of her death, he killed the bastard who'd fucked her."

Karin frowned, her brows pulling low. "Or maybe Kace killed the man who'd murdered his girlfriend."

"Or maybe Kace didn't kill anyone!" Bree snapped.

But they just stared at her as if she was insane.

Grayson's lips twisted. "The NOPD thinks he's buried more bodies than they can count. Like I told you, he doesn't handle betrayal well."

"I betrayed him. I went in under a lie to do nothing more than deceive him. And I'm standing right here. Alive and well."

Grayson's lips parted, but then he seemed to catch himself. He hesitated a moment, then, voice curt, asked, "Karin, give us a minute, will you?"

"Uh..." Her stare swept toward Bree.

"A minute, Karin." Now Grayson wasn't asking. He was ordering.

"Fine." Karin pointed at him. "But you'd better not drop any more bombshells while I'm gone. Because finding out that you have a history with our chief suspect *is* something you should have disclosed to the team sooner." Her high heels tapped on the floor as she headed for the door. "I'm going to find Dominic and bring him up to speed."

The door closed behind her with a click.

Grayson's jaw was clenched as he gritted, "You spent the night with him."

"Wasn't that the plan? You destroyed my room, I became the victim, I stayed with—"

"I mean you slept with him. Didn't you? In his bed?" He advanced on her.

Yes. But instead of answering, she evaded with, "Did you want me to do that? Because you sure threw me at him."

"I want you *close* to him. But I don't want you becoming one of his victims."

Now she laughed. "I can handle myself. I'm FBI, remember?"

"That's what I told Dominic. But he reminded me…we're sending you in alone. And Kace can kill you as fast as he can kiss you. Especially if you're trusting him. If you're falling for him. You won't see the threat coming, not until it's too late."

"I see the threat." She stared straight at Grayson. "It's you who can't see beyond the past. You and Kace have a history? Okay. Glad to finally get those details. I'm sure there is a whole lot more you're not telling me."

His eyes turned to slits. His hands fisted.

The body doesn't lie.

Bree fought to keep her emotions in check as she noted, "Because of that past, maybe you're not seeing clearly right now. Maybe you're not seeing the truth."

"The truth?"

"That someone else out there is setting up Kace. That someone else wants to destroy him. The perp is hurting these women because he thinks killing them will hurt Kace. He thought they were all involved with Kace. He was wrong."

Voice mocking, Grayson said, "Because Kace told you he didn't sleep with them—"

"Yes, because he told me that. The last vic developed an obsession with him. I documented the truth by questioning other staff members at Fantasy when I had the chance."

He blinked. Narrowed his eyes.

"Amelia told everyone that she was sleeping with Kace, but she wasn't. It was just *her* fantasy. The woman was using, and she went to a rehab clinic, a place that Kace sent her to, but she didn't get help. She broke out and went onto the streets." Where the killer found her.

A faint line appeared between his brows as Grayson finally seemed to consider what she was saying. "So, say Kace was never involved with them. Fine. Then who the hell *is* he involved with? Who do you think the killer is going to target next?"

Her lips parted. *Me.* But she didn't let that confession slip. Instead, the one word seemed to roll through her mind, again and again.

Me.

"Bree?"

Play this cool. "I'm the one in his house. To outsiders, I look like the one he's sleeping with." A plan began to form. "I'm the next victim."

"What? Oh, the hell, no, you—"

"I *am* the next victim," she argued back fiercely. "I have to be, don't you see? I can be the bait. I can draw the killer out. I can prove it's not Kace when we catch the real perp."

Grayson shook his head. "No, no—"

"It's already happening. The plan is unfolding, whether you like it or not. I've been seen with Kace at Fantasy. I've been with him on his motorcycle. I'm another blonde who fits the victim pattern. *And I'm staying in Kace's house.* If I'm not on the killer's radar yet, I will be." She'd make sure of it. "I'll stick to Kace like glue. I'll get the perp's attention. I'll make him come after me."

"And if Kace *is* the killer?"

He's not. "Then we stop him."

***

Kace walked into the Fantasy, flipping on the lights. He'd disabled the security system just moments before.

"You really think moving the FBI agent in your house is the best plan?" Remy demanded.

After Kace had turned off the security system, Remy had dodged his steps. Now, Remy was right at Kace's side.

"I think it's an epic plan. Destined for full success." He headed for the main bar area, turning on more lights as he advanced. The lights came on slowly, illuminating the interior. The chairs had been carefully stacked on top of the tables, and his cleaning crew had done their usual top-notch job.

His gaze slid toward the performance area. The silks dangled from the ceiling. Odd. They should have been secured, not left loose that way. Why did…

"I get that you like to keep your enemies close and shit," Remy grumbled, "but this is going too—"

"Why are the silks out? The aerials should have been secured Saturday night." His gaze rose to the ceiling and—

Blond hair. Falling just beyond the woman's jaw. Hanging over her face as she hung from the silks. Dressed in a black leotard. Her arms were twined in the silk. Her legs jutted toward the floor. Her neck—

The silks twisted around her neck. Over and over.

She hung from the silks, strangled by them.

Kace raced forward, fury and fear breaking within him as he roared her name. He grabbed for the silks, yanking them hard, wanting them *down.*

"Kace, fuck, man, *stop!*" Remy grabbed him and jerked him back. "We have to call the cops!"

Kace drove his fist into Remy's jaw. Remy staggered back, then slipped, falling on his ass. Kace whirled around and grabbed the silks, he grabbed her dangling feet and he yanked her down, pulling hard over and over again, pulling until—

Remy tackled him. "What the fuck are you doing, Kace?"

Kace looked up. From this angle, he could see her face.

That's not her.

All of the breath left him in a deep rush of air.

"We have to call the cops!" Remy snarled. "We're calling them *now!*"

CHAPTER THIRTEEN

The body hung in the middle of the silks. Her head was tilted forward, and her blond hair slid against her jaw. Bree stared up at the woman as horror snaked through her. Her team filled the scene, and crime scene techs were collecting evidence like bees in a hive.

"Marie Argeneaux," Remy said as he stood beside Bree. "Someone cut her hair shorter, but that's Marie. Shit. *Shit.*" He sounded shaken.

He and Kace had found the victim. As soon as her team had arrived, Grayson had immediately ordered the two men separated. Kace had been escorted to his office, while Remy remained at her side.

"Tell me again," Bree directed him. "Everything that happened. Leave nothing out."

His cheeks puffed before he gave a hard exhale. "I got a call from Kace. He asked me to meet him here. When I arrived, he was standing outside of Fantasy."

She licked her lips. "Can you swear that he hadn't entered before you arrived?"

Remy raked a hand through his hair.

Grayson walked closer to them, moving so that he'd be able to hear the interrogation.

Remy dropped his hand. "He unlocked the door, turned off the alarm, and…yeah, yeah, that means he hadn't been inside before I arrived. That's what it *has* to mean. And the way he reacted…" His voice trailed away as he looked up at the victim once more. "How long are you going to leave her hanging there? Someone needs to take her down."

"She can't be moved until the crime scene is secured. We have to collect evidence." Grayson's words were low.

"Kace's DNA will be all over the place. He grabbed the silks, grabbed her legs, tried to get her down." A rough sigh escaped Remy. "Even slugged me in the jaw when I tried to stop him."

She could already see the bruising along his jaw.

"Like a man possessed," Remy groused. "Never seen him like that. He was out of control."

Bree kept her expression blank. "I need you to tell me everything that happened *after* Kace turned off the alarm." The fact that the alarm had needed to be disengaged was an important point. The killer had known the security codes for the place. He'd gotten in and out too easily.

"We headed to the main bar area. We stopped a moment. Talked."

Remy didn't say more.

Grayson raised one brow. "About what?"

Remy's gaze cut to her. "Bree."

Her shoulders stiffened.

"I told him it was dangerous having a Fed so close, but he didn't care. That's the thing about Kace. He never listens to warnings. Always does whatever the hell he wants."

"Is he going to be pissed that you're talking to us?" Grayson wanted to know.

Remy appeared confused. "Why the hell would he be? I'm not spilling state secrets. We came in, we both discovered the body, and then Kace tried to pull her down." His hands fisted. "I'm about to do the same damn thing myself. Not right to leave her up there while people are taking pictures and *talking* around her body."

Voice low and calm, Bree explained, "The techs are just doing their jobs so we can catch her killer. If we take her down too soon, evidence can be compromised."

Remy grunted. "Doesn't mean I have to like it."

"No, it doesn't." She glanced over her shoulder at the vic. "I don't like it, either." When she turned back to Remy, she found him watching her with a hooded gaze. She narrowed her eyes on him. "Who realized the victim was

Marie? Who made the connection first? You or Kace?"

Marie. God, she'd seen the woman just nights before. Marie had been the original aerial performer in Fantasy. But Abby had said that Marie had texted in her resignation…

Did Marie really send that text? Or had it been her killer?

And the bastard had put her body in the silks, a deliberate act. Using the silks she'd loved as the instrument of her death.

"Kace made the connection." Remy rolled back his shoulders. "I tackled him because he wouldn't stop trying to get her down. When we hit the floor, he looked up, and he could see her face from that angle. He stopped fighting then. He said—" But Remy clamped his lips shut.

Too late. Grayson perked up, as if he were a shark who'd just scented blood in the water. "What did he say?"

Remy's expression turned mutinous, and she didn't think he'd reply.

"A woman is *dead,*" Grayson snarled. "A woman you knew. You need to cooperate with us. You need to tell us everything—"

"Kace said, 'It isn't her.' Okay? That's what he said. He saw her face, said that, and he stopped fighting. *'It isn't her.'*"

Bree fought to keep her breathing slow. Her heart was racing out of control, and her hand rose to brush back her hair.

Someone had cut Marie's hair.

Slowly, she made herself turn until she faced Marie. "That's the leotard I wore on Saturday night." The hair still fell over Marie's face. "And her hair has been cut to look *just like mine."*

Grayson swore. He surged forward, and his shoulder brushed against hers.

"She looks like me," Bree whispered. Marie had been *made* to look like Bree.

She'd come up with a plan to bait the killer. Grayson hadn't liked it, but he'd been willing to go along with her idea. Only it seemed she'd already caught the perp's attention...

But he wasn't supposed to go after another innocent woman. He was supposed to come after me.

***

"How long are you planning to keep me prisoner in my own office?" Kace demanded.

The guy standing near his door—an FBI agent named Dominic Grant—blinked owlishly a few times. "Uh, the special agent in charge will be in to see you soon and—"

Kace rose from his chair and stalked toward the fellow. "I'm cooperating. I found a dead woman, I called the police. I let you all into my club. I'm letting you tear my place apart without so much as a word of complaint."

Dominic stiffened and started to sweat in his cheap suit.

"But it's been over an hour since you *escorted* me in here, and I want to talk with someone higher up on the freaking food chain, got me?"

"Uh, you need to calm—"

"Get Grayson Wesley in here. Get Bree Harlow in here. *Now.* Or I will call my lawyer—or *five* of my lawyers—and you will find yourself in a world of hurt. You don't get to hold me prisoner in my own building."

Dominic was sweating more. He lifted his left hand, wiping his brow, and Kace caught sight of the tattoo on his inner wrist. A rose with thorns twisting around it. What the hell?

"G-Grayson will be in—"

A quick knock sounded at the door. Dominic jerked forward.

The door opened.

"Speak of the devil," Kace muttered as Grayson surged into his office.

And right after Grayson—

Bree.

Kace sucked in a deep breath.

Bree's gaze cut to him. Her eyes were so deep and golden. Her blond hair swung against her cheeks. She wore a pair of jeans and a white t-shirt. Definitely not clad in the standard and unimaginative FBI uniform of cheap suits. She looked young and beautiful and *alive.*

Not caring about their audience, Kace went right to her and hauled her into his arms. She was warm and soft against him. She smelled like lavender. She was *alive.*

Because when he'd first seen the victim in the silks…

"You thought it was me," she whispered.

He held her tighter. "For a moment, yeah, I did." A terrible moment he'd never forget.

Grayson cleared his throat. Kace ignored the asshole. He had more important things to focus on right then. "I think I went a little crazy." A truth that didn't make him comfortable. He'd have to analyze his reaction later. Have to fully understand why the whole world had seemed to go dark around him even as a killing fury had surged through his veins, maddening him.

Grayson cleared his throat again. "We have questions for you."

"Fuck off." Kace lifted his head so he could stare down at Bree. "You saw her hair."

She nodded.

"It was cut roughly, but it was made to look like *your* hair."

"I know."

"She wore your fucking leotard."

A shiver. "I…I know."

"You have to get away from me, Bree. Get out of New Orleans. Get the FBI to transfer you far away." *Let her go.* He made himself step back.

Grayson cleared his—

"Are you choking?" Kace demanded as he whirled to confront the guy. "Because if you're not, stop that shit. I'm talking to Bree and you're interrupting."

Now Dominic made a strangled sound.

Maybe they were all choking.

Figured.

Bree's hand squeezed Kace's arm. "We have to ask you some questions."

"I didn't kill her. I walked in with Remy. Found her body." He shrugged. "Then we called the cops. Just like any law-abiding citizens would do in those circumstances." He was staring at Grayson as he made that statement. And maybe he emphasized *law-abiding* a bit too much. So what? It had been one hell of a morning so far.

"That's not exactly what happened, is it?" Grayson pushed. "We talked to Remy. He was happy to provide us with full details about the events of this morning."

"Why you saying it that way? Trying to make it sound as if Remy turned on me and sold you secrets?" Kace gave a quick laugh, actually amused. "I told him to cooperate. If I had ordered him to tell you jack shit, he would have done that, too."

Now the sweating Dominic slid forward. "Why didn't you tell him to, ahem, tell us all jack shit?"

"Because Marie was *mine.*" He forced his back teeth to unclench. "She worked for me, she had a tie to me, and because of that, some sick sonofabitch killed her."

Grayson pursed his lips. His gaze raked over Kace. "Or *you* killed her. Maybe you're the sick sonofabitch who wrapped her in silk and choked the life from her."

Don't beat the ever-loving-hell out of him. Don't. Kace gave Grayson a cold smile. "I don't kill women. Don't you remember that from our time together before, Grayson?" Because, yes, he'd recognized the bastard. He'd just chosen to hold that secret a bit. "That's not really my thing."

"I think it's *exactly* your thing."

Bree's hold tightened on Kace. "Why did you try to get her down, Kace? Why did you touch the body? You had to know that would contaminate the crime scene."

Another bark of laughter came from him, and only Kace knew it sounded angry. Mean. He was feeling pretty mean right then. *She looked like Bree.* He glanced down at her. "I thought it was you. I wasn't fucking leaving you hanging from the ceiling. I wanted you down. I stopped thinking. Didn't care if it was a crime scene." His gaze traveled over Bree's beautiful face. "I was getting you down."

"Huh." Dominic had circled around him. The sweating prick was giving him an assessing, too-clinical glance. "It didn't matter that Marie was hanging from the ceiling. You could leave her up there. But Bree was something—"

"I would have taken her down." She'd *better* be down by now. "But Remy stopped me. After he tackled me, he told me that we had to call the cops. Had to leave her in case any evidence from the killer was up there. That if we screwed it up, the bastard might keep getting away with his crimes." He shrugged and focused his attention on Grayson once more. "Not like you've done a bang-up job of catching the guy so far, have you, *Grayson?* I mean, the victims keep dying, and you just keep looking at me."

Now Grayson stepped toe-to-toe with Kace. "Marie was murdered in your club."

"That's pretty fucking obvious, isn't it?" Kace bit out.

"Remy said you had to type in the code to get inside Fantasy. When the killer came in and murdered that poor woman, did you get any notice from your security company?"

"No alarm went off." He knew where the SOB was going with this one.

"How many people have access to your code?"

"Three. Me, Remy, and my floor manager, Abby Johnson."

Grayson gave him an arctic smile. "You understand, of course, I'm going to need alibis for you all."

"You won't have to look far for my alibi." Bree's hand had fallen away from his arm, but Kace cut a glance her way. "Special Agent Harlow was in my house last night. She can vouch for the fact that I didn't leave."

Bree's face appeared too pale. He didn't like that, not one damn bit.

"We haven't established time of death yet," Grayson told him, the dick's voice grating on Kace's ears. "Once the coroner does that, then we'll talk alibis."

Dominic shuffled closer. "We'll need to know the name of the individual or *individuals* who were here last."

"Remy. He and Abby were the last two here on Saturday. Probably left around four a.m. You'll need to talk with them." Tension had gathered in Kace's shoulders. "The club is closed on Sunday. No one should have been here then."

The killer had known that, dammit. He'd come in with Marie and the bastard had known that no one would bother him. He'd probably taken his time with the kill.

When I find him, I'll take my time with him, too.

"We want you to come to the station with us," Grayson murmured. "We have more questions that you need to answer."

"Bullshit. You just want some dog and pony show for the Press. You want to haul me out of Fantasy, you want everyone to see me being led away, and you want the world to think I'm a killer."

Bree inched closer. "Kace, we need your cooperation."

Wasn't he *giving* his cooperation?

"You *are* a killer," Grayson rasped. "This time, I'll prove it. You won't walk on some BS alibi."

Kace wanted to reach for Bree once more. Wanted to lock his fingers with hers. Instead, he just smiled at Grayson. "An FBI agent who can back up my whereabouts hardly counts as BS. I think you don't get a better alibi than that."

"We don't know what time—"

"Spare me the crap. You've got an estimate. So do I. Her body was cold and hard. Lividity, right? Isn't that the term?" He knew it was. He was always so much smarter than the cops had given him credit for being. Just because he'd been poor, they'd thought he didn't know shit.

So wrong.

"She's been dead for at least eight hours. No longer than twelve." Kace shrugged. "And Bree will alibi me for that time. So, you can throw out your accusations, but you won't stick this on me."

Grayson's body tensed. "Know a lot about death, do you?"

More than you can guess.

"You're going to the station," Grayson snapped. "And you're going now."

"Grayson," Bree cut in, voice strained. "He's cooperating. And he's right about the lividity—"

"He's a psychopath, Bree. Cold-blooded to the core. Didn't you hear what he said? The club was empty all day yesterday. The bastard could have killed her at any time he wanted. And if he really knows death as well as he says, then he could have staged the body to throw off the coroner. To throw us all off. It's not like he hasn't staged a crime scene before."

On that, Grayson was right.

Sighing, Kace pulled out his phone. He sent one fast text. "You'll have about an hour. Maybe less."

Grayson frowned at him.

"You can ask me your questions for an hour. I'll answer the ones I choose. And when that hour is up, my lawyer will make sure you don't get within fifty feet of me again." He gave a wolfish smile, and he *didn't* look at Bree again. Right then, he couldn't. Too much was at stake. "Shall we get the dog and pony show on the road?"

CHAPTER FOURTEEN

"You're not going in there," Grayson announced as he threw a hard glance at Bree. "Not when the jerk is using you as his alibi. Karin and I will handle the interrogation. You and Dominic can watch from the observation room."

She'd already figured he wouldn't let her inside. But… "Kace didn't do this. He's right about the lividity, you know that yourself. It's like crime scene 101. Maximum lividity always occurs between eight and twelve hours after death. I was in the house with him last night. He didn't leave."

"You're sure about that? Were you really with him every single moment?"

"I—"

"Or did you sleep, Bree? Did you fall asleep at some point last night? Because I'm betting you did. And I'm betting you don't know if he stayed in that house while you slept or if he crept away."

Crept away and killed another woman? Had he gone from comforting Bree after her nightmare, from making love to her…to killing?

"No." She shook her head. "He didn't. It's not—"

"This is why you're not going in the interrogation room. And why you're staying away from him. You're compromised." He motioned to Karin. "Let's go."

Karin mouthed *Sorry* as she filed out of the room behind him.

Dominic whistled. "Shit, that guy is *pissed.*"

Yeah, well, so was she. "He's wrong about Kace." She moved to stand closer to the observation window.

"Uh, maybe. Maybe not." Dominic pulled at his tie, loosening the knot. "Abby Johnson and that Remy fellow have also been brought in for interrogations. You want to take them?"

"I want to watch Kace first." She wasn't budging. This mattered. He mattered.

I thought it was you. She could still hear Kace's rough, ragged voice in her mind. Bree stared through the one-way glass. He sat at the table, appearing utterly calm. His lawyer was at his side, a stylish woman in an elegantly cut, blue blouse and a black, pencil skirt. Her coffee cream skin was absolutely flawless.

The door opened. Grayson barreled inside. Karin took her time entering. While Grayson took the chair across from Kace, Karin settled into a position near the wall.

"He's not going to learn anything," Dominic predicted as he stood beside Bree. "That lawyer—she's Deidre Shaw. She's the best criminal defense attorney in New Orleans. The woman has stone walling down to an art."

As Bree watched, Deidre gave Grayson a Cheshire-cat smile.

Grayson didn't smile back.

As for Kace, his gaze slid toward the one-way mirror. He stared at the mirror, seeming to stare straight at Bree and then—

He winked.

***

"Do you find these proceedings humorous in some way, Mr. Quick?" Grayson demanded.

The guy really needed to get the stick out of his ass. "I don't find anything about Marie Argeneaux's death to be humorous. I find it to be a fucking shame." Kace focused on the jackass and not on Bree. He knew she was watching. He could feel her.

I need to get her out of this city.

As much as he wanted to hold her tight, he would need to push her away, at least until he'd buried the bastard playing the sick games in Kace's city.

"How long had Marie worked for you?"

"About a month. Abby hired her when we first got the idea for the aerial act." He kept his voice flat, kept his posture relaxed. He knew how the game was played.

Grayson pulled out a notebook. Jotted something down like he'd just made some major freaking discovery.

He'd discovered nothing.

"Were you sleeping with her?" Grayson asked, not looking up.

Kace parted his lips to reply—

"You don't have to answer that," Deidre announced as she glowered at the agent across from her. "Really, must you push our courtesy to its limits? My client is cooperating out of the goodness of his heart."

Kace heard a snort. He was pretty sure it came from the female agent who was leaning against the wall. Petite, with red hair that she kept twisted in a bun behind her, the woman had sharp, intelligent eyes. Karin...hadn't that been her name? Special Agent Karin Miller.

Karin apparently didn't think he had goodness in his heart.

"So, you *were* sleeping with her," Grayson decided. "Were you also intimately involved with—"

Time to cut through the crap. "I wasn't sleeping with Marie."

Deidre's delicate jaw hardened. She'd give him hell for answering that question later.

"I wasn't sleeping with her, not with Lindsey, not with Ciara, and not with Amelia, either."

Grayson stiffened.

"I knew them all. Had employed them all. But if you ask around, you'll learn that I have a strict policy about *not* sleeping with my staff. There are lines I don't cross. That's one of them."

"Right." Grayson's expression called bullshit.

He could call whatever he wanted.

Once more, Grayson glanced down at the notepad before him. "Did you leave your house at any point last night?"

"I didn't. Shouldn't you know this? I mean, I figured the FBI was staking out my place."

Grayson's head snapped up. "You're certain you never left? Not even for a few moments?"

"I was tired last night." No, he'd been busy having the best sex of his life. "So, I didn't go out." A shrug. "I returned to my house around eight last evening, and I didn't go out again after that."

"Eight." Grayson pursed his lips. "What were you doing before you got back home?"

Deidre sighed. "Your questions have to be related to something. This isn't a fishing expedition. Oh, wait." She rolled her eyes. "It is. Because you've dragged my client in here for an interrogation when he's the *victim*."

But Grayson's eyes stayed locked on him. "Where were you last night before eight p.m.?"

"I had business that needed taking care of."

"What kind of business?"

"The kind of business that's mine." Kace offered him a very cold smile.

Grayson glared at him. Someone had an anger issue. "I'll find out. So why don't you just save us both a bit of time and tell me where you were—"

Deidre shook her head. Aw, so sweet. She probably thought he'd been up to something illegal. He hadn't been. Being kind, Kace revealed, "I was visiting with an old friend." He would have answered sooner, but he honestly enjoyed jerking Grayson around a bit. He needed to understand the guy's weak spots. Obviously, the special agent in charge had a short fuse. If he was pushed the wrong way, Kace was sure the fellow would explode. *I am so good at pushing.*

"A friend?" Now Grayson looked at the one-way mirror. A faint smile tugged at his lips. "A *female* friend?"

Was the dipshit trying to make Bree jealous? He should leave her the hell alone. "No, he's male. Jax Fontaine. Maybe you've heard of him." Who hadn't, in that town?

Grayson's whole expression tensed as his attention zeroed in on Kace again. "I thought he'd left New Orleans."

"He did." A good thing, too, because the town really hadn't been big enough for them both. "Shady bastard fell in love and followed his woman. But we keep in touch. Mutual interests, I guess you could say."

***

"I don't know that name," Bree said, frowning.

"Jax Fontaine…he's trouble. Bad news." Dominic rocked forward onto the balls of his feet. "He and Kace used to fight for power in New Orleans, but then Jax got out of the game. He married a woman named Sarah Jacobs a while back."

Sarah Jacobs. Okay, now *that* name mattered to Bree. "Murphy the Monster's daughter?" *Everyone* at Quantico knew about Sarah Jacobs. She was the only child of an infamous serial killer. When she'd been a teen, Sarah had walked in on her father and discovered his dark life. He'd wanted her to be like him. Instead, Sarah had become a profiler. She'd worked to unmask serials. But…she'd been in the private sector. She'd—

"Last I heard," Dominic mused, "Sarah was still working for LOST."

LOST. Last Option Search Team. Yes, yes…Bree had even thought about getting a job with that group herself, but she'd decided to join the FBI instead.

"I think she's still trying to find her dad." Dominic's voice was halting. "Because that sick perp is still out there."

Bree rubbed her sweaty palms onto the front of her jeans. "Kace went to talk with Jax..." He hadn't told her about that. Why not? Why did she feel like she was missing something?

"Wonder what they talked about." Dominic narrowed his eyes as he studied the interrogation scene.

I sure as hell wonder, too.

***

"Why'd you go meet Jax?" Grayson demanded.

"Oh, you know..." Kace waved one hand vaguely in the air. "To shoot the shit. Catch up on old times. Jax is only in the city for a few nights, and I wanted to chat him up." He gave the other man a cold smile.

"Was Sarah with him?"

Ah, so the guy knew all about Jax's Sarah. "I think she was." As if imparting a secret, Kace added, "He likes to keep her close."

Grayson grunted. "I can call Sarah. Have her on the phone within minutes. Jax might be an ex-criminal, but Sarah still works with the FBI from time to time."

He let his eyes widen. "Lucky for you. You need someone with sense to help you out."

Grayson didn't like that jab. Kace could see it in the guy's gaze. Too bad.

"Sarah will tell me what you discussed yesterday."

Kace laughed. "Doubt it."

"She's with the FBI as a freelance—"

"I don't care what freelance work she does for the FBI. All I know is that Sarah protects the confidentiality of *her* clients. Since I'm a client, she won't tell you anything." He was feeding the agent breadcrumbs. Only that. Nothing more.

"You hired Sarah?" Karin asked, breaking her silence and keeping her post near the wall. "You trying to get her to find someone for you?"

Not exactly. But the FBI could run on that tangent. It would give Kace some needed space.

"Another victim?" Karin pushed. "Is someone else in your life missing and you're trying to find her?"

"Fishing," Deidre announced with a sad shake of her head. "Without a license."

Karin surged toward the table. "If there is another potential victim out there, we can find her. We can put her face on every newspaper, on every website and TV—"

The agent's heart was in the right place. She seemed to care about the victims first, and the killer second.

"It's not related to this case," Kace murmured. He glanced at his watch. "Time's ticking away. You only get the hour."

Grayson slammed his fist down on the table. *"We both know that Marie was posed to look just like Bree!"*

And again, Kace thought...*someone has some serious anger and control issues.* That would work to Kace's advantage. There was a reason he'd agreed to this little chat, after all.

Seething, Grayson snarled, "You're going to sit there all smug when it's obvious that Bree is the next target?"

The last thing he felt was smug. Furious. Ready to kill. Ready to destroy. But Kace shrugged. "Bree's FBI. She's tainted."

Bree would hear those words. He hated that.

"Tainted?" Karin repeated as she stood near the table.

"I can't have her around me anymore. It was fine when the rest of the world didn't know who she really was. I do enjoy playing games with the FBI." He smiled, carelessly. "But now that the secret is out, you need to send Bree back to Quantico. Reassign her somewhere else, because she won't be close to me any longer. Consider her all-access pass revoked. Playtime is over."

"You sonofabitch." Grayson leaned close. "You fucked her, and now you want to walk away? When she's got a target on her back?"

***

Bree felt all of the blood leave her face. Her skin went icy, and she could not look away from the scene before her.

You fucked her, and now you want to walk away? When she's got a target on her back?

"That's not true, is it?" Dominic asked, voice stilted and awkward as hell. "Grayson is just trying to push the guy. Get him to spill something we can use."

"There isn't anything we can use on this case. I told you, Kace isn't the killer." She was still certain of him. Absolutely certain.

Even though he was apparently…done with her. Tainted. He'd called her *tainted?* Her hand fisted. She'd show him tainted.

"Did you sleep with him, Bree?"

She didn't answer.

Dominic let out a sad sigh. "People aren't always who you think, Bree." He pushed up the sleeve on his left arm, revealing his tattoo. A rose, encircled by thorns. "Got this to remind myself of that fact when I screwed up a long time ago. Trusted the wrong woman."

Her gaze lingered on the tattoo. The blood red rose. *Blood…*

He covered the tat. "With our job, we can't afford to take chances. We can't afford to cross the line. You might think you can trust someone, but you can't. People lie. They deceive. It's just who they are." He hesitated. "So, I'm gonna ask you again, did you sleep with him?"

"I slept in Kace's house." Her voice sounded brittle to her own ears. "After Grayson screwed me over and trashed my room." She returned her gaze to Kace, wondering just what he'd say next.

He'd told her he wasn't the type to kiss and tell. But this was his moment. Would he reveal their secret?

Grayson had a wild look in his eyes. He wasn't going to stop. He was pushing and pushing and pushing and pushing—

"Did you fuck Agent Harlow?" Grayson shoved that rough question at Kace.

Kace smiled at Grayson. And it was an absolutely chilling sight. "I believe *you* did that, Agent Wesley."

Her skin didn't feel like ice any longer. It was absolutely red hot.

***

Grayson's face purpled with fury. "You—"

"You fucked over your own agent," Kace continued smoothly. "When you set her up as a 'victim' at the bed and breakfast. You destroyed her room and forced her to turn to me for help. Then she stayed at my house, under your direction, no doubt."

"Oh, this is some *shady* bullshit." Deidre sniffed. "I will have a field day with this if any charges are ever pressed against my—"

"If the killer has turned his sights on Bree," Kace didn't let his voice alter a bit as he focused on Grayson, "it's entirely your fault. You sent her to me. You knew what would happen."

"Because she looks like Brittney Lang?" Grayson pushed silkily. "The first girl to be strangled…the girl you loved when you were still just a punk kid? Same blond hair. Same—"

"Appearances are skin deep. When I look at Bree, she is the only person I see." They needed to be clear on that. Bree wasn't a stand-in for anyone. Never would be. "You sent her to me because you've been watching me too long. Building your flawed profile. Studying me. Always hating me because you thought I'd tell your dirty little secret to the world one day. You thought I'd expose *you*."

Grayson shot to his feet. "This interview is over."

Actually, it wasn't. It was just getting started. He'd planned this moment perfectly, even arranged the audience he wanted. He could feel Deidre's avid attention.

And Bree's. Bree would be watching so carefully. She needed to hear this. Needed to understand all about the man she worked for.

"You thought I'd forgotten you." Kace laughed. "I don't forget faces. The minute I saw you with Bree, I recognized you from the old days. Only you didn't go by the name Grayson back then. Just your first name. Alton. You were a green uniform who tried to keep out of the spotlight during my trial, but I remembered you. And I did my checking when our paths crossed again." He was savoring this moment. Kace cocked his head as he studied the agent who wanted to destroy him. "You think I just forgot about Brittney? You think I didn't want to find her killer? Didn't want to know every detail about what happened back then?"

Grayson whirled for the door.

"You fucked her."

Grayson stilled.

Karin and Deidre were both avidly watching the scene. Sometimes, it was good to have an audience.

So he played to his audience, and Kace enjoyed the torment he saw in Grayson's gaze. "You were involved with Brittney Lang, too. It was the rage that gave you away. You had too much hate and fury whenever you'd come close to me."

"Shut up."

"And here I thought I was in this room so that I could talk." Kace laughed—and kept talking. "After I was cleared of her murder—you know, found *not guilty* by a jury of my peers—I did my digging. Sheldon Taggert? He was one of her lovers, all right. But so were you. A lover that the Press and the DA never heard about."

Grayson marched toward the small table and flattened his hands on the surface as he leaned toward Kace. "You are mistaken."

No, he wasn't. He could see the truth staring straight at him. "You're back in town, and women are dying in the exact same way as poor Brittney." Kace let out a low whistle. "One hell of a coincidence, don't you think, *Agent* Wesley?"

Grayson surged across the table at him. Kace didn't even let the guy get in a punch. He just wasn't in the mood for that shit. He grabbed the agent's arm, moving quickly, and he sent the fellow flying toward the one-way mirror.

Deidre surged to her feet. "You just attacked my client! I *will* be pressing charges."

Grayson pushed himself upright.

Kace stalked toward the SOB. He leaned in close. Grayson's control was back, Kace could see it right then. *Too late.* Kace had already used the guy's weakness against him. *That anger issue will bite you in the ass.* "You just screwed up," Kace said, grinning. "I think I might even be able to get your badge for this."

"You sonofa—"

"Take your best shot," Kace dared. "Bet we can get jail time if you try hard enough."

Grayson's breath heaved in and out. Karin shoved between the two men. "We're done here."

For the moment, they were.

"Kace, let's go. Now." Deidre was already at the door. "I'll be getting a restraining order, too, Agent Wesley. After that attack, you won't be able to get *near* my client again."

"The FBI should all stay the hell away from me." Now Kace's gaze rose, and he peered at the one-way mirror. "Stay away." That message was for Bree. Because, dammit, it wasn't safe for her to be near him.

He followed Deidre into the hallway, and as soon as he stepped onto that gleaming, tiled floor, the door to the right flew open. Bree stood there, glaring at him.

He drank her in even as he made sure a mask covered his expression.

Bree wasn't wearing a mask. Her emotions were clear to see as she strode toward him. "You lied to me."

"Uh, who is this?" Deidre demanded in a tone that could have frozen a desert. "My client is done—"

Bree poked her index finger into Kace's chest. "You never told me about your connection to Grayson. You knew who he was, I told you about our past, and you never mentioned a *word* to me."

No, he hadn't. "Wasn't part of my plan."

Her skin seemed to pale. "You used me."

"We used each other. That's the whole reason you came in Fantasy undercover, isn't it?" He kept his voice mocking. "Now it's time for you to leave. Get your sweet ass out of New Orleans, Bree. This isn't the place for you any longer."

A gasp came from behind him. "Are you *threatening* her?" Karin demanded. He hadn't even realized she'd slipped from the interrogation room.

"No!" Deidre snapped. "My client was absolutely not—"

"We're done," Kace told Bree.

Pain flashed on her face.

Every muscle in his body tightened. He wanted to grab her and hold tight. Instead, he didn't move.

"Sheldon Taggert." Bree dropped the name. "Did you kill him?"

The question caught him off guard. He stared into her eyes, the past surging up toward him—

"My client will *not* answer that question." Deidre pulled him away from Bree. "And, of course, he's not some killer. He's a respected member of the community. A businessman who supports an assortment of non-profit agencies and charitable causes. He works to help the down trodden and—"

Bree jumped in front of Kace again. "I'm not leaving this city."

Shit. *Shit.*

"And I'm not going to let someone else die. I've got his attention. The perp wants me? Then he can come and get me."

No, hell, *no.* "You're making a mistake."

She leaned toward him. "No, you are." Her words were low, for him alone. "And you'll regret it."

"Let him go, Bree." From Grayson.

That piece of shit didn't need to order her to do anything.

Kace spun to glare at the other man.

Grayson was straightening his shirt and coat. "We have other witnesses that we need to interview. We are done with Mr. Quick for now."

But Mr. Quick isn't done with you.

"Not another word," Deidre hissed to Kace. "We're getting out of here, right now."

***

Bree watched Kace walk away. He'd been using her. Keeping secrets.

"I warned you," Grayson muttered.

"Seriously? You just assaulted a suspect." He didn't get to act self-righteous about anything.

"I never touched him."

"Because he was too fast for you." She couldn't trust Grayson. He'd been holding back too much. So had Kace. "This is about the past for you. That's why you're so locked on Kace. You can't see other suspects because you want him to pay for a crime that was committed years ago."

"Fifteen years ago. *His* crime."

Bree could only shake her head. "You want to destroy him, and he's determined to do the same to you." But Kace had been keeping his intentions secret much better. "And while you two piss at each other, women are dying. Someone is *killing* them, and I'm done with innocent women hurting. You and Kace should just go kick the crap out of each other." Bree spun on her heel. "I'm taking interview room two." Remy was in there.

"I'm in charge," Grayson barked. "I can—"

"Uh, no." Karin's voice was crisp and very clear. "You're sitting this one out. I already sent in a text about what went down, and FBI Brass says you are to step back until we see if Kace Quick will be pressing charges. Until we hear otherwise, I'm in charge, and your ass is benched."

Bree glanced back at her. Karin and Dominic were huddled together. Both had their phones out.

"Do the interviews, Bree," Karin urged. "You're the one who's had more contact with Remy and Abby. Talk to them both. They'll tell you more than they'll share with anyone else."

She wasn't so sure of that, but Bree was more than willing to try and get to the truth.

***

"What in the hell was that?" Deidre's long, red nails bit into Kace's arm, penetrating through the shirt he wore. "When your lawyer tells you to stop talking, you stop!"

He smiled at her. "You know I don't follow directions for shit."

"This is serious! Women are dead! The last victim was found *in* your club—and with your DNA all over her because you grabbed the body. This isn't some joke! We have to play this case carefully or you could wind up charged with murder!"

"I didn't kill Marie. Or the other women."

"I didn't ask." That was always her rule. She never asked if he'd committed any crimes. She just defended him against every accusation. "And, Jesus, you let an FBI agent into your home? Knowing she was an agent?"

"Bree isn't a threat to me."

"She is the biggest threat to you! You can't go thinking with your dick. The woman will turn on you in an instant. Hell, that's her only job. To sell you out."

"She doesn't have anything that she can use against me." He was two steps ahead of the Feds, had been all along.

He'd known who Grayson really was. He never forgot a face. He'd just played along. When you played dumb, it was the cops who fucked up.

"Stay away from her, Kace. I'm serious. Stay away from the pretty Fed."

"Not a problem. The FBI should be shipping her back to Quantico now."

Deidre turned away with a snap of her Jimmy Choo's. "Don't be too sure of that. They'll probably promote the woman. After all, she did her job, didn't she? She got close to you."

He didn't follow her down the steps. "Bree has to leave." There wasn't an option. If the FBI didn't send Bree away, then he'd have to see to the deed himself. The town wasn't safe for her.

He would *not* let her be taken by the bastard after him.

Kace could still remember the fear he'd felt when he thought Bree had died.

She has to leave. I'll make her leave.

CHAPTER FIFTEEN

"Look, let's just save time on this thing, okay?" Remy tapped his hands on the old table before him. "I already told the Feds everything I know. I told you guys at the scene. I don't have anything else to add. So, I'm ready to get the hell out of here."

Bree pulled out the chair across from him. Dominic had tailed her into the room, and he sat next to her.

"Two Feds? Really? Because you both need to hear this story again?" Remy rolled his eyes. "Do I need to get a lawyer in here, too?"

"That depends," Dominic said quietly. "Have you done something wrong?" He opened the file he'd carried into the room and pushed the picture of Marie Argeneaux toward Remy. "Like kill this poor woman?"

Remy stared at the picture. No expression crossed his face.

"You *did* have access to Fantasy," Dominic continued. "You had a key. You had the alarm codes."

Remy sighed. He glanced up, but didn't focus on Dominic. Instead, he stared straight at Bree. "Is that the new idea? That I'm the bad guy? That I'm watching my boss, seeing the women close to him, then murdering them? Maybe framing him, too? Because—what? Why?"

"Because you want his power," Bree answered carefully as she studied Remy. "Because you're his right-hand man, but maybe you're tired of that position. Maybe you want to take over, and the easiest way to do that is to get Kace out of your way."

Remy leaned toward her. His gaze was cold and hard. "If I wanted Kace out of my way, wouldn't I just kill the guy? Seems a lot simpler than strangling women and trying do some frame-up job on him."

It did. "Where were you last night?"

Remy shrugged. "At my house. Sleeping."

"No one can vouch for you? You don't have a lover or a friend or someone who can alibi you?"

"No, I don't."

They stared at each other.

"My lovers don't stay the night. I'm not exactly the relationship sort. I like quick and dirty sex." He pushed the picture back toward Dominic. "Now are we done?"

"No." Bree's voice was hard. "We're not."

Remy's lips curled a bit.

"You know every aspect of Kace's life. You know *him*."

"I know what Kace wants me to know. I don't think anyone—not even you, Bree—will ever understand who he truly is."

Dominic shut his folder. "Was he sleeping with any of the victims?"

Remy shook his head. "No, not as far as I know."

On a hunch, Bree pushed, "Were *you* sleeping with any of the victims?"

His lips pressed together. "I don't think I'm going to answer that."

Holy shit.

"Actually, I think I'm done talking. My lawyer—Deidre Shaw—should still be close by. And I'm pretty sure that she will have me out of here in the next five minutes." He offered a shark's smile to them. His head turned toward Dominic. "Go get Deidre. I'd bet money she's outside the building, talking to Kace. They wouldn't leave without me. Not their style."

Dominic didn't move.

Remy started to rise.

"Sit down," Bree ordered flatly. She slanted a glance at Dominic. "Go get his lawyer." She hoped he could see the message in her eyes. *I want to be alone with Remy for a few minutes.*

Dominic's chair scraped across the floor, then he hurried out. She waited until he was gone and then—

"It was Marie. You were involved with her."

He stared back at her.

"I saw you when you realized Marie wasn't working at Fantasy any longer. You were surprised. You took out your phone, and I think you texted her. We're going to get her phone records. If you've called her, if you've—"

"Yes," he gritted out. "It was Marie. And you shouldn't have pushed. I *told* you no more questions. I asked for my lawyer, I—"

"I didn't ask you a question. I stated facts. You're the one who just made the confession."

His eyes narrowed. "You're better than I thought."

"I keep being underestimated. Story of my life." Her heart was racing, but her voice was utterly flat.

"You should stay the fuck away from him." He barely seemed to breathe the words.

"What?"

Remy didn't repeat his words.

But she'd heard them, and they just made her angrier. "Was that a warning? Or a threat?"

He leaned toward her. "I've been helping you, and you didn't even know it."

"Helping me? By searching my room? You did that, didn't you? Because you're Kace's *right-hand*."

No confession but… "I saw when you took your transmitter out of your bra the first night at Fantasy. I never breathed a word about it to Kace. You owe me."

"I don't owe you a damn thing." But she made a mental note. The guy was willing to deceive his boss. What else might he do?

"He's not rational when it comes to you." Again, Remy's voice was barely a whisper. "I saw that today. He lost it when he thought Marie was you." A swallow. "I was the one who'd fucked her, but he was the one who went crazy—*because he thought it was you*. You're going to get in the way, and I can't have that."

"It sure sounds like you're threatening me. You're going to want to watch yourself."

"No, you're the one who has to be careful. You're the one—"

The door opened. "I am tired of this," Deidre announced with a dramatic sigh. "My clients are being attacked by this department, and it's ending."

Bree didn't look away from Remy. "No one is under attack."

He was already on his feet. "Remember what I said."

How could she forget it?

***

"Don't worry." Remy climbed into the back of the SUV with Kace. The driver took off. "I didn't tell them a damn thing."

"I wasn't worried." Kace turned his head so that he could study his friend. "And I didn't tell them that you were fucking Marie."

Remy flinched. His hands fisted. "One time. It was once, and it was a mistake."

"Was it?"

Now Remy looked at him. "You think I did that? That I killed her?"

He let a slow smile curl his lips. "Of course, I don't."

Remy's breath released in an expulsion of air.

"The security cameras weren't running yesterday. Did you realize that? The Feds made the discovery first thing. My cameras are always set to run, but someone had disabled them."

"*Someone,*" Remy emphasized, "who knows too much about your business."

Yes.

"You think the person is tied to the club?" Remy hooked his seatbelt. His fingers trembled faintly.

"I think the person is tied to me. I think it's been about the past all along."

Remy glanced at his now fisted hands. "You haven't talked to me about your past. I've been working with you for almost a year, and you still haven't told me…you never told me about Sheldon Taggert or Brittney Lang."

Kace pushed a button near his seat, and a privacy screen rose, blocking the driver from hearing their conversation. "There isn't much to tell about Sheldon Taggert. The dead don't speak."

"It's me," Remy said baldly. "You can tell me. Dammit, my job is to protect you, but I can't protect you if I don't know the truth." His fingers flexed. Released. "Did you kill him?"

Kace laughed. "Haven't you heard? That man died in an auto accident. That's why you shouldn't drink and drive. Bad things happen."

Remy seemed to gather his thoughts, then muttered, "You are a bad thing."

"Yes, I am."

"What about Brittney?"

"I was tried and found not guilty of her murder." He exhaled slowly. "Such a keen interest you have in my past."

"If I don't know what you're hiding, then I can't do my job. I can't protect you from the threats out there." Remy's voice seethed with frustration.

"Maybe it's not about what I'm hiding." Kace let his smile stretch. "Maybe it's about what *you're* hiding."

Remy didn't move. Not so much as a flicker of an eyelash. Then…"I don't know what you mean."

"Do you know how I feel about people who betray me, Remy?"

"Probably the same way I feel. Fool me once, and you're dead to me."

"Exactly." He lounged back in his seat. "Do you have anything you want to tell me, Remy? I believe the old saying is that confession can be good for the soul." Provided, of course, that the person had a soul.

He wasn't so sure that Remy St. Clair owned a soul—or a heart.

***

"I don't understand." Abby gripped the mug of coffee in her hands. Mascara had dried on her cheeks. "You're…a Fed?"

Bree cleared her throat. "I was working undercover. Trying to find the man responsible for the murders of—"

"The New Orleans Strangler?" Abby cut in with a cracking voice. "But you didn't. You didn't find him. You didn't stop him. Marie is dead. I…the cops told me. Uniformed cops came to my house. They told me she was dead, and they brought me here." The coffee sloshed because her hands were shaking. "I thought she'd quit. *She just quit Fantasy.* She wasn't supposed to be dead."

Bree waited for Abby's gaze to rise. When the other woman looked at her, Bree said, "I need to know about Marie. What can you tell me about her?"

"She was quiet. Flirted a little too much with Remy, but not with anyone else. She…she's dead?"

Bree nodded.

"And you're a Fed." Abby's shoulders hunched. "Does Kace know?"

"He does."

Abby flinched. "He's not going to want me talking to you. I-I should call him."

"I just want to find Marie's killer. That's my job. If you have any information that can help me, then, please, *tell* me. Give me something, Abby." She was practically begging.

But Abby shook her head.

Dammit. "I don't want another woman dying."

Abby stared at the dark coffee.

"You knew the other women, too, didn't you, Abby?" Bree pushed. "You know all of Kace's employees at his clubs."

"I train most of them." Again, she was staring at the coffee. "I…knew the others, yes."

"What connected them, Abby? What was it about them—"

"They all looked the same. Blond hair. Like...you."

"But was there more? Something that went beyond the surface? Something that you noticed?"

Once more, Abby shook her head.

"You never saw any customers paying too much attention to them? Never heard of the girls having trouble with anyone?"

"The cops interviewed me and the wait staff right after Lindsey was found. Told them and I'm telling you, there was nothing."

But there had to be *something*. "The girls never mentioned feeling as if they were being watched?" Because she believed the killer had watched his victims. It wasn't some snatch and grab. The women had all been carefully chosen and that implied *stalking*.

"No, they never mentioned it. We didn't exactly have long conversations. They did their jobs. I did mine." She sniffed. "I think I should leave now."

"Wait." Bree curled her fingers around the other woman's wrist. "Tell me about Amelia Sanderson."

Abby stared at Bree's fingers. "Not much to tell about her. I had to let her go when she wouldn't leave the boss alone."

"But did Amelia make any threats when she was fired? Say anything that stuck out to you?"

A furrow appeared between Abby's brows. Her head tilted back as she finally met Bree's gaze. "She did. She…she said Kace would be sorry. That he'd regret what he'd done." Her tongue slid over her lower lip, and she leaned conspiratorially toward Bree. "I got the impression that she thought…Amelia thought she had something on the boss. Something that she could turn over to the cops. A woman scorned and all that—she can be a dangerous thing."

Bree didn't look away from Abby's eyes. "Do you know what she had on him?"

Abby pulled her hand away from Bree. "Kace has been a good boss. I don't have anything else to say."

But there was fear in her eyes. And Bree wondered…was she afraid of talking to the Feds? Or afraid of Kace?

***

Bree parked in front of the wrought-iron gate. She'd gotten a rental car, a small, blue sedan. She straightened her shoulders as she approached the gate. Lights illuminated the house and pushed back the night's darkness. There was a camera perched nearby. She suspected Kace was watching her through that camera.

"Open the gate," she told him as she put her hands on her hips. "Let me in. We need to talk."

The gate didn't open. The camera just kept staring at her.

"Kace, I'm not leaving. Just open up, would you? Just—"

A guard appeared. He walked from behind the house, and her eyes narrowed when he stepped under a light, and she recognized the tattooed form of Franco. He headed toward the gate with slow steps. His head ducked a bit. "Boss isn't here, Bree."

She curled her fingers around the bars. "Where is he?"

"Had some business to take care of. Asked me to stay and keep an eye on the place for him."

She'd tried calling Kace. He hadn't answered. Not overly surprising, but the hours had passed in a too fast blur. The day had vanished, and there'd been no contact from him. She *needed* to talk with Kace. They had a murderer to catch.

"You should leave." Franco didn't exactly sound friendly any longer. "Boss doesn't want a Fed hanging around."

He sure hadn't seemed to mind the night before. Bree crossed her arms over her chest. "And neither do you, huh?"

His stare swept her. "Liked you. Thought you were nice enough. But you don't screw over the boss."

He wasn't going to let her past the gate. Fine. "Tell Kace this isn't over."

Franco didn't respond.

Huffing out a breath, Bree spun and marched back to her car. She walked around the front of the vehicle, headed for the driver side door and—

Car lights flashed on. Bright lights that had her throwing up her hand. Night had already fallen, and the street had appeared deserted just a moment before.

But now those lights were on her, and an engine was growling, snarling, and she realized the other vehicle was coming straight for her.

Bree didn't bother yanking out the gun she had holstered at her side. What good would that do? Even if she shot the driver—the driver she couldn't see—the vehicle could still hit her. So, she focused on hauling ass. She leapt over the hood of her sedan.

Franco shouted.

She heard the terrible screech and crunch of metal. The sedan jolted as it was hit, and then the other driver was speeding away.

Bree had fallen to the ground, but she jumped up. She raced after the other vehicle. An SUV. Dark. No tag—

A hard hand grabbed her and spun Bree around.

"Are you all right?" Franco stared at her with wide eyes.

"Did you see the driver?" Bree bit out.

He shook his head.

She hadn't seen the bastard, either. But maybe the security footage had caught him. Kace had so many cameras around his house—they must have seen *something*. She yanked out her phone. Called Karin. "I need an APB on a SUV, heading north on St. Charles…"

***

Kace pressed the phone closer to his ear. "She's okay?"

"Yes, sir," Franco's voice was low. "SUV was waiting down the street. Didn't even see it in the dark. Came right for her."

A chilling numbness snaked through his chest.

"She's wanting your security footage so the cops can try and get an image of the driver."

"Give her the footage."

"But—"

"Give her whatever she wants. I'm on my way there." He ended the call. Turned and rolled back his shoulders.

Remy slumped on the other side of the room. Blood dripped from his lip, and several dark bruises had already formed near his jaw.

"Get him home," Kace directed the men who were nearby. "And get a cleaner in this place." Blood lined the floor.

Who would have thought that Remy was such a bleeder?

When the men went to him, Remy shoved their hands away. He staggered to his feet. "Don't need…help."

The guy was so wrong. Kace walked toward him, flexing his fingers. "I expected a better fight from you. Usually you're a much more skilled opponent."

Remy squinted at him. "And you usually don't try to take my head off when we spar. This shit was different."

Was it? Kace smiled. "Better be careful. You seem to be favoring your ribs. I hope I didn't break any of them."

"Liar." But Remy smiled—smiled through his busted lip, as if they were just sharing a moment of camaraderie. They weren't.

"That would be you, Remy." Kace stared at him. *You're the liar.*

Remy's smile slipped. "Kace?"

"Bree was nearly run down a few moments ago. I'm going to see her now."

Alarm flared in Remy's eyes. "I'll come, too. You might need—"

"No, Remy, you're not needed right now. Take care of those ribs." His hands flexed. "I'll be seeing you again very soon."

Remy swallowed.

Kace grabbed a towel on his way out of the gym—his gym. His driver was waiting for him at the door.

"Feel better, boss?"

He looked at his bruised knuckles. Thought about the fact that Bree had nearly been run down while he'd been punching the hell out of Remy. "Not even close."

The driver took one look at Kace's face and didn't say anything else. He yanked open the back door. Kace hurried inside. "Get me home. *Now.*"

The driver hauled ass getting him back to his place in the Quarter.

When they turned on the street to his house, police lights illuminated the scene. A swirl of blue. A tow truck was there, latching to a crumpled sedan.

And Bree stood near the sedan, her arms wrapped around her stomach.

"Stop the car," Kace ordered.

The driver stopped. Kace jumped out of the vehicle. Went straight to her. Bree turned as he approached, her eyes flaring wide, but he didn't stop. He closed the distance between them, wrapped his hands around her arms, then raked her with his gaze.

She flinched, and he lifted his left hand, seeing the red, raw skin near her elbow.

A growl built in his throat.

"Just a scratch," Bree said quickly. "I had to jump across the hood, and I—"

"Franco."

The guy rushed toward him. "Boss, shit, you got here fast. I, um, I gave them the footage and—"

Kace's head turned. He focused his fury on the other man. "She's hurt, Franco."

"I, uh, I just told her that she couldn't come into the house. Like you said, I—"

"Where were you, Franco, when the vehicle was coming toward her?"

"I was…I was behind the gate. I didn't realize—"

"Stop." Bree's shaking voice. "He didn't hit me. He rushed to my side as fast as he could, okay? So back off Franco."

He'd do no such fucking thing, and Franco knew it.

"I thought you were done," Franco mumbled. His head ducked. "When you said—"

"No one touches her again. No one gets close to her. As long as she's in this town, she's mine." The words tore from Kace. "Make sure everyone knows. You fuck with her, I destroy you."

Bree's mouth dropped in shock. "Kace, what—"

Franco nodded and hurried away.

"He didn't do anything wrong." Her voice was low. "Except not let me into the house, but that's on *you*. That's—"

He pulled her closer, being careful not to touch the scratch near her elbow. "You shouldn't be in this damn town. Don't you get what a target you have on your back?"

"I *want* the killer to come after me. If he really has got me pegged as his next victim, then I want it, I—"

"What. The. Fuck?" For a minute, his whole world went red.

"Bree?" It was a slightly nasally voice. One of the other agents. Dominic. The sloppy dresser. "Everything okay, Bree?"

"Go screw off, Dominic," Kace snapped. "We're talking."

"Hey!" Outrage sharpened his voice. "You can't—"

Kace spun toward him. "I can't what?" His voice was low. Too low for the cops milling around to hear. Bree would hear, but she should hear this. She should start to take off the blinders and realize what the hell was happening. "I can't tell you what to do? I can tell you any damn thing I want, *Dominic*. You owe over seventy-five grand at my casino in Biloxi."

Dominic's mouth opened, closed. "That's…you don't—"

"I sure as hell do. The way I figure it, I own you. Because I know all about your addiction. Your debt. I know just how desperate you've been to erase that debt. And I know what you've done so that you could keep going to the tables." He held the other man's stare. "Ready to lose your life? Or you want to keep playing *my* game?"

Dominic glanced at Bree.

Then he turned and walked away.

"What in the hell was that?" Bree demanded.

He pulled her closer. Stared down at her gorgeous face. "You're in so deep, and you don't get it, do you? Good guys, bad guys. They all want the same thing. To take me down. To destroy me, by any means necessary." The rage burned so hot inside of him. "And I fucking gave them all the means." Because he hadn't possessed better control. Because he'd thought he was the one in charge all along.

But he hadn't been.

Bree had shot his plans straight to hell.

"We're going inside."

Her hair slid over her cheek as she shook her head. "Uh, maybe you should stop giving orders—"

"We're talking, and I don't want every rookie cop in the NOPD gaping at me while we do it. It's not safe out here for you, don't you get that?"

"The killer—"

"I'm not talking about the freaking Strangler. I'm talking about all my enemies, Bree. We both know a hit and run isn't the Strangler's MO. This wasn't him. This was just someone…" He sucked in a deep breath. Tried not to hold her too tight. "Someone who wanted to hurt me."

"By going after an FBI agent? That doesn't—"

"By going after the one woman I'm insane to possess." This was Remy's fault. One of the reasons why he'd sparred the guy and hadn't held back. Why he'd beat the shit out of him.

And why he would destroy Remy.

Dominoes all fall down.

"Talk to your FBI team. Make sure your precious evidence is collected. It won't matter. *I'll* find the one who did this. I'll punish the driver."

But Bree had lifted her stubborn little chin. "You can't take the law into your own hands."

When would she get it? In that town, he was the law.

"I'll watch you while you check in with the others." Because he wasn't letting her out of his sight. "When you're done, we go in the house together."

"Oh, so first you can't be bothered to talk to me and now—"

"Now I have someone who thinks killing an FBI agent who got close to me will either piss me off, hurt me…or…" He tucked a lock of her hair behind Bree's ear. "Or gain my favor. Until I figure out what the hell is happening, I have to keep watch on you."

She stepped back. "I don't need your protection."

She did. Far more than she possibly realized.

"I need your cooperation, Kace. So, I'll check in with my *team.* I'll clear this scene, and yes, we'll talk. Because I've sure got plenty that I want to say to you."

Without another word, Bree walked away. He watched her go…because it was a fucking fine sight.

***

In order to destroy a man, you had to take what mattered most to him.

He watched the flash of blue lights as they illuminated Kace Quick's mansion.

Money. Power. Possessions. The bastard who'd been born with nothing had it all now. He'd stolen and lied and cheated his way to the top. Kace thought he was king of the world.

Even kings could fall.

In order to destroy a man…

You took away what mattered.

If it was the house, you burned the house to the ground.

If it was the money, you stole every single dime.

If it was the man's power, then you wrecked it. You took the king, and you made him into a criminal. Locked him away.

And if it wasn't any of that…if you planned and you plotted and you realized you'd picked the wrong target, then you went after the man's heart.

Bree Harlow hurried toward a uniformed cop.

You went after his heart, and you cut that bitch out.

CHAPTER SIXTEEN

"Want to explain about that crap between you and Dominic?" Bree tried to keep her voice at a reasonable level. A very hard act considering that she wanted to scream at the man standing so casually before her.

They were in Kace's study. He had a glass of whiskey in one hand. And he was giving off a major I-don't-give-a-fuck vibe.

Considering that she'd nearly been run down, Bree gave a fuck. Lots of them. Tons.

"It's simple enough. Don't trust your team. They'll screw you over in a heartbeat." He took a sip of the whiskey. "Good old *Dom* has been selling FBI secrets for the last year as he tries to pay off his debts. The guy is a talker."

"No. You're lying. That's *not* true."

"Oh, sure, I'm the liar." Another sip—no, correction, he just gulped down all the whiskey and slammed the glass against the top of his desk. The I-don't-give-a-fuck vibe had vanished in a blink. "And you're a saint, aren't you? No lies from you. Not from sweet, innocent Bree."

"Fuck you." Her hands went to her hips.

But Kace just laughed. "I'm telling you the truth about Dominic. Why do you think the guy got so sweaty every time he was near me? He was afraid I'd rat him out. Finally decided to do just that because he pissed me off."

"So, what—he's been on your payroll?"

Kace shrugged.

She lunged across the room toward him. "You said you haven't lied to me. I call BS. You omitted the truth. That's the same thing as lying."

"I don't think it is."

He didn't… She growled. "Sheldon Taggert."

Kace blinked at her.

"Did you kill him?"

He smiled at her. "Are you wired, Bree?"

She grabbed the hem of her t-shirt and yanked it over her head. It hit the floor a moment later. Then she kicked off her shoes. Shoved down her jeans. Stood before him clad in her panties and her bra. "No. Wire." Her breath heaved in and out. "Did you kill him?"

His gaze heated as it raked over her. "Taggert was no choir boy. You want to hear the whole story? Fine. I knew Brittney was screwing around. The thing is…I didn't care. We weren't what you'd call serious, and I had other priorities."

"But—the trial, it was—you were supposed to be in love with her. I read the transcripts, you said—"

"I lied to them, Bree. I'm not lying to you."

She felt goosebumps rise on her arms.

"Taggert was always sniffing around her. Always trying to come close. Fucking stalking her. Terrifying her because he wanted her all the time. So, I told him to back the hell off. Then I beat the hell out of him for her. That's why Taggert was so quick to testify against me at the trial. He wanted his payback. So he said that I was the jealous one. That I'd attacked him because I found out that Brittney was sleeping with him. And if I'd done that to him, gotten so physical and rough, well, imagine what I must have done to her."

"I don't have to imagine. I read the coroner's report."

He towered over her. She could feel the heat from his body coming toward her. "Are you afraid of me?"

"Are you a murderer?"

"Yes."

It took a moment for that one word to sink in. A moment too long.

"Going to put your clothes back on? Going to rush away and tell your FBI friends that you just got a confession?" A bitter laugh escaped him as he turned away from her. "Good luck with that. I just said yes, but you have no idea who I killed." He headed for the bar. Poured another whiskey.

"You killed Sheldon Taggert."

"Stop beating that dead horse." He stared into the glass of amber liquid. "He terrorized her. Brittney was shaking when she came to me and said the guy wouldn't leave her alone. I found bruises on her, and when I asked about them, Brittney told me they were from Taggert."

"*Why* didn't you tell the judge? The cops? The—"

"Because he was a rich, privileged kid, and I was a thug who already had a juvie record. But it was okay. I knew how to play the game." He swallowed the whiskey. "I just had to find a witness to match him. Someone who was just as rich and privileged. Someone who would provide me with an unbreakable alibi. And I did. I found the perfect person."

"Susannah Mills."

"Saw her name in the court files, did you? Yes, sweet Susannah was my alibi."

"How did you get her to go along with the story?"

"Simple enough." This time, he set the glass down without a sound. "She told the truth. I *had* fucked her that night. Brittney and I were done, and I wanted some fun. Some women have always liked the thrill that comes from screwing someone dangerous." Now he glanced at her. "Don't you love that same thrill?"

"No."

"Liar."

"I don't."

"Then why'd you fuck me?"

"Because I wanted you in spite of the danger. And the stories. In spite of *everything*. Even though I knew I was crossing a line that would cost me."

He gave her his taunting half-smile. "Cost you at the Bureau?"

"Cost me part of my soul. Because that's the kind of man you are, Kace Quick."

His gaze swept over her, lingering on her breasts as they thrust against the cups of her bra. "I am enjoying the show."

She grabbed for her shirt. "Fuck you—"

He was across the room in an instant. He snatched the shirt from her hand. "You did that. It should have been one and done, but it wasn't. Now we're both screwed." Then he shoved the shirt over her head. "Keep this thing *on*."

He was dressing her now? "Are you insane?"

A bitter laugh. "I think I absolutely am, at least where you're concerned." He stared at her. "Taggert drank his ass off. I watched him. A fucking rich frat boy who came looking for a good time on Bourbon Street. He was twenty-two, you know that? Twenty-two and didn't give a shit about anything. Thought he could come on my turf and push me around. He found me on the anniversary of her death, and told me, 'The bitch got what she deserved.'" His smile was cold. "I guess Taggert got what he deserved, too."

"Kace…"

"Not that I was in a bar back then. I mean, how could I have been? I wasn't twenty-one. Not that I could have watched him drive away. Not that I could have followed him on my motorcycle. *Not* that I could have watched the sonofabitch nearly take out a guy and his girlfriend who had the nerve to just be walking on the street when that drunk bastard was weaving all over the road."

Her heart thudded in her chest as her bare toes curled against the floor. *Not that I…*He was phrasing his statements so carefully.

"Not that I did any of that, my beautiful Bree."

Her arms wrapped around her stomach. She didn't know what to say.

"And *not* that I am freaking the hell out with every breath because we are screwed, and I'm trying to figure out a way to protect you." His hands fisted at his sides. "You should have just left New Orleans. If you'd left, then they would have thought Remy was wrong. That you didn't matter."

Her gaze had dropped to his fists. And for the first time, she noticed the bruising on his knuckles. A little gasp left her lips as she hurried to him and reached for his right hand. "What happened to you?"

"I beat the shit out of Remy."

Her fingers feathered over his bruises. "Why?"

"Because he put the target on you."

Her gaze rose to lock with his.

"He shouldn't have talked about what he saw. I played the game. I let him stay close. Then he talked. Told the cops. Told the Feds…"

"He didn't turn on you." She didn't understand, but she was trying hard. "He didn't tell anyone about your business—"

Kace laughed. "Screw the business. I'm talking about *you*. He told them all how I reacted when I thought it was *you* hanging in those silks."

She was still holding his hand. And remembering Remy's words. *I tackled him because he wouldn't stop trying to get her down. When we hit the floor, he looked up and he could see her face from that angle. He stopped fighting then.*

"I went crazy when I thought that was you hanging up there. A reaction that says you mean far more to me than just a quick screw." Kace's words were ragged. "Remy was the only one who saw how I reacted. He should have kept his damn mouth closed. He didn't. Now everyone knows that you matter. I was sending you away. Turning *away* from you so that you'd be safe, but Remy told the whole freaking world, and now..." His breath heaved out. "To hurt me, my enemies want you. To impress me, my friends want you. They want to hurt the FBI agent they think betrayed me."

She was caressing his hand. He was staring at her as if—*as if I'm the only thing that matters.* Why would he look at her that way?

Why was she still touching him?

Why? *Why?*

"Remy and I spar all the time," Kace admitted. "He's strong and he's quick, so I like to fight him."

She thought of how fast Kace had moved when Grayson had lunged at him.

"I usually hold back, though. This time, I wanted to tear him apart." A shrug. "And I'm not done with him yet. I will make him pay." His bright blue gaze was electric with fury. "He's put you at risk. Not just from the sick sonofabitch targeting women, the fucking Strangler, but now, you're in the sights of anyone who wants to—"

"Why do I matter to you?" Her words cut through his.

Kace frowned.

"Why do you care what happens to me? If you turn away, if you leave me on my own, won't that send a message to your enemies? And to your friends? Won't that show them that Remy was wrong?"

His jaw hardened even more. "You'll get hurt."

"I'm an FBI Agent. Being hurt is always a risk. I don't need a big, bad guy coming in to protect me."

Now his hand lifted to caress her cheek. "Maybe I want to protect you."

"Kace—"

His fingers moved, sliding under her hair and tipping back her head. "Maybe I lost everyone that mattered in my life, and then you appeared. I knew what you were from the word go, but I thought I could play you. I could do what I wanted, take what I wanted, then send you away." Each word was rougher than the last. "But I can't. I can't turn you loose. I can't let you go. You got to me, slipped right past my guard, and now we're both lost."

His lips lowered toward hers. She could stop him. Shove against his chest. Pull away. But she didn't do any of those things. Instead, she reached up, moving onto tip-toes, and her hands curled around his neck. Their mouths met in a hungry crush of need and desire.

He said she'd gotten to him.

He'd done the same thing to her. From the first...*from the word go*...Bree had known what he was. But she wanted him. She'd thought she could walk away, too. Only he haunted her.

He'd gotten beneath her skin. In her very blood.

The kiss was frantic and rough. Her heart thundered in her chest, and the lust that boiled just beneath the surface reached a fever pitch.

Want him. Didn't matter what would happen in an hour or even what would happen in the next day. For that moment, Bree just wanted *him.*

His hands slid over her body, moving to caress her breasts, making her breath come faster, harder. He yanked off her shirt. The shirt *he'd* put back on her. Kace threw it across the room, leaving her clad just in her underwear. The underwear didn't last long. He shoved her panties off, then he lifted her up, spun her around, and put Bree on his desk.

Her legs were spread, his hips between them. His hands had slapped down on the wooden surface of the desk, on either side of her. His eyes were so hard and deep. His jaw clenched. The stark need on his face took her breath away.

He had on too many clothes.

"I can't fuck you and walk away." His words were guttural. One hand lifted. Slid between her legs. Caressed her with sensual skill and savage possession.

"I'm…ah…not walking away." Her hands were on his shoulders. Her nails bit into his skin.

He unzipped his jeans. Grabbed a condom from his wallet and shoved it onto the long, stretching length of his cock. He yanked her closer to the edge of the desk. His cock pushed at the entrance to her body.

"I'd kill for you," he whispered. He kissed her. "I'd do *anything* to keep you safe."

He drove into her. Her sex clamped greedily around him even as her legs rose and locked tightly around his hips.

There was no more talking. There was only frantic thrusting. Panting. Moans. His fingers were on her clit, stroking her over and over again as he pounded into her. She was wet and hot, and she surged toward him as they fought for the wild rush of pleasure. He kissed her with a ferocious hunger. Bree strained against him, absolutely wild. She'd never been this way with a lover before. She'd never wanted someone so much that nothing else mattered.

The climax hit her, whipping through her whole body and tearing a scream from her lips. He thrust harder, rougher, his hands moving to clamp around her and arch her against him even more. Kace growled her name when he came. He held her in a grip that was tight and hard.

Their heartbeats slowed. The wild craving eased. She could breathe. She could think. And as for Kace…

His head lifted. For a moment, she could have sworn that she saw a flash of fear in his eyes. But he blinked, and it was just Kace. Kace with his power and his pride and his secrets. "I tried to send you away."

Bree's tongue swiped over her dry lips. "I'm not a thing to be sent somewhere. I'm here in New Orleans, I'm working a case, and I won't leave until the case is over."

He slowly pulled from her body. "Even if you *become* the case?" He grabbed a tissue from his desk, yanked off the condom, and tossed it in the trash. He was still aroused.

So was she. Bree tried to keep her breathing even. "I am the case now. We both know it. And I'm going to stay with you. I want the Strangler to see me."

"You want him to come after you." Kace zipped up and turned his back to her.

She remained, naked, on the desk. She wasn't going to frantically try and cover herself as if she was embarrassed by what had happened. She wasn't embarrassed. She didn't understand *them.* Their relationship, if they had one. If that's what it was. But she wanted him. Wanted the sex. And she wasn't going to pretend otherwise.

"If you stay with me, Bree, everyone will know that you belong to me."

"It's…not about belonging."

His shoulders stiffened. “Don’t you want to be mine?”

“I belong to myself, Kace. Always have. Always will.”

He turned his head to stare at her. “I think I’m yours. That’s part of the problem. I think you snuck inside, and I think you’re close to owning the last bit of a soul that I have.”

“Kace…”

“Good and bad. It’s all together. You’ll have to accept that, or you’ll have to leave me. Soon enough, you’ll make the decision.” Kace’s hand rubbed over his jaw, scraping against the stubble there. “You’re going to use yourself as bait for the Strangler, aren’t you?”

“I’ll be monitored by my team.”

A bitter laugh. “I got your team leader fired, remember? Or at least, he *will* be fired, before I’m done with him.”

She hopped off the desk. Her knees were a little jiggly but she didn’t let that weakness show. “Why didn’t you tell me the truth about Grayson?”

His gaze stroked over her body. “You are so beautiful.”

She kept walking toward him. Slow but certain steps. *“Why didn’t you tell me the truth?”*

“Because you didn’t ask for it. You didn’t ask if Brittney had been sleeping with someone else. You were only interested in the present, not my past." His hand rose, and his fingers lightly trailed over the scar on her side. "But the past marks us, and it doesn't let go. We think we've buried it, just to turn around and see the bastard coming for us again."

A shiver slid over her. "You think the Strangler is tied to your past."

His hand fell away from her. "Don't you, Bree?"

"Yes." She did.

"And what about the killer in *your* past, Bree? If someone found him for you, would you want him brought to justice? You want to stand up in court and face off against him?"

Why was he bringing up her past?

"Or do you just want him in the ground?"

Her lower lip trembled. For a moment, she could smell her parents' blood.

Kace scooped her into his arms and held her tight against his chest. "Don't answer. I don't need the answer. I understand you, baby, far better than you realize." He pressed a kiss to her temple.

Her body softened against his, but when he carried her out of the room, Bree gave a startled laugh. "There is no way you're getting me up the stairs."

His hold tightened on her. "I work out." A faint, possibly teasing note had entered his voice. "You should have more faith in me. I'm strong."

She knew that. "You had to be." To accomplish all that he had.

But he didn't need to carry her. She'd *never* been carried by a lover before. Yet…he carried her up the stairs. Didn't even seem a little winded. And he took her straight into his bedroom. With gentle hands, he eased her onto the bed. Kace removed her bra—she'd forgotten she still had it on. Then he stared down at her and stripped away the last of his clothes.

She caught sight of the faint bruise on his ribs right before he turned off the lamp. Her hand reached toward the mark. "What—"

"Remy got in one good punch."

Remy.

He climbed into the bed. Pulled her close. "You know…" Kace murmured. "There's a reason the cops can't link me to any criminal activity. No money laundering. No illegal gambling rings."

"No drugs?"

"No, baby, no drugs. I don't run drugs." Flat. Hard. "My mother OD'ed when I was a kid. A fucking year after my father did the same thing. I don't run drugs," he said again, the words even harder. Rougher. But his hands were gentle on her. So careful. "But I'd be lying if I said I hadn't ever crossed the line and broken the law."

He was confessing to her, in the darkness of his bedroom, with her still naked, with his body curled around hers, and his hands gently stroking her.

"But even a criminal can go legit, can't he? My friend Jax did it a while back. Changed everything up for his Sarah. You just need the right reasons."

What was he saying? That he'd change—

"The cops can't find anything because there's nothing to find. Not now. I've let them have their fun, but my patience is gone." Another kiss to her temple.

"Kace..."

"If you play bait, he'll come after you."

She turned toward him. Bree wished she could read his expression in the dark. "I'll play bait, and my team will *stop* him."

"Only if you catch him before I do. Because if I get him first, I will kill the sonofabitch." A kiss to her lips. Slow and sensual even as he spoke so easily about death. "Then the cops will have their evidence. They'll finally lock me away."

And he'd told her before...downstairs, he'd said he would kill for her.

Lots of men would probably say that to a lover. Say the words to sound strong and alpha. But Bree knew Kace wasn't making some empty threat. He was giving her a promise.

"Guess I have to find him first," she whispered.

"One way or another," Kace told her, voice a rumble in the dark, "this will end."

***

He watched his prey scurry through the streets. The man moved like a damn rat, furtive and fast. He'd run to the left, to the right, snatching up prizes as he found them hidden in the dark.

It hadn't been hard to hunt down Hank Cannon, Vietnam Vet. Hank had been in and out of the VA Hospital for the last twenty years. When he was off his meds, the man loved the streets. He scavenged for food, he hid in the shadows, and he saw things that he freaking shouldn't see.

Hank pulled a half-eaten banana from a dumpster and turned to flee—

You're not scurrying again, little rat.

"Hank," he called the man's name deliberately, wanting to get the show moving. He had places to be, after all. Things to do.

Hank let out a gasp and spun around. "Wh-who's there?"

He pulled out a twenty and waved it in the air as he slipped from the shadows. "Just someone who wants to help you."

Hank's eyes went to the cash. His tongue swiped across his lower lip.

Another twenty was waved at him, too. "Hank, I'm a reporter. I want to talk to you, and if you answer my questions, I'll pay you. Don't you want the cash?"

Hank sidled closer.

"I heard you saw a bad guy the other day." He kept to the darkness. A streetlamp overhead fell on his hand, though, like a spotlight that lit up the cash. "Want to talk to you about that."

"She died." Hank's voice was abrupt. He was flexing his fingers, as if he wanted to snatch the money and run. "Pretty lady in red died."

She hadn't been wearing red. She—

Oh, right. The blood.

"Lady died. He ran. I want the money now."

He pulled the money out of the light. "What did he look like?" Maybe he wouldn't have to kill the fellow. If Hank didn't know, if Hank couldn't tell anyone anything…

Well, why bother with Hank? Hank wasn't the prey he favored. No need to—

"Eyes like hell. Burning, burning, burning…" Hank sounded crazy. "Evil to see. Face was twisted. Evil."

He almost laughed. Hank wasn't going to be able to tell anyone a damn thing. The guy's mind was shot.

He put the money back in the light. "Thanks, Hank, you can—"

Hank bounded forward and grabbed the money. The bastard moved so fast—he yanked the money and they both slammed together.

The light fell on—

"Evil to see! Eyes like hell!" Spittle flew from Hank's mouth as he gaped in horror. "You, you, you! You, you, you—"

He drove his gloved fist into Hank's jaw. Hank tumbled back, fell, and his head slammed into the broken pavement.

He rolled back his shoulders as he glared down at the guy. "Just had to be a problem, didn't you, Hank?"

***

Her shoes were in the blood. The smell was all around her. Her mother was just staring up at her, and all of that blood—

Hard hands grabbed Bree, yanking her back even as she felt the knife press to her side.

"Isn't this what you wanted?"

"No!" She struggled and the blade bit even deeper into her skin. She looked down at his hand. Saw the blood and—

"Now you're free, Bree. Now you're free." For an instant, she could have sworn she felt his lips press to her temple. *"I did it for you. Killed them, for you."*

"No!" Her eyes flew open as Bree sucked in a frantic gasp of air. Her heart was racing, a film of sweat covered her skin, and his rough whisper played in her mind over and over again.

Just a nightmare? Or a memory?

Her hand flew to the left, reaching out for Kace, but he wasn't there.

She focused on calming her breathing. In and out. Slow. Easy. It had just been a bad dream. Not a real memory. Her past and present had gotten all twisted together. It was because Kace had said he was going to kill the Strangler if he got to the guy first. Yes, that was it.

Bree pushed the covers away and swung her legs over the side of the bed. She grabbed one of Kace's t-shirts from a nearby chair and pulled it on as she hurried for the door. When she cracked open the bedroom door, Bree didn't see Kace in the hallway.

But a light was on downstairs. She tip-toed down the hallway, then made her way to the first floor. She was careful not to let her foot press down hard on the fourth stair from the bottom.

The door to Kace's study was partially shut. Light spilled from the room as she crept closer. And then—

"I don't care what it costs. This is me, Jax. You think money matters to me? It's a means to an end. Nothing more. It gets me what I want, and in this case, I'll pay anything."

Jax. Was he talking to Jax Fontaine? Had to be him. What were they making a deal for?

"Sarah can talk to her. Yeah, Bree might balk. See what Sarah can find on her own first."

They're talking about me.

"I want the sonofabitch. Turn him over? Hell, no. I want him in pieces. I want to know exactly what happened." A bitter laugh. "Right, any price. And we make sure the cops never know."

She inched closer to the door.

"You get his location, you get any intel on him, and you come straight to me. I'll owe you." A rough bark of laughter. "I know you always collect."

Silence. Was the call over? She risked moving a few inches nearer to—

The door opened. Kace's hair was tousled. His eyes stormy. And he had his phone pressed to his ear. "The Feds are going to be looking for you," he told the person on the other end of the line. "I might have told them that you were my alibi. Yeah, well, shit happens." He lowered the phone, his finger sliding over the screen. His gaze drifted over her body, slowly. Lingering on the thrust of her breasts and the exposed expanse of her legs. "Listening in doorways? Is that something they teach in FBI 101 classes?"

"They tell us to listen anywhere and everywhere that we can. People can make easy mistakes, any time." She pushed back her shoulders. "Jax Fontaine? Is that who was on the line?"

"Yes."

"Why were you talking to him?"

"Didn't you hear enough to figure it out?"

She had. "You have him looking for someone. The killer."

He smiled at her. Only the smile didn't reach his eyes. "You have a team. Doesn't it make sense that I get one, too?"

"Jax Fontaine isn't part of any intelligence team."

"Don't be so sure of that. You know who is really, really good at collecting intel?" He leaned close to her and confided, "Criminals. We always know all the bad shit that happens in a town."

"You think Jax can lead you to the Strangler? He hasn't even been in New Orleans since—"

His phone vibrated, cutting through her words. Kace glanced down at the phone, at the text he'd just received, and his whole face hardened. "Fuck."

"What is it?"

"My club. It's burning." His head jerked up. "Some SOB just set Fantasy on fire."

CHAPTER SEVENTEEN

The firefighters had put out the flames by the time Kace roared up to the scene. A fortunate thing because the way all of those buildings were smashed together, the whole street could have gone up. The scent of smoke and ash filled the air as Kace braked his motorcycle. Bree's grip tightened on him for a moment, then she was hopping off the bike. She flashed her badge when some of the uniformed cops rushed forward.

He didn't get off his bike, not yet. Kace's gaze swept the scene. He was tired of this shit. No one fucked with what was his.

"Kace!"

His head slowly turned at the yell, and he saw Remy hurrying toward him. The street lights fell on the guy's face, and Kace saw the soot that marked him. And the bruises on the fellow's jaw. Remy glanced over his shoulder, staring back at the club. It looked as if most of the place had been saved. The firefighters had gotten to the scene fast. Black ash darkened the windows and the roof appeared singed.

"Kace..." Remy was almost on top of him. "We've got a problem. A big one."

"Yeah, I know." He shoved down the kick stand and slowly rose from his motorcycle. "Some jerkoff burned my place. And the security cameras better have been working."

Remy swallowed. "The fire started in the back of the club. Dammit, a guy's dead."

"What?" That was Bree's sharp response. Her hands were on her hips.

"They found a body," Remy announced starkly. "The guy was torched. Someone poured gasoline on him. *That's* how the fire started."

"Excuse me," Bree said, voice flat. She hurried for the line of yellow police tape that blocked the scene. Kace watched her flash her badge again, then she was ducking under the tape. His eyes narrowed, and he realized she'd headed for her team members—he recognized Karin Miller and Dominic Grant. And there was Grayson Wesley, too. What in the hell was he doing there? Grayson should have been thrown off the case.

"Who is the dead man?" Kace asked Remy.

"He, um, he was burned pretty badly. I don't know if the cops are going to be able to ID him." His hand raked over his face. "The cops are already asking for the video footage. The fire started in the back. We had two cameras back there. What should I—"

"Give them the footage. Let them see who the hell set the fire." He stared hard at Remy. "*After* you send that shit to me."

Remy pulled out his phone. "It's here, man. I had it linked to my phone. After what went down with Marie, I wanted to make sure I could get access to the system at any time."

Remy had an all-access pass to the club, to the security system. To everything. That would be changing very, very soon. Kace would make sure that the man wasn't in charge of his security any longer. "From now on, the security link comes to *my* phone, understand?'

Remy nodded. "I'll make sure that happens."

"You do that."

Remy lifted the phone.

And Kace watched the scene unfold. A man in a battered leather jacket and wearing a motorcycle helmet appeared. He dragged another fellow—a guy who appeared to be unconscious—toward the rear door of Fantasy. The man in the helmet dropped the victim, turned, and the camera caught the fact that the visor was pulled down on his helmet.

Right, you sonofabitch. Try to hide.

A moment later, the guy was back. And he was pouring gasoline all along the victim's body. Kace thought he would light the vic on fire then but—

The killer pulled a thick length of rope from his pocket. He wrapped it around the victim's neck. Tightened, tightened.

"Fucking bastard," Kace snarled.

The victim went totally limp. Dead. *Then* the bastard in the helmet lit him up and backed away.

"Kace, the jacket looks just like yours," Remy mumbled.

Yeah, it did. Exactly like the one he was wearing. And the helmet looked just like the one he kept with his motorcycle. The one that he'd had Bree wearing moments before. The one that was behind him on the bike right then. "Still setting me up," Kace announced grimly. Fury pounded through his blood. "And ten to one…ten to freaking *one* that the poor fellow in that video was the witness."

Remy's brows furrowed. "Witness?"

Ah, Remy. Don't play dumb. "The homeless man from the Canal Street Station. The guy who interrupted our killer when he was attacking Amelia." The rage was almost choking him. "The poor fellow's clothes were three sizes too big. His shoes didn't match. Didn't you see that in the video?"

Remy's gaze cut away from him. Seemed to focus on Bree and the Feds with her. "Is she going to back up your alibi this time?"

"I was with her when we got the text about the fire. She'll back me. This piece of shit can try all he wants to set me up, but it won't do any good when I've got my very own FBI agent protecting me."

When Remy looked back at him, Kace caught the glint of rage in the other man's eyes. *Careful, there, Remy. Your mask is slipping.* But he didn't say those words. And he didn't act on the fury he felt. There were too many eyes on them. The cops were ready to jump on Kace at any moment. They wanted an excuse.

Not happening.

"So, I guess you aren't using her any longer? Did the hit and run at your place change your mind?" Remy's voice was low.

Not low enough. Bree was walking back toward them, and Kace saw her shoulders stiffen. He smiled at Remy. "I'm going to find the piece of shit who tried to run down *my* Bree, and I'm going to make him…regret his actions."

Remy rocked forward. "The way you made Sheldon Taggert regret his?"

"Kace." Bree reached out and touched his arm. "I told them that you were with me. I told them all there is no way you were involved with what happened here tonight."

She was protecting him. He'd make certain he protected her. "Remy just showed me the security video from Fantasy."

Her gaze cut to Remy.

"The killer wore a leather jacket just like mine." The one that was a heavy weight around him. "And he made sure to keep a motorcycle helmet over his face when he got close to the security cameras. I think he killed the witness from the trolley tracks."

Her eyes widened. "We interviewed that witness. He was—he wasn't making any sense. Kept talking about eyes of evil. The poor fellow was off his medications. Hank couldn't describe anything to help the investigation."

It hadn't mattered to the killer. The guy had thought the vic was a loose end. And he'd eliminated him.

Grayson stalked toward him.

"What the hell does he want?" Remy demanded roughly. "Thought you said he was benched."

Grayson glared at Kace. "Another death at your door."

"Grayson," Bree began, with a warning edge in her voice.

Kace raked his gaze over the jackass. "Maybe with the jacket and the helmet…Maybe it was you." He pursed his lips. "You sure as hell hate me enough, don't you?"

"What?" Grayson barked. "What are you—"

"I'm saying that you hate me. You hate so much that you'd do just about anything to get me locked away, wouldn't you? Even kill. Kill women who were your informants. Kill women you were using in your quest to take me down. Kill the one man who *saw* you in the act...because you were afraid he'd let your secret out."

"You're insane." Grayson shook his head. "I'm an FBI agent, I'm—"

"Where were *you* when the poor bastard was being torched?" Kace reached out and slid his fingers down Bree's arm. "Because I have someone who can vouch for me. Can you do the same?"

Grayson's furious stare narrowed on Bree's face. "Can you vouch for him? Every single moment? Can you *swear* he didn't leave your sight?"

"Sure, she can," Remy cut in. "They were fucking. Why the hell do you think they're standing so close to each other now? They're lovers. You can see that shit."

Bree went statue-still beside Kace.

Kace turned his head to stare at Remy. "Fatal mistake."

Remy blinked. "Boss?"

But then Grayson blasted, "You weren't supposed to fuck him, Bree. The job was to get close, not to become a freaking whore who—"

He didn't get to finish because Kace had lunged toward him. Kace didn't put his hands on the jerk. He knew how to play the game. Didn't touch him at all. But Kace smiled, and he knew it would be a chilling sight. "You don't talk to her that way. You aren't her boss any longer. You're nothing to her."

Fury hardened Grayson's face.

"You are nothing," Kace continued in a cold, lethal tone. "And you'll see that…because I'm going to take away everything that you care about. You'll be in the street, begging, before I'm done with you."

"Is that a threat?"

Kace just laughed.

"You're laughing," spittle flew from Grayson's lips, "while a man just burned behind your club."

"I'm laughing…because I can't wait to destroy you."

"Oh, yeah? You think you're so big and bad? Do it."

"*Don't.*" Bree grabbed Kace's arm. "He's trying to make you take a swing. He wants you to attack. It's the same shit you did to him at the station."

Kace already knew that. "I don't make mistakes." A definite warning to Grayson. And to Remy. Remy's mouth was too damn big. Someone was going to shut him up.

"You're choosing the wrong side, Bree." Grayson's words were a fierce snarl. "You're supposed to put the criminals away, not fuck them."

The guy was trying to antagonize him. Trying to push Kace into making a mistake.

It would be so easy to punch the fellow.

Kace opened his mouth, ready to tell the jackass where to—

"He was a much better fuck than you," Bree said calmly.

Oh, damn. Kace's gaze swung to her.

Bree lifted one brow as she stared at Grayson as if he were a piece of shit that had gotten stuck to her shoe. "Kace didn't torch this place. He didn't kill the vic. He's done nothing wrong the whole time I've been with him, and, yes, I've fucked him. Several times. And I plan to do it again. So how about you maybe stop the sex shaming and actually find the real killer? Does that sound good to you? Oh, wait, it doesn't matter if it does or not. You're not on the case. You're suspended. Since you are, get the hell away from *my* crime scene."

Shit. *Shit.* That woman was amazing.

Without another word, Grayson turned on his heel and stalked away.

"*Dismissed,*" Remy muttered, and he sounded impressed.

"I'm going to get more details from Dominic and Karin." Bree started to rush past Kace.

He held tight to her. "You are insanely sexy and beautiful."

She blinked. "You realize, of course, my career is probably about to be torpedoed because I just told—"

"Your career won't suffer at all."

A broken laugh. "I don't care. You aren't the man he thinks."

And you're a woman I could love.

Oh, no. That thought shouldn't have been there.

"I took this job because I wanted to protect people. Because I wanted to make a difference." Bree nodded. "That's what I'm going to do."

She shouldn't be with someone like him. He would never deserve her.

"I'm going to be here for a while. There will be lots of questions. You'll probably want to get that lawyer of yours on stand-by." She squared her shoulders.

He kissed her. Leaned in close and kissed her right there on the street. Screw whoever was watching. He was staking a claim and letting the whole world know.

She is mine. I'm hers. You go after her, I wreck you.

He held the kiss, let it linger, and then he pulled back and watched her walk away.

Remy gave a low whistle. "I didn't realize…like that, is it?"

Kace didn't speak.

"I…I thought you were using her. Throwing her up as bait for the killer."

"Bree isn't bait."

Cocking his head, Remy studied Kace. "Then what is she?"

Everything.

***

"What just happened over there, Bree?" Dominic asked her, his voice low. "Because Grayson sure looked pissed."

Yes, he had. "I'm plenty pissed myself. I thought Grayson was suspended."

"He is." Dominic sidled closer. "Karin told him to get his ass away from her crime scene."

She was really liking Karin more and more.

"Your, ah, your boyfriend…you sure he was with you—"

"Kace didn't leave the house." She'd only slept for about twenty minutes before her nightmare had woken her. That wouldn't have given him enough time to leave and commit the horrible murder.

"Then you did your job." Dominic nodded. "We sent you in to find proof of his innocence or guilt. He's not our guy, you've got proof, and now we can—"

"Now we can see what mistakes this bastard made." She took a pair of gloves from the crime scene techs. "I want to survey the kill area." Bree glanced over her shoulder and saw Kace still huddled tight with Remy. Remy's lip was busted, and his jaw sported some serious bruises. She would be asking more about that later. *Sparring, my ass.* Bree made her way through Fantasy, her gaze sweeping the place. Not much damage inside. The fire had been contained at the rear of the building. She headed to the back. The vic was still there.

Jesus.

She flinched and jerked her gaze away, even as nausea rolled through her stomach. The horrible smell of burnt flesh filled her nose—

"Don't gag," a woman barked at her. She looked down to see a beautiful, African American woman kneeling near the remains. "If you contaminate my crime scene, I'll be pissed."

Bree kept her breathing shallow. *No deep breaths. Don't inhale this.*

"You'll never forget the smell." The woman's gaze softened with sorrow. "You'll wish you could. But it'll just be something that stays with you forever." A sigh. "Poor bastard. He was still wearing his dog tags. They melted to—" She broke off, shaking her head. "I'm the coroner, Dr. Angela Craword. I'll be running a full autopsy, and I'll get you my report ASAP." She pointed behind her. "Fire marshal is already here, too. But you can tell by those marks on the building, our killer was slinging accelerant as fast as he could."

Because he'd wanted his victim to go down in flames.

Why?

"What in the hell?" Angela leaned forward. "He's holding something in his hands. Something…it's not burned."

The vic's charred right hand was clenched tightly around something.

"Money?" Angela questioned. "Why is he gripping—"

"You want a homeless man to come close, you tempt him with money." Bree braced her legs apart. She knew why the guy was gripping money even in death. "There are going to be fingerprints on that money."

Angela glanced up at her. "Probably hundreds of prints."

True, but… "A hundred prints or five prints…whatever is on there, this is a start. It's a real lead for us." Because even if the perp had been wearing gloves, he might have been carrying the money around for a while. If that was the case, the guy could easily have touched the cash at some point *without* his gloves.

Hell, yes, *yes*.

Angela's lips pulled down. "Too bad this fellow had to die for the lead."

Yes, it was.

***

Kace Quick was a fucking *bastard.* Grayson paced around the confines of his apartment. He was on the top floor of an old, converted antebellum home in the Garden District, a home not too far away from Kace's place. He'd picked the location deliberately, wanting a space that would allow him to keep watch on his prey.

Grayson stormed into the bathroom. Ash covered him, and he needed to get that crap off. He stripped, then climbed under the hot spray of the shower. As the water thundered down on him, the fury he felt just grew.

Kace had screwed him over at the station. Got him to react when Grayson knew he should have kept his cool in place. The guy had pushed his buttons. After all of Grayson's careful planning, he'd been so sure—

He heard the click of a door closing. A faint sound, one that he barely caught over the blast of the shower, but Grayson stiffened.

What the hell was going on? He yanked off the water, sending it into a fast *drip, drip, drip* before he shoved back the shower curtain. "Who's there?" Grayson called.

Nothing.

He grabbed a towel and looped it around his waist.

There was one person who had a key to his place. She should know better than to come right now, though, not after the shit she'd pulled. Water trickled down his chest as he grabbed for the bathroom door.

He heard the creak of the floor in his bedroom. The wooden floor was always creaking and groaning. A dead giveaway that he had company.

"Dammit, Abby," Grayson thundered as he shot into the bedroom. "You shouldn't be—"

A hard fist hit him in the jaw, sending Grayson stumbling back. His eyes widened in shock when he got a good look at the man who'd been standing near his bathroom door. Just waiting for him to appear.

Kace Quick.

Kace's blue eyes were icy. "I didn't like the way you were talking about Bree."

Oh, fuck.

"So, I decided it was time for a little visit."

CHAPTER EIGHTEEN

Grayson tried to run for the door. Seriously, the freaking idiot who only had on a bath towel tried to run. Kace rolled his eyes as he threw out his foot and tripped the fool. Grayson slammed into the floor, hitting with a thud. "Get that dumbass up," Kace growled.

Franco rushed to obey. Franco was always good at this kind of work. The fellow showed a true talent for generating fear. As for the other guy that Kace had brought along for this friendly little chat…

Remy wasn't looking so good. He was still standing by the bed, his hands loose at his sides.

Franco grabbed Grayson by the shoulder and yanked him up. The FBI agent—the *suspended* FBI agent—came up swinging. He drove his fist into Franco's stomach, but good old Franco didn't even grunt. The guy could certainly take a punch. But before Grayson could swing again, Kace was there.

He caught the jerk's fist in his hand. "I'm not here so you can pound on my crew."

Grayson's head turned. He smiled. "You're going to jail. You just screwed yourself, buddy. You broke into an FBI agent's home. You *assaulted* an FBI agent, you—"

"You dropped your towel, dumbass. And your dick is tiny."

Grayson's head snapped down as he tried to look at his own dick. *Too tiny to find.*

Kace used that moment of inattention to his advantage. He drove his fist at the creep again, slugging him a hard right. Grayson gave a pain-filled grunt.

"Get his ass in the chair," Kace ordered.

Remy finally moved. He grabbed one of Grayson's arms. Franco grabbed the other. They shoved the guy into a nearby desk chair and held him there.

"You're not getting away with this!" Grayson yelled. "You're not going to—"

Kace sighed and pulled out a gun. He'd had it hidden beneath the back of his leather jacket.

Grayson's eyes doubled in size. He immediately shot a frantic glance at Remy.

Like help was going to come from that end.

Voice mild, Kace told him, "I'm going to ask you questions. You're going to answer me. And if I don't like what you say, I might just shoot off your tiny dick."

Grayson blanched.

"Right. Here we go." Kace rolled back his shoulders. "I believe you called for…Abby, was it? When you realized someone was in your bedroom?"

Grayson pressed his lips together.

"I think you meant *my* Abby. Abby Johnson, correct? Because it only makes sense. Someone had to be feeding you information about me. And I've learned about your style. You like to manipulate women in order to get what you want. You seduce them, make them promises, and then you use them." Kace gave a sad shake of his head. "Hardly the behavior of an upstanding FBI agent."

"Fuck you!" Grayson shouted as spittle flew from his mouth. He tried to lunge forward, but the grip of the other two men held him in check. "Like you didn't do the exact same thing with Bree! You knew what she was! You seduced *her*. You used—"

Kace had no patience and no fucks to give. "Say Bree's name again, and I'll shoot you in the knee."

Grayson's eyes went wild. "Y-you won't. You won't do it, you—"

Kace had to laugh. "You've been telling the world that I'm a monster all this time, and now you think I won't shoot you?" He leaned toward the fellow. "Don't you get it? I'm not worried about you reporting this little chat. Because if I wanted, I could just snap my fingers and make you vanish. No one would ever find you—there wouldn't be anything left to find."

Grayson's frantic gaze darted around the room.

"Bree isn't your concern, Grayson. She's *mine*. So you'll treat her with the respect she deserves. By the way, it's a hell of a lot of respect. In case you were wondering."

Grayson wasn't speaking. He was staring at the night stand drawer.

Inspiration. Kace tucked his gun back into his waist band. He headed for the nightstand drawer. He still had his gloves on, so he opened the drawer without worrying about leaving any finger prints. As he'd suspected, Grayson's gun was waiting inside. He had to laugh. "Maybe I will let the authorities find your body. Easy enough to make it look as if you shot yourself with your own gun." He glanced back at his enemy. "A disgraced FBI agent. Not like it would be hard for many people to make the leap and assume you took your own life."

"Fucking sonofabitch—"

"Abby was feeding you intel on me. And before Abby, it was Ciara, right? When Ciara came to me, warning me that the FBI was closing in, it was because you were working her."

Grayson gave a jerky nod.

"Sorry." Kace inclined his head toward Franco. "I couldn't hear you."

Franco shoved down on Grayson's shoulder. Hard.

Grayson bellowed.

"Oh, feel free to scream. These walls are thick as fuck. No one will hear you. I made sure of that. I don't leave things to chance." Not ever. A wave of his hand had Franco easing his attack. "Now, where were we? Ah—Abby."

"She's working with me. I'm—we're fucking." His breath heaved in and out. Lines of pain bracketed his mouth.

Kace just waited.

"She…gave me names of women who might turn on you. Abby and I—we go back to the old days. I knew her when I was young in New Orleans."

"She gave you Amelia." That made sense. It also connected more dots that he didn't like.

"She wanted you and she hated you, so it seemed like Amelia would be good to turn on you." Grayson huffed out a breath. "But then she wound up dead."

Now they were getting some place. "Every woman that *you* tried to use against me…they all were victims of the New Orleans Strangler."

Grayson blinked. Over and over. "Wait, *wait,* no, shit, it's not—"

"You know what I see as the connecting piece in all of these murders? I see you. I see a man consumed by hate. A man who couldn't get the evidence he needed, so he decided to work a frame job. You killed those women. Maybe they were all coming to tell me the truth about you—Ciara certainly wanted to let me know about the Fed on my trail. But then someone stopped her from talking. Someone strangled the life out of her. Out of Amelia. Out of Marie."

"It's not me!" Grayson bellowed. "You can't possibly think—"

"I think I'm staring at a dirty Fed. A guy who had access to the witness who saw Marie's killer—the homeless man who was torched less than two hours ago. Maybe you killed him so he couldn't tell the world what he knew...about you."

"I interviewed him! Sat with the guy for an hour! If I was the man he'd seen, don't you think he would have said something?"

"Maybe he did. Maybe he said something in that interview, and you knew you had to get rid of him. Not like you could do it at the station with all of those eyes on you. So, you waited for the perfect opportunity. You told everyone he had shit info to give, and then you offed him."

"No." A frantic shake of Grayson's head. *"No."*

"And why should I believe you? Bree asked for an alibi, but you didn't have one, you didn't—"

"I was with Abby! Trying to fix the mess she made!"

Kace didn't let any emotion show on his face. This was what he'd waited for.

Sweat slid down Grayson's cheek. "Abby was freaking in love with you. Did you know that?" Grayson gave another shake of his head, this time in disgust. "The other women… Ciara turned on you for money. Marie was talking because her brother is in jail and she wanted a deal. Amelia—that one was just screwed in the head."

Disgust had his lips curling into a sneer. "You are such a freaking class act."

Grayson's chin notched up. "You never looked at Abby. She hated that. Now, she hates the one you can't take your eyes off. I was trying to make her see reason. I was trying—"

Kace's spine stiffened. Another puzzle piece had just snapped into place. "Abby drives a black SUV."

Franco twisted Grayson's shoulder.

Grayson bellowed.

Kace ignored the man's cry of pain. Bree had nearly been run down by someone driving a black SUV. *Abby drove a black SUV.*

"Ease up," he ordered Franco. Then he pointed to Grayson. "Talk. Or that arm gets broken."

"Love can make people do crazy shit." A bitter laugh from Grayson. "When she found out that Bree was a Fed, that she was working for me and you didn't care, Abby lost it. You still wanted Bree, you still were just as obsessed with Bree even though—"

Kace's left hand drove into the guy's ribs. "I told you not to mention her name again."

Grayson's face flushed.

"You knew Abby tried to run down Bree? You knew it, and you didn't turn her in?"

Grayson coughed. "What...what did you want—"

"You're a worthless piece of shit. You're done with the FBI. I'm going to make sure of it. You're done in this town. You're *done.*" He lifted the gun.

"I didn't kill those women!" A desperate yell. "Ask Abby—she can alibi me! I didn't kill—"

"I'll ask Abby. I'm going to see her next. I'll get her to tell me everything." He smiled. "I'll have my men watching you. Every single moment. You won't see them, but believe me, those guys are in the shadows, and they are watching *you.*" He waved to Franco and Remy. "Let's go. The other team won't let him out of their sight." The men he'd already stationed as lookouts just beyond Grayson's place.

As they headed for the door, Grayson called out, "I'll have you locked up for this!"

Kace didn't look back. "No, you won't. Because my men here will swear that you instigated this meeting. That *you* were the one to attack me when I walked in the door. I just had to defend myself." Grayson's gun was still in Kace's hand. "And I'll be keeping this…" Like he was going to leave the guy armed when Kace's back was turned. Besides, the agent's gun might come in handy…in case he needed to frame the SOB.

What better way to take down a Fed? Show the world he's dirty. *Your turn to be the criminal.* He wasn't done with Grayson, not by a long shot.

Franco led the way as they left the building. Remy was pulling up the rear. Kace inclined his head as he saw two of his men waiting across the street. Grayson would go nowhere. Not without him knowing.

"Get back to Bree," Kace told Franco as they stood on the street corner. "I've got men watching her, but I want you there." Franco had never been afraid to get rough. "Anyone comes at her, and you make the fool sorry."

Franco nodded. Without a word, he headed for his car.

"You don't trust me with Bree?" Remy asked quietly. "I thought I was supposed to be your right-hand man."

Kace smiled at the guy. "Of course, I trust you. That's why you're about to help me do the dirty work."

***

The coroner's office was ice cold. Located near the police station, the short, squat building reminded Bree of a freezer. She'd gone there to see what info she could get from the coroner. But now she was just cooling her heels as she waited for—

Bree's phone rang. She yanked it up, frowning when she saw the caller. She put the phone to her ear. "Grayson? What do you—"

"You were supposed to bring him down, Bree." His voice was angry. Muffled. "Instead, he brought you down. Down into the mud with him." Static crackled, distorting his voice.

"Look, Grayson, I don't have time for your—"

"Meet me at the cemetery, Bree. St. Louis Number 1. I'll give you all the proof you could ever need."

"You think I'm meeting you in a cemetery? Are you insane?"

"Your *boyfriend* has his men watching my place. I have to sneak out. I can't let them see me. *We* can't be seen together."

And he was picking a cemetery for a meeting spot? That didn't sound ominous *at all*. "You got something to say, meet me at the station."

"I'm *suspended*. Shit, do this, okay? Give me a chance to plead my case. Meet me there. Thirty minutes." He hung up.

"Jerk." Her gaze darted to the coroner's closed office door. She hurried forward, knocking before she pushed inside. "Dr. Crawford? Do you have any—"

Angela turned toward Bree. Amelia Sanderson's body was on the table before her. Her skin was pale. Her hair had been brushed away from her face. The deep stab wound on her body puckered up her flesh.

The blood is all around me.

"It's going to be a little while longer," Angela told her, voice brisk. "I *did* recover a dark hair from the victim, but it could have just come from someone at the hospital. I won't know for sure until we do DNA analysis. And I'm afraid that's going to take some time."

Time they didn't have. "I have to go for a meeting." Bree grabbed a pen and scribbled down her number. "Text me if you discover anything I can use."

"I will." A pause. "I'm going to begin work on Marie next. Maybe I'll find something on her remains that will help us. The dead can often reveal many secrets."

A line of lockers waited to the right. Bree knew bodies were in those lockers. Victims. "I hope Marie tells you something we can use." Something that could stop the killer out there. It wasn't right that Marie was trapped in one of those cold lockers while the man who'd hurt her still hunted on the streets.

Bree rushed away, her shoes squeaking over the tiled floor as the scent of antiseptic chased her from the lab. As she hurried out, Bree bumped into Dominic.

"Bree!" He caught her shoulders in his hands. "Where's the fire?"

Bad joke. Bad.

He winced. "Sorry. That's not what I..." He let her go. "Did you learn something?" His gaze jumped to the lab doors. "Did Dr. Crawford find a link to our killer?"

"She found a hair on Amelia. But you saw that circus at the hospital. The hair could have come from a doctor or a nurse or—" Bree exhaled in frustration. "We won't know until the tests are done. For now, though, I've got Grayson calling me, telling me that we have to meet up because he's got evidence I need to see. And he wants to meet in a damn cemetery of all places."

Dominic's eyes immediately narrowed. "What? I'm coming with you."

"No, I've got this covered." And if Grayson was going to throw out some shit on Kace, she didn't want Dominic there for that scene. "You stay with Dr. Crawford. She's going to start on Marie soon."

He nodded, but still seemed worried. "If you need me…"

"Don't worry, I'll call in the cavalry at the first sign of trouble." Bree briskly strode the hallway. It was edging close to one a.m. The coroner was pulling an all-nighter, everyone was working around the clock on this case, and now Grayson was demanding they meet at a freaking cemetery?

Like that didn't smell like the worst kind of plan ever?

Bree pushed open the glass doors and hurried outside. The air was crisp, strangely so for New Orleans, even in October. She ran down the steps, catching sight of the two men that Kace had left to keep an eye on her. She was an FBI Agent with her own body guards. And right then, she was absolutely going to use them. Bree pointed to the men. "You're coming with me."

A meeting in a cemetery? In the middle of the night? Trouble. Absolutely. She didn't trust Grayson as far as she could throw him. So, if he tried anything with her, she'd have back-up. And if he did have evidence against Kace…

No, I don't believe it. Grayson doesn't have anything on him. Despite everything…maybe because of it…

Bree had started to trust her lover. She'd let Kace past her guard and into her heart. He wasn't a cold, dark killer. Not Kace. Not him.

***

"You're a fucking cold-blooded killer, aren't you?" Remy demanded as they braked in front of Abby's home. A small, quiet house on the outskirts of town. "You're going in there to kill that woman."

"She tried to kill Bree."

"You're going by *Grayson's* words? His accusation? We both know the guy is a dipshit!"

Kace turned his head. He'd driven them over while Remy had ridden shotgun. "Are you in this with me?"

"What?" Remy's eyes were huge. "In to killing Abby? Shit, *fuck.* Let's talk to the woman first. See what she has to say. Because from where I'm sitting, I buy Grayson being the bad guy, not her."

"We'll see." Kace climbed from the vehicle. He didn't go to the house's front door, though. Instead, he headed around back, moving toward the garage that he'd paid to have installed for Abby last year.

Her SUV waited inside.

He flipped on the garage's light. Stared at the scratched and crumpled front end of Abby's vehicle.

Behind him, Remy swore.

"How's that for proof?" Kace asked. He'd worked with Abby. Given her a chance. Hell, they'd known each other for years. They'd come up on the streets together. They'd known each other since…

Fucking hell. I knew her back when I dated Brittney.

Abby had been friends with Brittney. Grayson had even admitted to knowing her, too. Saying they'd gone back to the old days.

"She couldn't have done it on her own." Kace's hands fisted as his mind whirled. "No fucking way. She wouldn't be strong enough to move the bodies. Not on her own. And I *saw* the guy in the video. Abby isn't that big."

"What are you talking about?" Remy demanded. Then his eyes widened. "You think—no, Abby isn't the Strangler! The killer is a man." He was adamant. "We both saw him in the video. No way Abby is strong enough to drag Hank Cannon the way the killer did. She couldn't!"

Kace shoved past him and ran for the house. At the door, he didn't even slow down. He just kicked it open, and the door flew back against the wall. "Abby!" Kace bellowed her name.

She wasn't there. A fast and frantic search of the house showed that the place was empty. The house was quiet and still and…

Kace turned toward her bedroom. He stalked inside.

"What are you doing?" Remy rushed to keep up with him.

"When I was getting her to tell me about serials, Bree told me that they often keep souvenirs from the kills."

"Trophies," Remy muttered. "They're called trophies. Not fucking souvenirs."

Kace slanted him a fast glance.

"I watch Investigation Discovery, okay? So I know some shit. And Abby isn't the killer. We're looking for a man. We're looking for—"

Kace opened the closet door. Turned on the light. Saw all of the clothes that were carefully arranged on the right. Clothes he'd seen Abby wear at the club. But to the left…those clothes were different.

A woman's scarf. One with a C on the bottom. *Ciara.* A leotard covered with faux diamonds. The same leotard that Marie had worn at Fantasy. A black blouse—a waitress's blouse like the one that Amelia would have worn, back when she'd worked at Kace's other club, Nightmare, and—

A black box was under the clothes. With his gloved hands, Kace reached for the box and opened it. Blond hair was inside. Chunks of sawed off blond hair. *Marie's hair.*

"Holy shit," Remy exclaimed. "But, but—"

"She's not doing it alone." A man *had* been in the video with Hank. A man *had* been seen at the tracks. Abby was involved with the killings, but it wasn't just her. It had never been just her. "She's got a partner." He yanked out his phone. "And we fucking just left the sonofabitch." He called one of the men he'd left stationed at Grayson's place. The fellow answered on the second ring. "Get inside," Kace blasted. "Make sure the bastard is still there!"

***

"Wait! Hold on!"

Bree turned at the call. She'd been getting ready to slide into her car, but Franco approached her, breathing hard. "I'm coming with you, Bree."

She frowned at him. "I've got two guys already tailing me. I don't need—"

"Kace told me to stick with you. If you're going somewhere, then I'll be with you every step of the way."

Bree checked her weapon.

"It's the way it's gonna be," Franco said, looking uncomfortable. "I mean, if you're going to be with Kace. This is his life. He doesn't want to risk you."

"I can protect myself."

He nodded but said, "I don't doubt it, but if Kace finds out I let you leave without me, he'll kick me out onto the street. I'm not kidding. We both know it. I'm fired if I don't stay with you."

Hell. "Get in the car."

He gave her a giant grin and rushed around the vehicle.

She climbed inside. Slammed the door.

"Where are we going?" Franco asked. "Who are we meeting?"

We? They weren't exactly a team. "Grayson."

"*What?*"

***

"He's gone, boss."

Kace nearly crushed his phone.

"I don't know how he slipped away, and I'm so freaking sorry, but the Fed's place is empty and—"

"Search the neighborhood. Find him." Fury crackled in each word. He hung up the phone and immediately called the person who mattered most—the woman he feared was in the most danger. "Come on, baby, pick up." He stood in that closet, the evidence right in front of him, and Remy watching him with narrowed eyes.

Bree's phone rang. Once. Twice—

"Kace, this isn't a good time," she told him briskly.

"*Bree.* Fuck, baby, you're in danger."

"I'm not alone." She sounded utterly calm. "Don't worry. But I have to meet Grayson and—"

"*He's* the danger! He's the—"

Bree gave a sharp gasp. "What the hell? Why are you—*Gun!*"

The line went dead. He called her again. The phone rang and rang and—went to voice mail.

Remy coughed. "Uh, Kace..."

He could feel pinpricks on his skin as a cold, killing rage filled him.

"Kace, is everything okay?"

No, nothing was okay. Not a single thing.

Bree. Baby, I'm coming.

CHAPTER NINETEEN

"*Gun!*" Bree screamed out the word because she needed Kace to know what was happening.

The gun jabbed harder into her side. "Just shut up and drive, Bree."

"Franco." Her hands tightened on the wheel. After she'd screamed, he'd cut her Bluetooth connection, then he'd thrown her phone out the window. "What are you doing?"

He laughed. "You know what I'm doing, *Agent* Harlow."

"You're supposed to protect me. You work for Kace. You—"

"Kace should be working for me. What the hell makes him so special? *Nothing. Nothing at all.* The guy doesn't even have a killer instinct. Not anymore. The fool started going legit a year ago. Transferring all of his holdings, burying the past. But you don't get to do that. You don't get to just *throw* all of that power away, not when I've been waiting in the wings. Doing every grunt job he tossed at me. Not when it's my turn."

Her gaze cut to him. "You think you're going to shoot me?" They were almost at the cemetery. She could see the heavy wall. The gates. *Open.* They should have been locked. Grayson must already be inside.

Franco yanked her gun out of the holster and shoved it inside the glove box. "I'm not going to shoot you. Don't you worry about that."

"You're lying. When Kace finds out what you've done—"

Franco just laughed. "He's not gonna find out. He doesn't know it's me. Doesn't have any clue." His voice was thick with satisfaction. "Stop the car. We're going inside to see dear old Grayson."

She shut off the car. Turned toward him. "Why are you doing this?"

His phone started ringing. Kace. She knew it had to be Kace.

"It's my turn to rule this town. Kace Quick will go down in flames. He'll burn because of you."

No, he wouldn't.

"Get out of the car, Bree. Grayson's gonna be inside, you told me that yourself. Can't have him waiting."

This was her chance.

She shoved open her door. Heard him doing the same with the passenger side door. This was her best shot, his moment of inattention…

She ran.

"Bree!" Franco yelled her name.

She expected to feel a bullet slamming into her. But he didn't fire.

"Bree!"

She rushed through the open cemetery gates, her shirt getting caught on the old wrought iron and tearing. Bree didn't stop. She lunged forward. If she could find Grayson, he'd have a weapon. Or a phone. Something. They'd get out of there.

The cemetery was a maze. Everywhere she turned, tall, old mausoleums stretched taller than Bree. As she ran, she saw flickering candles near some of the graves. Those candles cast faint, sinister lights in the darkness. She wanted to scream for help, but Bree didn't want to give away her location, not with Franco hunting her.

Her heart raced in her chest. She rounded another mausoleum and sank down, ducking for cover. Running blindly wasn't going to work. She needed a weapon, and she needed one right then. Her hands fumbled against the wall of the old mausoleum. One of the bricks felt loose and she grabbed it, yanking hard, pulling with all of her strength.

A bright light hit her. "Hello, Bree."

She lifted the brick.

"What in the hell are you doing?" Grayson muttered. "I asked you to meet me here so we could talk without Kace's men watching, but you're holding that brick like you're about to bash my head in."

On the phone, Kace had said Grayson was the danger. But *Franco* had been the one to shove a gun into her side.

"Bree?" Grayson stepped closer. The light swept down her body, finally moving away from her eyes. "What's going on?"

"Franco." She licked her lips. "He has a gun. He's after me."

"Kace's goon? Shit." His hand reached for her. "Come on. We need to get moving."

"Give me your gun," Bree ordered, her voice a low whisper. She didn't take his offered hand.

"I don't have a gun. Karin made me turn in my official weapon, then your asshole boyfriend took my backup." Frustration rolled in his quiet voice. "Come on, Bree. We need to move. If Franco is here—"

Footsteps rushed toward them. Bree stiffened.

"It's okay," Grayson said quickly as his light swung to land on the other woman who'd just joined them. "It's only Abby. I asked her to meet me here. It's where we always meet."

In a desolate cemetery? Yeah, great meeting place.

"I want her to tell you the truth about Kace. But we can't do it now. If he's sent Franco to end us, then we all have to get out of here."

Bree rose to her feet. Voice still a whisper, she told him, "Turn off the flashlight. You'll give away our location." Three of them. One Franco—but he was armed. The bullets would mow them right down, so it didn't matter that they had the numbers advantage. "And Kace didn't send him. Kace doesn't know a thing about him."

"Bullshit," Grayson rasped as he shut off the light, plunging them into darkness. "He's been pulling strings all along. I told you, Bree, you can't trust—"

"They're here!" Abby suddenly yelled. *"Franco, right here! Shoot!'*

"What the fuck—" Grayson began, but those were the only words he got out. In the next instant, a gun was blasting. A powerful thunder that shook the night even as Grayson stumbled to the ground.

Bree lunged for him.

"Stop." Abby's voice was flat. "Move another inch, and I'll have Franco put a bullet in your head."

Bree froze.

"Drop the brick. You aren't going to hit me with it."

Footsteps pounded toward them. And then Franco was there, holding a flashlight right over his gun. His breath heaved in and out. The light hit Bree. "Bitch," he snarled. "I don't like chasing your ass."

Grayson let out a low moan.

Bree's frantic gaze swept from Franco to Abby. They were behind the light, so she couldn't see them clearly. But she could feel their hate. Their fury. *Franco is the one with the gun. I don't think Abby is armed.*

"I told you to drop the brick," Abby snapped.

If Franco wanted to shoot her, he would have done it by now. He sure hadn't hesitated to shoot Grayson. And he hadn't shot her in the car, either. Whatever was happening, there was a plan in place. So Bree didn't drop her brick. She also didn't waste time answering Abby. Instead, she threw the brick at Franco, aiming for the hand that held the gun.

Bree didn't bother to see if she'd hit her target. Instead, she was already rushing for the nearest mausoleum. She sprinted behind it just as another bullet thundered out. The bullet hit the edge of the mausoleum, sending stone flying. A chunk of stone hit Bree in the arm, and she hissed out a breath as she kept running.

No way was she stopping. She had to get out of there. Or get a better damn weapon than a brick.

"Bree!" Abby screamed after her. *"Bree!"*

***

Kace threw open the doors to the squat, brick building that waited behind the police station. He'd never been to the coroner's lab before, but according to his men, it was the last place where Bree had been. Jerome and Douglas had told him that Bree rushed out of that building—right before she left with Franco.

Franco had sent the other men a text, ordering them to stand down and stay put. He'd said that he'd be taking care of Bree.

Traitorous sonofabitch. You hurt her, and you're dead.

Kace rushed into the hallway, with Remy right on his heels. He figured Bree must have been talking to the coroner just before she left. Hopefully, the coroner should be able to tell him where Bree had gone. He could see the lab. He reached for the doors.

Dominic stepped out of the lab. The FBI agent frowned at Kace, suspicion immediately appearing in his eyes. "What are you doing?" The guy's hand went to his hip, lingering near his holster. "You coming to tamper with the evidence?"

Kace grabbed Dominic and shoved him back through the lab's doors. The coroner—clad in green scrubs, wearing a mask and gloves—gave a quick gasp of shock as Kace pinned Dominic to the nearest wall. "Where is Bree?"

"Get your hands off me! Dr. Crawford, call for security, call for—"

"I was talking to Bree on the phone. She told me that she was going to meet Grayson, but then someone cut her off. I can't get her on the line. I can't get Franco. He was with her, and it's as if he just fell off the face of the earth. I need her. Fucking now. Because Abby Johnson has a twisted ass trophy collection in her bedroom. She's got keepsakes from all of the Strangler's victims. Abby is missing. Bree is missing. Franco is in the wind. I need to know where Bree fucking is, right now!" The last part was shouted.

Dominic flinched.

"Tell us where she is," Remy cut in, his voice hard but a little less insane than Kace's. "You're on her team. You've got to care about her safety."

Dominic's Adam's apple bobbed. "She…she is safe. She was going to meet Grayson."

Kace's hands tightened on Dominic. "She's not safe with him."

"She was taking back up! Your men! She said she'd be fine. She was going to the cemetery—"

Fuck, fuck, fuck. "Which one?"

"Ah, I don't think she said. I-I didn't ask. She said it was weird he wanted to meet there, but that she had it and I should stay with the coroner—"

Kace let the guy go and spun to face Remy.

"We can send teams to every cemetery," Remy said at once. "You have enough men on your payroll. We can search every cemetery in the area."

Kace nodded. "Get the men moving." He rushed past Remy.

Remy grabbed his arm. "Where are you going?"

"St. Louis Number 1." An obvious choice. The Strangler had been leaving victims in locations designed to catch the public's attention. St. Louis Number 1 was *the* tourist spot for all the haunted tours because Marie Laveau was supposedly entombed there. What better place to leave a body than in an infamous cemetery?

But not Bree's body. Not Bree.

"Wait!" Dominic yelled from behind him. "If Bree is in danger, I'm coming, too!"

Kace didn't give a shit what the guy did. As long as Dominic didn't get in his way.

Hold on, Bree. Baby, I'm coming. And if she was hurt…

No, no. He'd get to her in time. Bree would be fine.

But an image flashed in his head. For just a moment, he was back at Fantasy. Staring up at the blond woman who hung from the silks. And feeling as if his whole world had just imploded.

He couldn't lose Bree.

Couldn't.

Because he loved her too much.

***

Bree ducked behind a mausoleum. She could see light up ahead, the sputter of candles that had been placed near the bottom of another tomb. Her breath seemed too loud, the ragged inhales and exhales obvious in the silence. She needed to get to the cemetery's outer wall. She could scale the wall, get out of there, and get help for Grayson.

Or maybe…maybe she should circle back to him. Make certain he was still alive. She didn't even know where the bullet had hit him. She just knew that he'd sunk like a stone.

Bree began to inch away from her hiding spot. The candles up ahead flickered and—

Someone was there. Someone wearing a black hood. Someone leaning forward to etch something onto the side of that tomb. The person eased back and the hood fell.

It's just a teen. Some kid with piercings that glinted in the light. A girl, young and—

Teens always have phones on them. Bree sprinted toward the girl—

Franco appeared. He grabbed the girl. Put the gun under her chin. "Stop, Bree."

She stopped.

The girl was struggling. Twisting and crying and screaming.

"Shut the hell up," Franco snapped at her. "Your dumbass shouldn't even be out here."

Abby burst onto the scene, breathing hard. Then she saw the girl in Franco's arms. "What in the hell?"

"Consider it a two-fer," he grunted. "We can dump her body with Bree's."

The girl screamed.

Abby slugged the girl in the jaw. No, she didn't slug her. She hit her with a gun. *Shit.* Bree hadn't thought Abby was armed.

She'd been wrong.

Bree surged forward, but Abby brought her gun up—and aimed it at Bree. The teen had slumped back in Franco's arms, knocked unconscious.

"I am not playing with you," Abby spat at Bree. "So, let me just tell you what's going to happen, *Bree.* You're going to do exactly what I say, or Franco and I will take our time and carve up that girl."

"Aw, Abby," Franco mumbled. "I don't like cutting. You know that. I don't like the blood. It's too messy. Don't like the fire, either. It's not the same. You know I like to feel it when I squeeze the life away."

Every muscle in Bree's body was tight with tension.

"Don't worry, Franco," Abby assured him. "You'll feel plenty. Tie up the girl. She should have stayed her ass home and not gone creeping through a cemetery at night, asking for some freaking charm from a dead voodoo queen."

He dropped the girl's body. Reached into a bag—Bree hadn't even noticed the bag, but he'd slung it over one of his shoulders. He pulled rope out of the bag and quickly bound the girl. Her hands and her feet. Then he slapped duct tape over her mouth.

Franco looked toward Bree. The candles were still sputtering around the tomb. Marie Laveau's supposed resting place. She could see all of the X's that had been marked on the tomb.

"This is where you'll die, Bree," Abby told her, voice triumphant. "The cemeteries are supposed to be closed at night. No one gets in because the cops patrol. But hey…guess what? The cops won't be patrolling tonight. I made sure of it. Or rather, Kace did." A little laugh. "Franco there, he told the cops on Kace's payroll that the boss wanted everyone clear of this place tonight. When the boss says jump, the uniforms say how high."

Bree slipped back a little.

"Don't!" Abby blasted. "Don't try to run! I told you, if you give me trouble, I will make that girl over there *beg* for death. You don't want that, do you, Bree? That's not what an FBI agent

should want. You should want to protect her." A laugh. "You should want to offer up your life for hers."

"You're going to kill us both anyway." She wasn't dumb enough to think that Abby would let the girl escape. Not when the girl could give a description of her attackers. And there'd been just enough candle light there for the teen to see—

"I planned to kill you. She wasn't part of my plan. I'm improvising right now."

Franco kicked the girl. The slumped figure didn't even grunt. How hard had Abby hit her? Franco pulled back his leg to kick the girl again.

"*Stop*!" The cry tore from Bree.

"Get the rope over here, Franco," Abby ordered. "Tie Bree's hands. Tie her feet!"

He yanked more rope from his bag. Rushed toward her. She realized he'd put on gloves. Abby wore gloves, too. Because they'd done this before. Killed. They were about to set their crime scene.

Abby was obviously the boss. A killing team. Abby gave the orders, and Franco scrambled to obey.

He grabbed Bree's arms and yanked them behind her back. She felt the thick, rough rope cut into her wrists. Then he bent low, his hands sliding up her legs as he tied her feet. If she tried to move, she'd fall flat on her face.

Abby bent and grabbed Franco's bag. She shoved the gun into her waistband and pulled out a long silk. "Recognize this?" Abby taunted as she came closer to Bree.

Yes, she recognized the silk. It looked like part of the set that had hung in Fantasy.

Abby looped the silk around Bree's neck. Once, twice, then she began to pull the two ends.

"I get to do that," Franco whined. "That's my part."

Abby was still staring straight at Bree. "So it is." A laugh. "You're going to die right here, Bree. Franco is going to choke you—"

"Just like he strangled all of the others?" Bree asked. She wanted a full confession.

"Someone had to do it." A shrug from Abby. "He was tired of taking orders, and instead of Kace giving Franco a chance to take power, the guy actually started trying to go legit. Can you believe that crap? He was going to change everything."

"It was my turn to be boss," Franco growled.

Bree swallowed. The silk was tight against her throat.

"We thought about killing him," Abby confessed. "But Lindsey heard us talking."

So she had to die. Hell. Grayson's profile had been so wrong.

"She was screaming for help," Franco cut in. "I just stopped her screams." He moved to stand next to Abby.

Abby still gripped the edges of the silk. "When she was dead, I remembered dear old Brittney Lang. Everyone had thought that Kace killed her. And since Lindsey worked for him—"

"You got the idea to set him up," Bree finished.

Abby jerked on the silk. Bree gave a desperate gasp.

More laughter from Abby. The bitch thought death was funny.

Franco's hands rose. He took the silk from Abby. Yanked hard on the silk as Abby backed up a step.

Not getting your hands dirty, Abby?

Abby told her, "The Feds came sniffing around hard. It was easy for me to figure out what Grayson wanted. So, I gave him intel on Kace. I worked with him. And I kept the bodies coming. The bitches who'd been in my way over the years became useful. When they died."

Franco's body brushed against Bree's. "When you die, your face is going to turn all purple."

Abby had pointed the flashlight right at Bree.

"Your eyes will go red. You'll gasp and shudder. And your tongue will flop out of your mouth." He started rolling the silk around his fists, making the noose tighter on Bree's neck.

"You'll be so fucking ugly before I'm done with you."

The light didn't waver from Bree's face.

"Grayson finally did some actual detective work," Abby muttered. "He realized I was the one who tried to run you down at Kace's place. I just couldn't help myself. I'd been talking to Franco, planning our next move, and then you were right there. If you just hadn't moved so fast, I would have gotten you."

Bree was desperately weighing her options. There weren't a whole lot of them. If she didn't get free, she was dead. Her hands jerked hard on the ropes behind her, and she felt the blood trickling down her wrists as she struggled.

"To buy some time, I fed Grayson some BS sob story about being in love with Kace. About losing control and trying to hit you with my car. But the truth is…fuck Kace. Fuck you. I don't care about either one of you. It's time for Franco to rule this town, and I'm going to be right at his side."

"You'll… be at his…side…." Bree had to gasp out the words. "In…jail…"

Abby just gave a wild laugh. "Kill her, baby," she urged Franco as she pressed a kiss to his shoulder. "Kill her, and we'll set up her body. The tourists can find her in the morning, and Kace will lose his shit when—"

Bree slammed her head into Franco's. Hit him as hard as she could and heard the crunch of bones. *That had better have been his nose breaking.* She staggered forward, then hunched her upper body as she drove her shoulder straight into his mid-section. The air left his lungs in a whoosh of sound as they slammed forward. And when they hit the ground, there was a very distinct *thud* as his head connected with the nearby mausoleum.

Her breath heaved in and out. The freaking silk hung around her neck, but Franco wasn't shoving her off him. Franco wasn't moving at all.

"What did you do?" Abby's frantic voice. She ran closer. "What did you do to Franco?"

Before Bree could answer, Abby had grabbed the ends of the silk. She was behind Bree, standing up, and the other woman yanked hard on the silk, choking the breath from Bree.

CHAPTER TWENTY

The cemetery gates gaped open. Kace had grown up in that damn city. He knew the gates were locked at sundown. They had to be. If they weren't, then tourists or teens would slip inside. Too many times, the graves had been desecrated. Kids would pull out Ouija boards and try to summon the dead during drunk parties. Or they'd go to Marie Laveau's grave and leave bloody chickens as some kind of dumbass offering. People who didn't understand jack or shit would wreck the place.

"Bree?" Kace called her name even as he pulled out his gun. No way was he going in that place unarmed. But there was no answer to his call. He'd taken a flashlight from the car, and he hurried inside. The mausoleums rose, the tall, white stones appearing like ghosts in the dark. Because New Orleans was below sea level, the dead weren't buried in the ground. If they were underground, then when the city flooded, the bodies would just float away. So, the folks there had adapted. They put their dead in the heavy tombs. Places where the dead would *stay*. They'd made their own cities of the dead.

His light shone over the ground even as fear ate at his guts. When he saw the blood, Kace felt his heart stop. A too thick pool of blood waited near one of the tombs. Fresh blood. Fuck. "Bree!" Kace roared her name.

There was a trail of blood. Heavy spots that led through the darkness. He kept his light on the blood, and he raced through the maze of the dead.

***

Her throat was on fire. Her lungs were burning. Bree's head jerked back at a rough angle as Abby pulled the silk tighter and tighter.

"You aren't going to get away, Bree. I'll finish you myself. You think I can't? You think I won't? You think—"

"Get…away…from her…" A rough shout.

Grayson's shout.

And then Abby was letting Bree go. The silk was still tight around her neck, but Bree found herself slumping over Franco's prone body. She sucked in desperate gulps of air even as she rolled her body, twisting so that she could see what was happening and breaking free of the silk.

Abby and Grayson were facing off. His hand was on his side, and he staggered forward.

Abby jerked up her gun, yanking it from her waistband. "I don't need you any longer, Grayson."

"Put…the gun…d-down."

Bree rubbed her wrists and the rope that bound them against the side of the mausoleum. Could she saw through the rope this way? Would it cut loose? Was the brick sharp enough?

"I'm not putting the gun down." Abby aimed the gun at Grayson's chest. "Why the hell would I do that?"

"I…helped you."

"No, you just took the bullshit stories I gave you. You were more than ready to frame Kace even without me. I simply told you what you wanted to hear, and you *never* questioned me. Hell, even when I told you that I'd nearly run down Bree—you didn't balk. I think you were going to try and cover for me." Laughter. "But I don't need you covering for me. See, I have a plan in place. I'm just going to say that you did it all. *You* stole my car. You went after Bree when she wouldn't help you lock up Kace. And in your fury, you killed her. Franco found you here in the cemetery. He shot you because the brave man was trying to save Bree, but it was too late—"

"Dead men can't shoot anyone," Bree threw at her.

Abby's hand jerked. "He's not dead."

"Yes, he is," Bree told her as she kept struggling to cut through the rope around her wrists. "He hit his head on the tomb when he fell. Didn't you hear the sound of his skull cracking? He's not unconscious, Abby. He's *dead.* Don't believe me? Look for yourself." The rope around her wrists gave way. *"Look for –"*

Abby swung toward Bree.

Grayson attacked. He slammed his body into Abby's, but she fired. The bullet thundered in the night.

Now that her hands were free, she clawed at the ropes around her feet. The knots started to loosen. She was almost out and – *Yes!* The ropes sagged around her ankles as Bree surged to her feet. Hell, yes.

Abby was upright, towering over Grayson as she aimed her gun.

Before she could fire again, Bree was on the other woman. Rope still dangled from Bree's wrists, and she threw her arms over Abby's head. Bree locked the loose rope around Abby's neck, and she jerked as hard as she could.

Abby gave a desperate gurgle as her hands flew up. The gun dropped to the ground, and Abby clawed at Bree's hands.

"Oh, hell, no," Bree growled at her. "I'm not letting your ass go. Abby Johnson, you're under arrest."

Abby twisted her body and kicked out at Bree.

Bree dodged the kick and then shoved Abby forward, ramming the woman toward Marie Laveau's tomb. Abby's shoulder hit the side of the tomb, but then she shoved back against Bree, succeeding in getting the rope off her neck.

Bree punched Abby. Twice. Busted her lip. Sent her head whipping to the side. Then she went in for a third punch—

A gunshot blasted.

Bree and Abby both froze for an instant. One instant. Then Bree's head whipped to the left.

Franco was on his feet, a gun gripped in his hand. He stared at Bree, the faint candlelight showing the shock on his face before he looked down. His lips parted as if he'd speak.

Instead, his knees gave way, and Franco slumped to the ground.

And Bree could see Kace. Kace, who'd been standing behind Franco. Kace, who'd just fired his gun and saved her ass. A wide smile split Bree's lips even as Abby let out a guttural scream.

Fuck that. Bree punched Abby in the stomach, and the other woman balled over, crying. "Told you," she snarled. "You're under arrest." *And I think your boyfriend is dead.*

All of the struggle seemed to leave Abby in a rush. Her body slumped as sobs shook her. Bree wasn't about to let her guard down. She knew

Abby could be acting. The woman was a cold-blooded killer. A manipulator to her core.

"Check on the girl, Kace," Bree said, her words tumbling out quickly. "Make sure she's okay." The girl on the ground hadn't moved the whole time. "And Grayson—I think he was shot twice. He needs help!"

Kace bent near the girl. Put his hands to her throat.

"Bree!" A bellow. A familiar one. Dominic burst from the darkness, with uniformed cops right behind him. He took one look at the scene—and saw Kace with his gun and his body close to the unconscious girl. Dominic whipped up his weapon, aiming it at Kace.

"No!" Bree let Abby go and lunged toward Kace. She put her body in front of him. "He saved me! Kace isn't the killer! *He. Saved. Me.*"

Dominic didn't lower his gun.

"Abby did it. Abby Johnson and Franco Wyels. They were behind all of the murders. They confessed everything." She realized that her voice sounded a little broken. Probably because she'd been freaking strangled. "Get her cuffed. I don't even know if Franco is still alive."

"He's not." Kace's flat voice. "I killed him."

Her gaze darted to the ground. To Franco. His mouth hung open, and his body lay slumped on its side.

"The girl's alive," Kace added. "Haven't bothered to check on Grayson."

The uniforms had closed in on Abby. "Franco was supposed to have it all. It's his turn!" Abby's head whipped up as she glared at Bree and Kace. "His turn!"

"It's your turn to get your ass thrown in jail," Bree rasped back.

Abby tried to lunge for her, but the cops hauled her back.

Dominic had finally lowered his gun. Karin rushed from the side of a tomb and joined the team working on Grayson. "Still alive!" Karin called out. "But we need an ambulance. He's losing too much blood."

Bree hurried to kneel beside him. She put her hands over Grayson's wounds, applying pressure. "He helped me," she said, hating the blood that poured through her fingers. "If he hadn't appeared and distracted Abby, she would have choked me to death."

The scene was chaos. Uniforms. Agents. Crime techs. A thousand lights soon lit up the place even as Grayson and the injured girl were rushed away in screaming ambulances.

Blood stained Bree's hands. Her throat ached. And when she looked to the right, Franco's body was still sprawled on the ground.

Kace hadn't said much since the others had arrived, but he'd stayed close to her. As the madness reigned around them, his hand lifted, and he brushed back a lock of her hair. "God, baby, I wish I'd gotten here sooner."

She leaned into his touch. "I didn't even realize Franco was still a threat. I managed to knock him out earlier. He hit the side of a tomb really hard. I didn't know he'd gotten back up. Didn't know he'd grabbed the gun." She swallowed and felt the burn in her throat. "They would have killed me. If you hadn't come—"

His lips brushed over hers. "No, baby, I'm not so sure of that. I think you might have just fucking killed *them* both."

But it hadn't come to that.

"I'm sorry." His voice was so low. So rough.

She wanted to grab tight to him, but she'd didn't want to touch him with blood on her hands. Her fingers balled into fists. "Sorry?"

"Franco was right beside me the whole time. I didn't see him for what he was."

"Kace—"

"I can't lose you, Bree. You matter to me, more than anything else."

Her heart was racing so fast and hard in her chest. His lips pressed to hers once more.

"Bree!" Dominic called.

There were questions to be answered. Dozens and dozens of questions. But she didn't want to leave Kace.

"Come to me when it's all over. Come to me when you want to crash. I'll be waiting on you." Kace stared into her eyes. "I love you, Bree Harlow."

What? "Y-you don't get to make a confession like that at a crime scene."

He smiled. "Of course, I do."

"Kace…"

"The cops are gonna want to haul me downtown so I can answer their endless questions. I'll play their game. Then they'll let me go." His words were low, only for her. "When you're done with your job, you'll come to me. I'll tell you my secrets. You'll tell me yours. Then you'll have to decide…can you stay with me, knowing all that I've done? Or will you turn me in?"

Before she could answer, he pressed another kiss to her lips. "Either way, Bree, I'll fucking love you until I die."

"*Bree!*" Dominic yelled.

Kace turned away. Started to walk through the crowd. He didn't get far, though. As he'd predicted, the cops and agents closed in.

I'll fucking love you until I die.

He hadn't asked her if she loved him. He hadn't asked her how she felt at all. If he had, she would have told him…

I'll fucking love you until I die, Kace Quick.

***

"Kace!" Remy shouted his name as Kace was led out of the cemetery. Reporters had already gathered. Hardly a surprise. After all, not one killer, but *two* had been found that night.

Franco. Freaking Franco. A betrayer who'd been right under Kace's nose, just as Abby had been. He should have seen the truth sooner. But he'd been distracted by other things. He'd failed. And that failure had almost cost Bree her life.

"Kace, what happened in there?" Remy asked as Kace was pushed toward a patrol car. "Why are they arresting you?"

Kace smiled at him. "Because I killed a man."

Remy's jaw dropped.

"Shot him, and if I had to do it all over again, I'd do the same fucking thing." He slid into the back of the vehicle. The cops were being ever-so-courteous. Mostly because those two were on his payroll. Not that he'd give away that detail to anyone.

"Don't confess," Remy muttered. "Jesus, man, I'll get your lawyer. She'll meet you—"

"Confessing is easy on this one." He rolled back his shoulders as he relaxed into the seat. "Sometimes, you kill and you become the hero."

Remy's eyes went wide.

The cop slammed the back door before Kace could say anything else. That was okay. He didn't have much else to say to Remy.

He'd killed a man. Hadn't hesitated. But this time, the Press wouldn't paint him as the sick killer. Franco and Abby—they'd been the ones strangling the women in New Orleans. He'd just stopped a rabid monster when he'd shot Franco.

The patrol car's blue lights flashed on as the siren wailed.

Sometimes, you kill and you become the hero.

His own words slipped through his mind as the car drove away, and unease slithered through Kace. He glanced back. Saw the entrance to the cemetery. Bree was still inside.

He'd killed to protect her. He would do it, over and over again if necessary.

And Bree had stared at him like he was a hero. Then she'd put herself in front of him. Protected *him* from Dominic.

Sometimes, you kill…

He thought of Bree's past. Of the nightmares that haunted her.

And you become the hero.

***

"Did you give Franco a warning before you fired?" Dominic stared straight at Kace as he threw out the question.

Kace didn't know how many hours had passed. Didn't really care, either. He'd been at the station, Deidre had been raising her usual lawyerly hell, and Bree…

He hadn't seen her.

She's okay. She's alive. She's safe.

And she would come to him. He knew it.

"My client didn't have time to yell out a warning," Deidre's voice dripped ice. "The attacker—a *serial killer*—was preparing to shoot at a federal agent. He did the only thing that he could. He took out his gun, and he fired it. It's a lucky thing that Kace Quick is such a fine shot. He saved not just Bree Harlow, but Grayson Wesley, and that young girl, Maureen West. If he hadn't stopped Franco, they could have all died."

Kace kept his relaxed pose.

Dominic's considering gaze swept over him. "Maybe you fired because you didn't want Franco to have the chance to tell the world about your involvement in the crimes. Maybe you were—"

"How dare you accuse my client—" Deidre began as she jumped to her feet.

Kace sighed. This was getting old. "I know you found the evidence at Abby's house. And now that Franco's on a slab some place…" Kace shrugged. "I'm betting that Abby is telling the world her story. She and Franco have been a couple for years. I just didn't realize that they were the couple that killed together."

Dominic's lips flattened. Karin stood behind him. Watching. Waiting. Judging.

Kace offered a thin smile before saying, "I'm not tied to any of the murders they committed. I shot Franco to stop him from hurting Bree, plain and simple. I wasn't trying to save anyone else. It was just about her." He hadn't even seen the others there. He'd only seen her. "If I'd realized what he was sooner, what he and Abby were doing, I would have stopped them."

"You would have *killed* them, you mean," Dominic clarified as his brows lowered.

"Is that what I mean?" *Yes, it was.*

Deidre grabbed her briefcase. "You have an eye witness. I know that Bree Harlow has already given you her sworn statement, attesting to the fact that my client saved her life. Now, unless there is anything else that we need to cover, we're done here."

Dominic's lips parted.

"We're done," Karin said softly. "Mr. Quick, thank you for your cooperation."

Taking his time, Kace rose from his chair. "Always happy to cooperate with the authorities."

Karin's lips twitched. "I'm sure you are."

He headed for the door, but stopped near Karin. "Where is Bree?"

"Getting checked at the hospital. I insisted on it. There was too much bruising on her neck. Told her either she went willingly or I'd have a patrol team cuff her and take her in."

"Thank you."

Karin inclined her head. He stepped into the hallway. Deidre was already up ahead, her elegant heels clicking on the tiles. The middle of the night, and she was still dressed to kill.

"I misjudged you." Karin's quiet voice stopped him.

Kace looked back. "No, you didn't."

Her lips parted, but he was already walking away.

***

The morning sky was blood red as the sun slowly rose to begin its trek across the sky.

"Ah, you sure this is where you want to be, Agent Harlow?" The uniformed cop nervously edged closer to her.

She gave him a distracted smile. "I'm sure. Thanks for the ride."

She strode toward the gate, and as she approached, it swung open for her. Bree knew that Kace was inside his mansion. Watching. Waiting.

Good.

She climbed the steps leading to his home, and the front door opened as soon as she put her foot on the sweeping front porch. He stood in the doorway, clad in a pair of jeans and a black t-shirt that stretched across his powerful chest. He held out his hand to her, and, not hesitating at all, Bree's fingers reached for his. Kace pulled her closer, got her to step over the threshold and into his home, and even as the door shut behind her, he was tipping back her head.

Her lips parted because she was so ready for his kiss—

"The bruising is bad, Bree."

He wasn't kissing her. His fingers were feathering over her neck.

"I'm so fucking sorry I wasn't there sooner."

She pulled her hand free of his. Put her fingers on his hard jaw and stared into his eyes. "You were there exactly when you needed to be."

His blue stare was electric with intensity. "They were going to kill you. I always think I know who is next to me. Always think I check people out, but I missed them. I didn't see *them*."

"Neither did I. Neither did any of the other agents or the cops. Because they were making you out to be the monster. They were setting you up too well." She rose onto her toes and pressed her mouth to his. "But you're not the monster."

For a moment, he kissed her back. His tongue thrust into her mouth as he kissed her with a ravenous need. His arm locked around her waist as Kace hauled her closer to him. She could feel the thick length of his erection pressing against her. She could feel—

"I killed him, Bree." He pressed his forehead against hers.

"I know. You did it for me. You—"

"Sheldon Taggert was in *my* bar. And, yeah, I know a nineteen-year-old punk kid isn't supposed to own a bar, but let's just say I did a ton of shit then—and since—that maybe I wasn't *supposed* to do. The law and I haven't always been close." He exhaled. "The bastard was drinking his ass off. Talking about how he killed Brittney. He confessed. On the anniversary of her death, he just flat out said what he'd done." Kace pulled from her. Turned and stalked down the hallway.

Bree followed him even as her stomach twisted.

He entered his study. Headed for his desk. His hands slammed down in the surface as he braced himself, with his back to her. "He had a wreck. The dumb SOB had drunk too much. I'd followed him. I'd followed him because from the minute he walked into my bar that night, I knew I was going to kill him."

Bree didn't speak. She just waited.

"I saw the crash. I climbed off my motorcycle. I went to him. I could have gotten him out, Bree. I could have done that. I didn't. Because when I stared at him, I saw her. I found her body, you know. Hell, of course, you know. You've read all the files on me." His head sagged forward. "I looked at him, tangled in the seat belt, trapped, and I saw her. The way she'd been when I found her body. She looked the same to me, at first. Her eyes were closed, her face so beautiful. Like she was just sleeping. Until you looked at her neck. Until you saw the circle of deep bruises around her neck." He pulled in a shuddering breath and turned toward her. His gaze went straight to Bree's throat. "Her neck looked just like yours. Same damn bruises. They tried to do the same thing to *you*."

Bree slowly walked toward him.

"I watched Sheldon die. I could have stopped it. Could have picked up the phone and dialed nine-one-one, but I didn't. That sonofabitch had killed Brittney. He killed her because she laughed at him in bed. Can you believe that shit? That's what he said…what he muttered at the bar when he was drunk off his ass. He'd gotten mad. Squeezed her neck to stop her laughing. He killed her, then he let me face a murder trial. He set me up by wrapping *my* shirt around her throat. I could have gone to jail. Could have lost my life." Kace shook his head. "I decided it was only fair for Sheldon to lose his life."

She tried to keep her breathing slow. Easy. But she failed.

"I'm not a *nice* man. I tried to warn you about that before. I didn't grow up easy. And to get power, to keep power, I've done things..." Now he looked at his hands. "Kill or be killed. Isn't that the law of the jungle? It's the law of my world, too." His hands fisted and fell to his sides. He slowly lifted his head until he was staring at her. "You can pick up the phone, and you can call in the FBI. They can haul me away, and I'll give them this same confession, too. They've been working for years to bring me in. Couldn't get me on other crimes, couldn't find where my secrets were buried, but for you...for *you,* I'll confess. I don't want to be the same man with you. I don't want to be the monster, but I'm afraid I don't know how to be anything else."

"You saved me today."

"I killed a man for you. Because that's what I'm good at."

Bree shook her head.

"Don't make me into a hero. Franco was dead, Bree, the minute I found out that he'd tried to hurt you."

"Kace—"

He surged toward her. Grabbed her. Pulled her against him. "Look at me, baby. *Look* at me. Even if I'd gone into that cemetery and he hadn't been armed...if he hadn't been about to shoot you, I would still have ended him. He wasn't walking out of there alive."

"But…you let Abby walk out alive."

"I don't kill women." His eyes blazed. "Didn't kill her, but her life is still over. If the cops hadn't arrested her there, I would have made sure they found evidence for others crimes. I would have made sure that she was locked up and tossed away, with no chance of getting out ever again."

Her gaze searched his. "What do you want me to say?"

He didn't respond. Maybe he didn't know.

"You told me before that you were trying to go legit with your businesses. That's why Franco said he was setting you up. You were changing everything, and he didn't have a place in that new world. He wanted to rule in the dark, but you weren't staying in the shadows any longer."

Kace gave a slow nod. "But you're a Fed, baby, and when it comes to right and wrong…"

"I'm not here to arrest you for any crimes you committed in the past. I was sent here to find out if you were the New Orleans Strangler. You're not. *You're not.*"

"But I'm a criminal. And you're…you."

Her eyes stung with tears. "You said you loved me."

"I do. Why the hell do you think I'm confessing? Because I don't want you living with what I am. I'll go away…*for you.*"

"And I'd lie to protect you!" Bree's words erupted as an angry scream.

He blinked.

"Don't you get it? You matter. You. You matter to me more than anything else. When my parents were murdered, I had nothing. No one. All I could think about was getting revenge. Finding the killer who'd hurt them. Making *him* pay." A wild laugh escaped her. "You wanted Sheldon to pay. You punished him. I wanted the man who killed my parents to pay. If I'd had the chance…" This time, it wasn't a laugh that escaped her. It felt like a sob. "I would have killed him, too." A tear slid down her cheek. "We're not so different, Kace. I knew that, felt that, from the beginning. You did, too. You told me we were the same." He'd been right. "You think I'm scared of any darkness you carry? I'm not. Because *I'm the same*."

He wiped away her tear. "We're not the same, Bree. You're a thousand times better than I'll ever be. And I'm terrified that if you stay, if I'm the selfish bastard I've always been and I try to keep you with me, I'll just drag you down."

She licked her lips. Tried to steady her heart. "It's not your choice." Her chin lifted. "Being with you is *my* choice. It was from the beginning. I read the files on you. I knew all the suspicions. And I still chose you because people aren't just good or bad. We're all more than that. *You* are more than that."

"Baby, I'll never be worth you."

"Don't! Don't you say that! Because I love you, and you don't say that about—"

He kissed her. Hot and hard and deep, and she could feel his emotions crashing over her. The desperate hunger. The hope. The fear. The love. So much love. Powerful and consuming and complete.

They weren't perfect, would never be. But he *was* exactly what she needed. He was the man she loved. The only one she wanted. His secrets, his twisted past—everything. He was hers. If she wanted to be with him, she had to accept it. Just as he had to accept her.

"You can't…you can't do it if we're together." She pulled her lips from his, but still tasted him. The heavy length of his arousal pressed against her, and she wanted to arch into him and forget everything else. But this had to be said. She'd made her choice. He had to make his. "I can't be an FBI agent while you're—"

"I may kill again."

Her breath caught. *Not* what she'd expected or wanted to hear.

"I'm going to find the sonofabitch who killed your family, Bree. I've already got people working on it. You are a part of me. You're mine, and I protect what's mine." His gaze pinned her. "I'll find him, and I'll kill him."

No, I will.

"But I'm done with the life I had before. My businesses are all legal, and…the cops I have on my payroll—"

"Kace…"

"It's for protection, baby. I need to know which enemies are coming for me. But if it means I can keep you, if you'll stay with me, I won't cross lines. I can leave my past behind."

Sometimes, the shadows from his past might try to reach out to him. She knew that. Wasn't naive enough to believe it wouldn't happen. And if those shadows came, they'd deal with them, together. They could deal with anything, if they were together.

"You are what I want. You are what matters. For you, I'll be more," Kace promised her.

"You are more. You are everything." She stared straight into his eyes. "I will fucking love you until I die." She gave him the same words he'd given to her.

His smile lit up his face. His dangerous face became so handsome and sexy. Then he was kissing her again. Shoving her clothes off even as she pushed his away. The need to be skin to skin overwhelmed her. They'd survived a nightmare, but they had each other. No, the future wasn't going to be easy. But if she'd wanted easy, she never would have fallen for Kace Quick.

She kicked away her shoes. He yanked down her jeans and underwear. Then he was lifting her up and sitting her on the edge of his desk. Bree gave a husky laugh. "God, I love your desk." It was quickly becoming her favorite spot.

His hands were on her thighs. He pushed them apart, and she expected him to plunge into her. Instead, Kace went to his knees before her. He pulled her toward him and put his mouth on her.

Her head tipped back as her palms slapped against the desk's surface. He licked her, sucked her, and pushed two fingers into her eager sex as she moaned his name. He was feasting on her, driving her wild, and she loved every single second of it. His tongue lapped at her, he stroked her clit, and her thighs quivered because her climax was so close. She was going to come against his mouth. Right there.

Right—

There.

"Kace!"

And he kept kissing her, tasting her pleasure. The orgasm rolled through her, contracting her delicate, inner muscles, and before it ended, the head of his cock was against her body. He stared down at her. So much hunger burned in his eyes.

"Condom," he gritted out. "I need—"

"Birth control is covered." This time, she wanted him. Only him. "I'm clean."

"Me, too. Me..." He pushed into her. "God, I love you."

She arched toward him as he sank deep, filling her. For a moment, they just stared at each other. He braced himself on his hands, making sure to keep the weight off her body as he pounded into her, over and over again.

She was slick and so sensitive. Her nails raked over his shoulders. She kissed him frantically, and she came again, her body primed for him.

He was with her. She felt the hot burst of his release inside of her. Her legs tightened around his hips, and Bree held on to Kace with all of her strength.

Just as she'd always hold on to him. When you found someone in this world worth loving, you didn't let go. You fought like hell to stay together.

No matter what.

***

Bree's nightmare came again. Kace hadn't been sleeping. He'd been in bed with Bree, thinking about how lucky he was that she'd survived. The bruises around her neck infuriated him, and he wished that he'd made Franco's death slower.

So much slower…

Then Bree whimpered. He felt the tension sweep into her body. Her fear.

He didn't want Bree afraid. So Kace pulled her closer. He wrapped his body around hers. "It's okay, baby. You're safe."

Her eyes didn't open, but her body relaxed. She turned toward him. Snuggled closer. Mumbled softly.

"What was that, baby? Say it again."

He kept holding her even as tension snaked through his body. He hadn't lied to Bree. When he'd told her that he would kill the bastard who'd turned her life into a nightmare, Kace had meant those words.

His hand slid down her side. Touched the scar that marked her. He would make her nightmares end.

And though he'd told Bree that he'd turn his back on the past, Kace knew that if anyone ever threatened her again…if she was put in danger because she was close to him…

I'll destroy the bastards.

Because nothing mattered more than she did. Nothing ever had, and nothing ever would.

CHAPTER TWENTY-ONE

"It's not going to help, Kace." Bree squared her shoulders and looked straight ahead as the elevator rose, heading for the top floor in the pricey hotel. "You think I haven't talked to psychologists before? You think I haven't tried to remember more about that night?"

He caught her hand in his and brought Bree's fingers to his lips. Kace pressed a kiss to her knuckles. "Sarah isn't just any psychologist. You know that."

Sarah Fontaine—*formerly* Sarah Jacobs— was one of the absolute best profilers in the country. Kace had hired her to help him find the man who'd murdered Bree's family.

"I know all about Sarah. Everyone does. When your father's Murphy the Monster, the guy at the *top* of the FBI's Most Wanted List, there isn't an agent alive who won't know who you are."

The elevator dinged. The doors opened.

"She's going to try getting into my head," Bree muttered.

"Is that a bad thing? I rather like your head."

She stepped off the elevator. He followed right beside her. "In my dreams, he says it's what I wanted. What if—"

He kissed her. "You aren't the bad guy, Bree. That's me, remember?"

"That crap's not funny. You're legit now."

He was. Mostly.

He guided her toward the penthouse. A guard waited outside, but the guy recognized Kace and opened the door for them. When he stepped inside, Kace saw Jax first. The infamous Jax Fontaine.

The tattooed guy had supposedly given up his wicked ways for Sarah. Kace might have to ask the fellow for some tips.

Or not.

Jax shook Kace's hand. "You convinced her to come."

"She wants closure. It's time."

Jax offered his hand to Bree. "Sarah knows killers better than anyone I've ever met. She already has some ideas for you but…"

"But I'm not sure you will want to hear what I have to say," a stylish brunette announced as she headed toward them. Dark eyes assessed first Bree, then Kace. A slow smile curved her full lips. "I'm Sarah."

Bree stiffened. "I'm Bree Harlow."

"*Agent* Harlow," Sarah said, inclining her head. "It's a pleasure to meet you. I have a few friends at the FBI. They tell me that you are expected to do great things." A pause. "I hear you also work at profiling."

"Nothing like you. I'm just getting started."

"Yes, well," Sarah gave a slow roll of her shoulders. "I started very young. Kind of have to, when you find out dear old dad is a killer."

"Do you know where he is?" Bree's voice held a crisp edge.

Sarah's smile stretched. "I have no idea." She began to hum a little as she turned away. "But I suspect he's always closer than I'd like." Sarah made her way to the couch. Sat down. Crossed her legs. Jax immediately took up a position behind her. A rather protective position, Kace noted. What did the guy think? That they were some kind of threat?

Bree didn't move, so Kace didn't, either.

"You've profiled *your* monster," Sarah said as her gaze stayed locked on Bree. "I know you have. You must have worked on his profile a thousand times over the years."

"Yes."

"Why don't you tell me what you think?"

But Bree shook her head. "I want to hear something new. I want to get out of my own head and look at this case from a new angle. There's no way he killed my family and just stopped. Never hurt anyone else. That doesn't happen. He has to still be out there. Still be—" But she broke off.

"Hunting?" Sarah finished.

Bree nodded.

"Yes, I think he is still hunting. I don't think he'll ever stop on his own. Men like him have to be stopped."

Jax's hand moved to her shoulder.

And Bree slowly crossed the room. She sat in the chair near Sarah. And Kace—he decided to take up his own protective position right near her. If things got uncomfortable for Bree, he'd take her the hell out of there.

"After I came to New Orleans, my dreams changed," Bree blurted. "In the dreams, after I found my parents, he spoke to me. He said…he said that I'd gotten what I wanted. That I was free." Her hands fisted in her lap. "I didn't want that. I never wanted my parents to die. I *loved* them."

"You were suspected in their murder," Jax said. The guy never pulled his punches.

Kace flipped him off. "Watch your ass."

Jax just shrugged. "She was. So, let's hit the elephant in the room." A pause. "Did you ever ask any boyfriend or *anyone* to off your parents?"

"No."

"You wouldn't have needed to ask," Sarah noted, her voice soft and sad. "This person would have done it on his own. This person would have wanted to separate you from the ones you loved because he wanted you for himself."

Bree gave a brittle laugh. "Yeah, that's what I thought, too. He had the chance to kill me, only he didn't. He *marked* me." She rose, lifted her shirt, and showed Sarah the scar. "Everywhere I go, no matter what I do, I carry his stupid mark. And I *hate* it."

Sarah nodded. "He wanted to own you. To possess you."

And Kace wanted to tear the bastard apart. *I will. I'll find you. It will happen.*

"It's been years." Bree lowered her shirt. Sat back down. Reached for Kace's hand. "I keep looking for him. I'm stronger now. I'd *kill* him if he came after me again, but he's never been there. I've never seen him. I've—"

"I think he's always been there, Bree." Sarah's face showed her worry. "I think this man has made a point of staying with you. He would always want to know what you're doing."

Bree's hold on Kace's hand tightened. "I would know."

"He wasn't face-to-face with you the night of your parents' murder. You never saw his face, but you felt him. You remembered his voice. You remembered his smell."

Bree shuddered.

"He knew all of that. So he stayed away. Deliberately. You didn't see him, but whenever he wanted, he's seen you." Sarah leaned forward. "That's *my* take because a man like him, a man who killed your family, marked you with his knife, and then *let* you slip away…he's a man who planned everything. He's a man who saw something he wanted, and he made sure that the object of his desire was alone. You've been alone, haven't you, Bree? All of these years?"

"Yes. I don't let friends close. As for lovers…" Her gaze flickered to Kace, slid away. "I don't stay with them."

"You do now," he growled.

Sarah nodded. "This is the same profile you developed, isn't it, Bree? You always feared he was watching you. You feared he would target anyone you got close to, so you kept them away. To protect them."

A nod.

"What changed?" Sarah asked.

"I met someone that I didn't want to keep at arm's length." Again, her gaze slid to Kace. "And I met someone who wasn't going to shy away from any danger that I might bring to him."

"Because Kace is as dangerous as the killer you fear has always been in your shadow?" Sarah's words were careful.

But Bree gave a hard, negative shake of her head. "He's not dangerous. Not to me."

"I sure as hell am to the man who hurt you." He leaned forward and kissed her. "Count on it."

"I can fight my own battles."

"That's what changed," Sarah murmured. "You got tired of running. You came into your own and decided you had a man worth fighting for."

Bree glanced back at Sarah. "Then my nightmares changed. Did he really say those words to me so long ago? Or did I imagine them?"

"I don't know. I doubt we'll ever know. But I think your dreams mean something else." A slow exhale. "I think they mean that you suspect—deep down—that he's close to you now. He's with you. Someone in your life. He's there. You just have to unmask him."

If that jerk really was in her life...

"I haven't told you anything that you didn't already know," Sarah continued. "But sometimes, it helps to hear the words from someone else, doesn't it?"

Bree hadn't let go of his hand. "Why hasn't he killed again?"

"He may have killed other people. But he isn't functioning as a typical serial killer. If there even is such a beast." One elegant brow rose. "You are his obsession, Bree. It started when you were young. Somehow, he found you. Locked on you. He saw your parents as a threat, so he eliminated them. There haven't been any other threats to your affection, so he hasn't needed to act again." Now her stare focused on Bree and Kace's joined hands. "If you two stay together, he will act."

Jax cleared his throat. "Sarah means he's gonna try and kill you, Kace."

Kace just laughed. "Let him." *Bring it.*

"No." Bree's sharp response. "I won't let that happen. I need Kace."

Not nearly as much as he needed her. "Give us something here," Kace snapped. "Something to work on. A way to bring the bastard out."

"You want him to come out? Really?" Sarah smoothed her already smooth skirt. "Get married. Forge a permanent tie with Bree. Do something to set him off. He'll come, though you might not see him coming until it's too late. Is that a risk that you really want to take?"

He didn't want to take any risks where Bree was concerned.

Sarah's face was focused with intent. "I want to go back over your life, Bree. This is what we need to do…you need to make a list of the men in your life—men in your life *now.* We need to see if those men ever lived in the same city you did before you came to New Orleans. If they ever *visited* the cities you lived in previously. If they had any ties to your job. If you came upon them in a setting that, at first, seemed like chance, but then later, that same man showed up again in your—"

"I met Grayson Wesley at a bar over a year ago." Her voice was wooden. "I turned around, and he was watching me. He bought me a drink. I-I slept with him. I don't usually sleep with strangers but I'd just finished a case that wrecked me. I'd found a missing girl, too late. A fifteen-year-old girl who'd been abducted and killed. When I saw her, when I saw the blood on her body, it just—" Bree stopped. "I wanted a night to forget. I was working on that case provisionally while I finished my training at Quantico. It was my first time to see the kind of work I'd really be doing. The first time to see that I wasn't going to always stop the bad guys. Not like I'd planned."

Sadness flashed on Sarah's face. "Sometimes, it doesn't matter how hard we try."

Bree inclined her head in agreement. "I needed to forget. Grayson gave me the chance to do that. I thought I'd never see him again. Then I walked into a workshop on profiling at Quantico, and he was there."

"Did you feel like...Grayson knew who you were before the two of you met in the bar?"

If Grayson was the bastard who'd done this to her...

"He looked as shocked as I was when we faced each other in the workshop, but he covered his surprise faster. Then he stayed away from me. I stayed away from him. Until...this case." Her tongue slid over her lower lip. "Grayson was the one to request me. I thought it was a chance to prove myself. He sent me to work undercover at Fantasy."

Jax gave a rough laugh. "Let me guess, the bastard was dead set on proving that Kace was the killer, huh? And I bet he didn't like it when you started fighting for the man you were supposed to destroy."

No, the prick hadn't liked it. And Kace sure as shit didn't like him. "We have a past, Grayson and I. We go back to the early days here in New Orleans."

"Grayson's FBI," Bree murmured. "It couldn't be him." But she didn't sound certain.

"We need to analyze your life," Sarah urged her. "Go back over everything. Grayson sticks out right now, yes, but sometimes, it's not the obvious person. Sometimes, the things we see…the things we think…a good killer will twist reality. A good hunter will make you not even realize you were ever his prey, not until it's too late."

***

"Marry me."

Bree stiffened. They were back at Kace's house. She'd spent the day with Sarah, pouring over details, going back as far as she could to try and find links in her past with the man who'd killed her parents.

She slowly shut the refrigerator door. "Say that again. Because it was very much *not* the dream proposal that every woman longs to hear."

His jaw was locked. "If Sarah is right and this prick will come out if we get engaged, *marry me.*"

He wanted to put a giant target on his back? "Okay, I get that you're trying to help me, but I'm not marrying you so that you can lure out a killer."

He stalked toward her. Took her hands in his. "Then marry me because you love me."

And still put a target on his back? Bree shook her head.

His bright gaze narrowed. "You love me. You—"

"Of *course,* I love you. Despite this seriously shitty proposal. And, FYI, I expect so much better next time. Like...I want flowers and champagne and maybe even a riverboat involved in this thing."

His brows raised.

"But I'm not going to risk you. Sarah and I have this. We're working on finding him. We *will* find him." She hadn't felt this hopeful in...well, ever. Because she had something to fight for. Kace. A life. She wasn't going to be afraid any longer. "Kace—" Her phone rang. Dammit. She yanked it out of her pocket. "Hold the thought."

Karin's face appeared on the screen. She swiped her finger over the screen even as she put the phone to her ear. "Karin, what's up?"

"Get down to the station—Abby Johnson is dead."

Her lips parted, but no sound emerged.

"The guards found her in her cell. Looks like she hung herself with a bed sheet. *Shit.*"

Strangled. Just like her victims.

"I need you down here, Bree. Now."

"On my way." She hung up the phone and found Kace watching her with an intense, worried stare. Bree rolled back her shoulders. "Karin thinks Abby killed herself. She used a bed sheet and—I have to go. I'm sorry. Karin wants me there now." She rushed around him.

His arm looped out and curled around her waist. He pulled her close. "I love you."

She could feel his warmth and strength pouring into her. "I love you, too."

"Come back to me when you can." His lips brushed her temple.

"Always." She grabbed her keys and her gun and headed for the front door. As her fingers closed around the doorknob, Bree glanced back. He'd followed her, and Kace stood just beyond the stairs. His eyes were stormy. She wanted to go back to him. To hold him. "Yes."

His brow furrowed.

Abby was dead. A person's world could change in an instant. Blink, and you might lose everything. So why not grab for happiness while you could? "I'll marry you, but I still want a redo on the proposal."

A faint smile curled his lips before she left him.

CHAPTER TWENTY-TWO

Abby's body had been lowered to the cell floor. The sheet had been removed, and Bree could clearly see the blue and red band of bruises that covered her throat.

"Happened sometime around eight p.m., judging by the lividity," the tech said. She lifted one of Abby's fingers. "That's…odd."

Bree leaned closer. Abby's pinky finger was also red and blue. Swollen.

"She broke her finger?" Karin said.

Now Bree was looking at both of Abby's hands. The ring finger on her right hand was swollen, too.

Holy shit. Those could be defensive wounds. "Who was the last person to see her?" Bree demanded.

Karin blinked. "Ah, I need to check the log, but…I think maybe her lawyer came to see her earlier in the evening?"

Bree was already hurrying toward the guard's desk. He gaped at her when she grabbed the log, but, sure enough, only Abby's lawyer's name was written there. *Susan Hall.* She slammed the log shut. "Did *anyone* else come to see Abby this evening?"

The young guard's eyes widened. "Just…just the agent…he flashed his badge. Said he had to see her."

Karin's footsteps thundered forward. "What agent?"

***

"You got here faster than I expected," Kace said as he opened his door to Dominic Grant. The guy stood on his porch, his shoulders hunched, and his face tense.

"You shouldn't have called me." Dominic was sweating. No big surprise there. "Does…hell, does Bree know?"

"Know that you're a gambling addict who sold out the FBI? Yes, have you forgotten already? She was there when I dropped that bombshell."

"I meant did she know you'd asked me here." Dominic licked his lips. "I thought we were even on those old debts. After I gave you the information that you needed…"

Kace backed up and motioned Dominic inside. "We are even." He shut the door then turned his back, aware of Dominic following behind him, but the other man drew up short when he caught sight of Remy.

Remy lounged on the sofa in Kace's study, a whiskey in his hand. When he saw Dominic, Remy gave a toast. "Guess it's a party now."

"Hardly," Kace muttered. Then he waved his hand between the two men. "I believe that you've met. Probably in an interrogation room some place."

"I-I can't talk with him here," Dominic said as he raked his fingers over his face. "We need to be alone. *Now.*"

"You can't talk with him here?" Kace faked a look of mock surprise. "Why the hell not? I mean, you're both FBI agents."

Remy choked on his whiskey.

"Oh, sorry, was I not supposed to know that?" Kace gave his right-hand man a very cold grin. "I'm afraid I knew from the beginning. Dominic here—he was very helpful, you see. He let me know that I couldn't trust you. He came to me, offering to sell out FBI agents who were working on my case, in exchange for the forgiveness of some gambling debts."

Remy's face mottled with fury.

"Wait!" Dominic cried. "Wait just a minute—"

Remy surged to his feet. "You *knew* what I was? All along? You—"

Kace shrugged. "Keep your enemies close…" He turned his back on Remy as he stared at Dominic. "And those you want to kill…even closer."

Dominic's mouth opened. Closed. Opened—

"Grayson Wesley grew up in New Orleans. He lived here when Bree's parents were being murdered in North Carolina. I know because I kept an eye on the bastard. He hated me as much as I hated him. So even though I'd love to wipe him off the face of the earth, he's not the man I need to kill." He pulled the gun from beneath his leather jacket. "You are, Dominic."

"Kace!" Remy's voice broke with shock. "What are you doing?"

"I know what you did, Dominic. I put the pieces together. I put the pieces together because Bree talks in her sleep. She doesn't always remember her dreams, though. I think because they're too painful for her. But do you know what she said last night? In her sleep, she turned to me and she whispered…thorns."

Dominic pulled down the sleeve of his coat.

"I noticed your tattoo the other day. Interesting design, with the rose and the thorns wrapped around it."

Dominic whirled and marched for the door. "This is insane. I'm not—"

Kace grabbed the bastard and threw him against the wall. Then he put his gun under the guy's chin. "I'm not insane, but thanks for asking. I'm just a pissed as all hell man who will do anything for the woman he loves." He jabbed the gun harder into his prey.

"Kace…" Remy was right behind him. "He's a federal agent. You don't want to do this."

"I do. I want to do it very much. I want to squeeze this trigger, and I want to blow his brains out. Boom." He smiled at Dominic. Sweaty Dominic. "There's not going to be some long trial. I'm not putting Bree through that. Your life is going to end now."

Kace felt a gun shove into his back.

"Let him go," Remy snapped. "I can't let you do this!"

"Remy, I didn't ask you here to stop me. I asked you here to be a witness."

"He's crazy!" Dominic yelled. But the SOB's fingers were reaching for his gun.

So Kace grabbed those fingers with his free hand, and he broke them.

Dominic howled as his left hand dropped to his side.

"Jesus, Kace!" Remy cried out. "Let him go, now! Don't make me do this!"

"He killed Bree's parents. He's stalked her for years. The fucker met her when he was at her high school doing some drug safety talk. He picked her out of a crowd and then he destroyed her life." Because Kace had made the connection.

Bree had been focused on Grayson but as soon as she'd said *Thorns*...He'd started ripping into Dominic's past. With the right money changing hands, it had been easy enough to get what he needed.

He hadn't told Bree, though...

Because he didn't want the blood on her hands.

"There's no way he did that." Remy's gun stayed pressed to Kace's back. "He's FBI."

"An FBI agent who sold you out. Who was ready to risk a dozen other agents, too. He offered to give me anything I wanted, as long as I made his debt disappear. You see, he's had a hard time holding his shit together over the last few years. Ever since he wrecked my Bree's life."

"He's lying!" Dominic's voice cracked. "Get him away from me! Shoot him, shoot—"

"If he shoots me from this angle, the bullet will probably just go into you, too." Kace gave him a wild smile. "And I'll still squeeze this trigger. Boom go your brains."

"You're a sick fuck! You're—"

"I'm going to marry Bree. She loves me. And she said yes."

There it was. He saw the flicker in Dominic's eyes. The tell that he'd wanted to see. The evidence hadn't been concrete, but it had been enough to push Kace to act.

His phone rang, but he didn't answer it. He didn't look away from Dominic. "You don't have her any longer. She's not alone. She'll be with me. Always."

Dominic's head gave a slow shake.

"Kace…" Confusion thickened Remy's voice. "What's happening?"

"You're a witness," Kace said again. His finger tightened on the trigger. His phone had stopped ringing.

"You *can't* kill a Fed in cold blood!"

"I'm Kace Quick. I can do anything I want." And he wanted to pull the trigger. "Admit it," he snarled at Dominic. "Tell me what you did. *Tell me!*"

But Dominic's eyes had gone cold. Hard. "You're crazy. You assaulted a federal agent. You belong in a cage. Just like the one that bitch Abby is in."

Abby…

Kace's phone rang again. And…shit, that ring tone. *Bree?*

His head jerked down.

And Remy acted. He yanked Kace back and tossed him across the room. Kace hit the desk, the sharp edge cutting into his side, but he didn't drop his weapon. He surged right back toward his prey.

Remy was positioned in front of Dominic. Remy's gun pointed at Kace. "I can't let you do this!"

"It's not about letting me. It's—"

Dominic shoved Remy forward. He yanked out his gun, and, using his non-broken right hand, Dominic fired.

Kace had grabbed for Remy. He took the guy down, but not in time. He heard the thud as the bullet sank into Remy's shoulder. "Dammit!" Kace looked up.

Dominic was smiling. And he had his gun aimed at Kace's head. "You won't marry her."

Fucking hell. Kace had his gun, too. But would he be able to lift it and get a shot off in time?

"I didn't *wait* this long so that she'd wind up with you. I found her. Beautiful Bree. I knew she was meant for me from the first moment. She was smiling at me. Asking all kinds of questions. Her gaze was on *me*. I got her message. I understood. I followed her home. Saw her fight with her parents. I went to them when she left…I killed—"

The front door crashed open. "Kace!" Bree yelled.

Dominic stiffened. Then he fired his gun. He shot it right at Kace even as Kace tried to get his weapon up. *Too late. Too late.*

Dominic's bullet had lodged into his chest. He felt muscles and bone explode. He tried to call out to Bree but—

Dominic fired again.

CHAPTER TWENTY-THREE

"Kace!" Bree ran toward the thunder that had to be a gunshot. She burst into Kace's study.

Blood on the floor.

She could see it pooling near his body. Too much red near Kace's still form. And Remy was right beside him. Remy lay crumpled near Kace, and Remy's eyes were closed. Kace was—

Dead. Dead. They're dead. Mom and Dad—

No, this wasn't her parents. This was Kace. Remy.

Her past and present were blurring together.

She started to run forward, but instinct kicked in, and instead of running to Kace, Bree whirled around—and she found Dominic backed into the corner of the study.

His eyes were wild. "Bree! Oh, God, Remy shot Kace! Just *shot* him! I came to talk with Kace. He called me…shit, I've got some gambling debts, and I told him Remy was an undercover agent!" His words tumbled out in a mad fury. "When Remy found out that Kace knew the truth about him, the guy went crazy! He shot Kace. I-I tried to help. I fired at Remy, but it was too late. It was—"

"Drop your weapon." She had her gun trained on him.

Dominic blinked, as if surprised to see that he still had his weapon. He was holding it with his right hand, which was weird because the guy was a left-hander.

He didn't drop his weapon.

"Lower it, *now.*"

Where was Karin? She'd been right behind Bree on the way over.

Dominic started to lower his weapon. "Remy must have been undercover too long. He let that world get to him. I-I couldn't believe it when he shot Kace!"

She kept her gun on him and backed closer to Kace. Bree knelt and her left hand went to his neck. *Be alive. Be alive. Be—*

His pulse fluttered beneath her fingers. "He's still alive. He's going to be okay." He *had* to be okay.

Dominic's face hardened. He still gripped his gun, and it wasn't pointed at the floor. *It's pointed at me.*

And Bree's gun was pointed dead center on him. "According to the guard at the jail, you were the last person to see Abby Johnson tonight."

"She wanted to confess to me…wanted to tell me that Remy had been working with her and Franco, too—"

Lie. "You killed her."

He blinked. "Bree…"

"Why? She was in jail. But you killed her. I saw the defense wounds on her. You screwed up. You left evidence behind. You *killed* her." Bree could only shake her head. "Why?"

He took a step toward her. "I did it for you."

I did it for you.

Her body started to shake.

"I always did it for you. Look what you've become, because of me. I freed you from a life that you didn't want. I made you better. I made you stronger. I made you—"

Bree fired. One bullet to the head. *For my mother.* One bullet to the heart. *For my father.*

Blood poured from him. His body crashed onto the study's floor, and the blood was everywhere. Just like it had been that long ago day. Just like it had been when her parents died.

"*Baby…*" Kace's rasp.

Her head whipped toward him. His eyes were open. "I was…gonna do…that part…"

"No." She dropped her gun and rushed to him. Put her hands over his wounds. Prayed. "He was mine to kill."

Remy let out a groan. He tried to sit up, but slumped back down. "Fucking…witness…"

She didn't understand.

There was so much blood.

"*Exactly* what…you are…" Kace's voice was weak, but determined. "No matter what…happens…me…you say…he f-fired at her…"

What?

"Kace, you're going to be okay." She grabbed for her phone, smearing blood across the screen. Where the hell was Karin? Bree dialed nine-one-one and demanded help.

"Witness…" Kace whispered.

"Just focus on living!" Bree yelled at him. "Stop talking! Save your strength! You—"

His eyes had closed.

"Kace?"

Footsteps pounded into the house.

"Kace, you stay with me! You don't dare die, do you understand? Don't you—"

A swarm of people entered the room. Karin had come with plenty of back-up. And all of those people were trying to pull Bree away from Kace. She fought them, yelling that pressure had to be put on his wounds. Yelling that he needed help.

Yelling…that she needed him.

CHAPTER TWENTY-FOUR

"You can't sleep forever."

Kace cracked open one eye. He felt like shit. No, worse than that. But…that was Bree's voice. She was beside him. Smiling?

Crying?

He tried to talk—

"Easy. You had a tube shoved down your throat until about ten minutes ago. Drink this. The nurse said it would help."

A straw was pressed to his lips. He sucked and ice-cold water chilled the burn in his throat.

"If you hadn't almost died, I swear, I would kill you."

His beautiful Bree. Now both of his eyes were open and on her.

"How did you know it was him?" Bree asked.

"You…talk in your sleep."

A furrow appeared between her brows.

"Thorns. Last night…you mentioned thorns."

"It wasn't last night. It was two nights ago. Because you've been out that long. I've been terrified that I was going to lose you for that long." She sat on the edge of the bed, and her hands rose to frame his jaw. "Why didn't you tell me?"

"Didn't want you…having blood on your—"

"I wanted to kill him."

He knew. "Couldn't let you…go to jail."

Her expression was tender and soft. "You can't always protect me."

Yes, he could. "Remy…witness…"

"Yeah, Remy is a great witness. Because you set that crap up. Remy said he heard Dominic's confession. The guy confessed to killing my parents. To stalking me. Karin found more evidence at his place. He had pictures. *Videos* of me that he'd taken over the years. The guy specifically requested this assignment, and then *he* was the one who convinced Grayson to bring me on. He's been in the shadows of my life all along, and I never knew it." She released a ragged breath. "His name was in the old police reports. He'd been at my high school, doing some kind of outreach that I don't even remember. When my parents were killed, he inserted himself in the investigation. Said he wanted to help, according to the notes in the files. I didn't even think about him as a suspect. He was just—*God, he was right there.*"

The worst danger could be right beside you. "Dead?"

She nodded. "He's definitely dead. I'm a good shot."

His head turned. Kace pressed a kiss to her palm. "Marry…me…"

A broken laugh came from her. "This is *not* more romantic than your last proposal in the kitchen. A hospital is not romantic."

He gazed into her eyes. Talking was still hard, but… "Love…you."

She leaned forward and kissed him. A gentle, sweet kiss. He could taste her tears in that kiss. "And I love you, and walking into that room, seeing your blood on the floor—it was like walking straight into my worst nightmare."

His beautiful Bree…

"But the nightmare ended differently. He didn't win this time. This time, I won. He's dead, and I have you, and I'm going to be happy. *We're* going to be happy."

Hell, yes, they would be. He'd do anything necessary to keep her happy. Anything.

"I love you, Kace, and as soon as you get out of this bed, yes, I'll marry you."

***

"I can't believe you want me to be your best man." Remy adjusted the sling on his arm. The bullet had torn into his rotator cuff. "I'm surprised that you're even still talking to me."

Kace slowly pulled on his tux. The stitches in his chest ached, but he ignored the pain. He was about to marry Bree. She was all that mattered.

"You knew all along?" Remy pushed. "Is that why I couldn't find evidence against you?"

"You found evidence. You just didn't use it." He headed closer to Remy. "That's why you're the best man."

Remy's eyes narrowed. "You set me up. You had me in that room because *you* were planning to kill Dominic. You thought you'd force a confession out of him, and when I heard the truth, I'd back you up."

"No, I thought that when you heard the truth, you'd take your gun out of my back. You'd let me kill him. *Then* you'd drag my ass to jail." He shrugged. The stitches burned with the movement. Whatever. He could deal with the pain.

"You were willing to go to jail?"

"For Bree? Hell, yes." But things had worked out differently.

Remy whistled. "You have fallen far and hard."

He sure had. "Be careful, my friend…" And he actually meant the term. "You might find yourself falling one day, too."

Remy appeared horrified by the very notion. "Hell, no. Not me."

"Lie to yourself if you want." Kace smiled. "Trust me, you'll fall when you never expect it."

Music started to play. Shit. It was time. He had to get out there. No way was he leaving his Bree waiting. He made it to the altar. The St. Louis Cathedral was filled with his friends…

And some enemies.

Even a few FBI agents. *Not* Grayson Wesley. He hadn't gotten an invitation to the event of the season. Too bad for that jerk. But Kace had dropped his charges against the guy. Since Grayson had helped to save Bree at the cemetery, Kace had decided to be kind. For the moment, anyway. He wasn't quite done with Grayson…

"How'd you score this place on such short notice?" Remy asked in a hushed voice as he stood beside Kace.

Kace looked down the long aisle and saw Bree slowly approaching him. "I know the right people."

"You *bribed* the right people, you mean."

How insulting. "I'm not a criminal, Remy. I'm an upstanding member of the community."

Bree was almost upon them.

She was freaking gorgeous.

"You're one lucky bastard," Remy told him, the words barely above a whisper.

Yes, he was.

Kace took Bree's hand and knew he'd hold her forever. She was the one thing that mattered to him, the one thing he couldn't live without.

He'd lie for her, fight for her, and kill for her in a heartbeat.

Maybe those should be his wedding vows…

"You're smiling." Bree's voice was husky. Sexy. She smiled back at him. "You're happy?"

Happy wasn't the right word.

He was complete. His life was whole. He didn't have to struggle, didn't have to fight, didn't have to possess everything because he had nothing.

He had Bree, and with her…he had everything he'd ever need.

He had the entire world.

The End

A NOTE FROM THE AUTHOR

Thank you for reading DON'T TRUST A KILLER.

I had great time writing about Kace and Bree, and I really hope you enjoyed their story. New Orleans is one of my favorite cities, and I'm already at work writing another tale that will be set in the Big Easy. If you liked DON'T TRUST A KILLER, please consider leaving a review. Reviews help new readers to find great new stories.

http://www.cynthiaeden.com/newsletter/

Again, thank you for reading DON'T TRUST A KILLER.

Best,
Cynthia Eden
www.cynthiaeden.com

ABOUT THE AUTHOR

Award-winning author Cynthia Eden writes dark tales of paranormal romance and romantic suspense. She is a New York Times, USA Today, Digital Book World, and IndieReader best-seller. Cynthia is also a three-time finalist for the RITA® award. Since she began writing full-time in 2005, Cynthia has written over eighty novels and novellas.

For More Information

- *www.cynthiaeden.com*
- *http://www.facebook.com/cynthiaedenfanpage*
- *http://www.twitter.com/cynthiaeden*

HER OTHER WORKS

Romantic Suspense

- Secret Admirer
- Don't Trust A Killer
- Don't Love A Liar

Lazarus Rising

- Never Let Go (Book One, Lazarus Rising)
- Keep Me Close (Book Two, Lazarus Rising)
- Stay With Me (Book Three, Lazarus Rising)
- Run To Me (Book Four, Lazarus Rising)
- Lie Close To Me (Book Five, Lazarus Rising)
- Hold On Tight (Book Six, Lazarus Rising)

Dark Obsession Series

- Watch Me (Dark Obsession, Book 1)
- Want Me (Dark Obsession, Book 2)

- Need Me (Dark Obsession, Book 3)
- Beware Of Me (Dark Obsession, Book 4)
- Only For Me (Dark Obsession, Books 1 to 4)

Mine Series

- Mine To Take (Mine, Book 1)
- Mine To Keep (Mine, Book 2)
- Mine To Hold (Mine, Book 3)
- Mine To Crave (Mine, Book 4)
- Mine To Have (Mine, Book 5)
- Mine To Protect (Mine, Book 6)
- Mine Series Box Set Volume 1 (Mine, Books 1-3)
- Mine Series Box Set Volume 2 (Mine, Books 4-6)

Other Romantic Suspense

- First Taste of Darkness
- Sinful Secrets
- Until Death
- Christmas With A Spy

Paranormal Romance

Bad Things

- The Devil In Disguise (Bad Things, Book 1)
- On The Prowl (Bad Things, Book 2)
- Undead Or Alive (Bad Things, Book 3)

- Broken Angel (Bad Things, Book 4)
- Heart Of Stone (Bad Things, Book 5)
- Tempted By Fate (Bad Things, Book 6)
- Bad Things Volume One (Books 1 to 3)
- Bad Things Volume Two (Books 4 to 6)
- Bad Things Deluxe Box Set (Books 1 to 6)
- Wicked And Wild (Bad Things, Book 7)
- Saint Or Sinner (Bad Things, Book 8)

Bite Series

- Forbidden Bite (Bite Book 1)
- Mating Bite (Bite Book 2)

Blood and Moonlight Series

- Bite The Dust (Blood and Moonlight, Book 1)
- Better Off Undead (Blood and Moonlight, Book 2)
- Bitter Blood (Blood and Moonlight, Book 3)
- Blood and Moonlight (The Complete Series)

Purgatory Series

- The Wolf Within (Purgatory, Book 1)
- Marked By The Vampire (Purgatory, Book 2)
- Charming The Beast (Purgatory, Book 3)
- Deal with the Devil (Purgatory, Book 4)

- The Beasts Inside (Purgatory, Books 1 to 4)

Bound Series

- Bound By Blood (Bound Book 1)
- Bound In Darkness (Bound Book 2)
- Bound In Sin (Bound Book 3)
- Bound By The Night (Bound Book 4)
- Forever Bound (Bound, Books 1 to 4)
- Bound in Death (Bound Book 5)

Made in the USA
Middletown, DE
16 November 2018